"I like you, too, Heidi."

Heidi's gaze shifted at Jackson's words, became deeper, sharper, hotter. "But you don't like me *that* way?"

He felt his jaw go slack. How could she not know how he felt? The evidence was clear. He could fix her doubt with one kiss, right now. Just a taste. A feeling swept over him, an eager hunger that made him feel surpris̶i̶n̶g̶l̶y̶ ̶l̶i̶v̶e̶. He pulled her close and kissed h̶e̶r̶ ̶̶̶̶̶̶̶̶̶̶̶̶̶̶̶d herself arou̶n̶d̶

Slow down, ̶̶̶̶̶̶̶̶̶̶
reassure her, ̶̶̶̶̶̶̶̶̶̶̶̶̶̶̶̶̶̶e he let the kiss go on and on and on. His hands itched to touch her in secret places.

She made a needy sound that threatened to push him over the edge. If they kept this up, he'd start ripping off her clothes – and they were sitting in the convertible in the driveway, the traffic a white-noise roar that made this seem like a hot dream.

Catching the tail end of his sense before it slipped away, he pushed back, holding her by the upper arms. "I think that's enough." His voice felt shaky and he knew he was holding on by a thread.

"Oh, no, that's not even close to enough."

Dear Reader,

Imagine packing up all your worldly goods and setting off for a new life with hope, excitement and jitters all a simmering stew in your stomach. Will you love your new life or hate it and run home, tail between your legs?

As if that isn't scary enough (can you tell I like security?), imagine losing everything you dragged with you – money, belongings, car. Talk about starting over again. Stark naked. Almost. The idea makes my heart pound and my hands go clammy. That's what my heroine, Heidi, faced.

I'm so proud of how she handled it. She struggled, she worried, but she kept at it and made her own way. With a helping hand from hunky Jackson McCall, of course. He offered a boost when she stumbled on her borrowed stilettos.

I hope you enjoy Heidi and Jackson's story. Drop me a line at dawn@dawnatkins.com and watch my website for upcoming releases – www.dawnatkins.com.

All my best,

Dawn Atkins

TEASE ME

BY
DAWN ATKINS

MILLS & BOON®

To my Aunt Wanda, Your generous spirit will
live forever in my heart.

*First published in Great Britain 2007
by Harlequin Mills & Boon Limited, Eton House,
18-24 Paradise Road,
Richmond, Surrey TW9 1SR*

© Daphne Atkeson 2005

ISBN: 978 0 263 85564 7

14-0307

*Printed and bound in Spain
by Litografia Rosés S.A., Barcelona*

1

MY NEW LIFE STARTS NOW, Heidi Fields thought, pulling up to the darling sky-blue town house with white gingerbread trim, her heart so happy it almost hurt. She braked her new Outback with such force her beautician's kit slid forward and bumped the back of her head.

She'd filled the SUV her brothers had given her floor-boards to moon roof, trunk to dash, with everything she owned, which made her exodus from Copper Corners, Arizona, all the more dramatic.

Leaving her old life completely behind, she'd bid farewell to her overprotective brothers, her station at Celia's Cut 'n' Curl, where she served as amateur therapist, and headed off for a future she chose, not one she just fell into.

She wanted to counsel people face-to-face, from a sofa or chair, not looking into a mirror, wielding a ceramic curling iron, blinking against the flash off the foil squares of a weave or shouting over the dryer roar.

She'd helped many a hair client through child-rearing hell, marital strife and personal crisis, and more than one came in for unnecessary touch-ups just to get Heidi's take on a new development, but she wanted a degree—proof that she knew the science behind her art.

She'd had to leave, before she got stuck in a limited life. She wasn't going to end up like Celia, who'd sold herself short in a tiny salon in a tiny town instead of becoming a Hollywood stylist, as she'd dreamed when she was Heidi's age. Sure, college would be hard and it was tough to make a living as a psychologist these days, but Heidi was giving it all she had.

She was on her way at last. Sweaty and stiff from the three-hour drive up from Copper Corners to Phoenix—fried-egg-on-a-sidewalk hot at the end of July—but happy because right outside the factory-tinted window of her brand-new car was her brand-new home.

Which she could no longer afford. She flinched at the thought. Her friend Tina had the lease on the place and Heidi had intended to rent the second bedroom and small bath. Except Tina got a great job offer in L.A. she just *had, had, had* to take—Tina was so dramatic. She'd left to do just that three weeks ago.

Heidi had decided to take over the lease. She'd get a roommate or work more hours at the new salon where she'd snagged a part-time slot. She had no spare cash at the moment. She had a cashier's check in her wallet from emptying out her savings account on the way out of town that she would sign over to Arizona State University for tuition in three weeks.

If she had to find a cheaper place, she'd do it. She wasn't waiting a day longer to start her new life. She was too afraid she'd lose her nerve altogether. She hadn't told her brothers about Tina's exodus because they liked and trusted Tina and that made them feel better about Heidi being in the city. She was twenty-four, but they treated her as though she were twelve.

Their parents had died when Heidi was just six, her brothers thirteen and sixteen. Though they'd grown up with their aunt and uncle, Michael and Mark had clucked over Heidi like parental stand-ins, and they saw no point in her leaving the safety and comfort of Copper Corners. She had her associate's degree from the nearby community college. What more did she need? Small-town boys inside out, neither brother had attended a four-year university.

Mike, Copper Corners' mayor, had offered to hire her as his secretary, and Mark, a real estate broker, wanted to train her as an agent. Mainly, they wanted her close to home.

And she wanted to get away. She wanted her own place and a private life. A sex life, frankly. No more hurry-up-before-your-brothers-get-home sex with guys intimidated by her brothers' physical size and political importance.

She'd convinced them she'd worked out the details and they'd accepted her plan. No way was she backing out now. She would solve the rent money problem on her own.

There was a slight slope to the street, so she yanked her steering wheel sharply to the right so the tires bumped the curb. Wouldn't that be awful? Letting her car slide downhill into traffic or a mesquite tree or a house? Talk about one mistake ruining everything….

She loved the car—a going-away gift from her brothers. High safety ratings and terrific value, they'd told her somberly. If they could have dressed her in combat gear and a flak jacket and trailed her all the way here, they would have. She'd wanted to refuse the gift, but they were so anxious to do something for her that she'd given in.

She smiled, thinking of her brothers' smothering love, feeling fond of them and a little homesick already, but relieved to be free at last.

She looked out at her new home, gleaming in the bleaching sun. Tina had e-mailed digital snaps, but they hadn't given the whole fabulous effect. The paint was grayed with age—maybe more of a slate blue than a sky-blue—and the white trim needed touching up. Hell, it had flaked so much it looked like a failed antiquing job. But who cared? It was her place. She already loved it.

The houses on either side looked as bad. Weeds clumped in the patchy grass of both yards, which were filled with weather-beaten kid toys—a swing set on the right, a faded vinyl play pool covered with grass clippings to the left. Both porches were loaded with stuff—bikes, a stack of newspapers, abandoned coffee mugs, beer cans and lots of plants. People spent time there, it seemed.

Not that different from Copper Corners, where every-one gathered on porches in the evenings to gossip and throw back Buds or Country Time. People were people, big city or tiny town.

Take the kids playing basketball in the street behind her. Just like in Copper Corners, she'd had to drive slowly to give them time to get out of her way.

She pushed her bangs off her sweaty forehead and grabbed the sack of goodies from Cactus Confections she would give the leasing agent, Deirdre Davis, for agreeing to meet her on a Saturday. Cactus Confections, Copper Corners' claim to fame, made jelly, syrup and candy from prickly pear cactus fruit.

Deirdre should be inside, but just in case she hadn't picked up her voicemail with Heidi's arrival time, Heidi grabbed her cell phone from the outside pocket of her purse.

The purse was stuffed too tightly under the seat to re-move, so she left it, opting instead to free the ficus she'd nestled onto the passenger seat, its top branches bent against the ceiling. She would get the garage open so she could pull in and unload her belongings more efficiently.

She tucked the candy under one arm, braced the heavy pot against a hip and made her way up the sidewalk, her muscles protesting the strain. On the porch, she set down the ficus and examined it. A few top branches had snapped, but the greener twigs had sprung back just fine. She and her tree had survived the drive—a little ragged and bent, but recovering nicely and ready to settle into their new home. Sheesh. She was getting sentimental about a house-plant.

She tugged down the top Celia had embroidered as a go-ing-away present. It showed too much midriff and was too little-girl for Heidi's taste, with eyelet trim and ivy stitched in a pattern Celia had designed herself. Heidi had had to wear it out of town because Celia had insisted on waving her goodbye as she hit the road. The top symbolized the sweet innocence Heidi wanted to leave in the desert dust, but it had love in every stitch, so she wore it cheerfully.

Ready, she pushed the buzzer and waited for the door to her future to open, a big smile on her face, a bag of candy in her hand.

Nothing happened.

Maybe Deirdre hadn't arrived yet. She glanced behind her, but no car approached. Two young men stood across the street staring. They tore their gazes away fast, proba-bly embarrassed to be ogling the new neighbor. Something else that didn't change from village to metropolis.

She gave a little wave, then turned back to buzz again. This time she leaned on it for a long, noisy blast.

She was rewarded by the thud of heavy footsteps head-ing her way. Whew. She stepped back and smiled, candy sack at the ready.

"Just hold your water," someone mumbled. Some-one male.

The door opened and there stood a big guy who'd obviously been grumpy when he grabbed the knob, but softened when he saw her. *Well, well. What have we here?* She got a little thrill at the blatant male interest. That was something she wanted—to date a man whose social security number, work history and drinking habits her brothers didn't know.

This guy's handsome face was soft with sleep, his longish black hair stood out in all directions, and there were pillow creases on his broad, square cheeks. His coffee-colored eyes were foggy. He looked like a bear dragged early from hibernation. He wore a holey black tank top and gray jersey shorts over muscular thighs, the waistband sagging so low her breath caught.

A tingle of attraction interfered with her alarm. Why was this guy—this hot guy—sleeping in her town house at eleven in the morning?

"Yeah?" he said.

"I'm Heidi Fields. For Deirdre Davis. To get the key?"

"The key?" He scratched himself embarrassingly low.

Heidi averted her gaze. "The key to this place—3210 East Alexander? Right?" She feigned a confidence that was trickling away like water in a cupped hand. "I'm renting it?"

He blinked and ran broad fingers across his bristled jaw. "I live here."

"You what?"

"This is my place. I'm Jackson McCall."

McCall. Ah. The owner of the building, she knew. Tina had said he was a nice guy—reduced her rent for letting him keep some tools in the garage and he'd sent someone to evaluate the AC and furnace just for her peace of mind.

"I guess there's been a mistake." Heidi held her tone

steady, fighting panic. "Tina Thomas holds the lease, but when she left, Deirdre promised I could take over."

"There's your mistake. Believing Deirdre. Mine, too, since she walked off with three months of your friend's rent. I hope you didn't give her any deposits."

"Security and cleaning," she said miserably. "And first and last months' rent." She hadn't signed an agreement. Deirdre had been so *nice*. So informal. Just like people in Copper Corners.

"Bummer." The guy seemed to feel sorry for her.

Deirdre had taken her money? And now the town house owner had moved in? Ice water raced along her nerves, making her go cold even in the pounding heat.

"Don't feel too stupid," Jackson said. "I'm the one who hired her. She'd had some bad breaks in Vegas and needed money, so I took her word and gave her the job." He shrugged. "Come in." He backed up and motioned for her to enter.

What was she going to do now? Absently, she stepped over the threshold into the living room, where she was assailed by the scent of pizza-drenched cardboard, stale beer, dust and man. Jackson McCall had been here a while, evidently.

A visual sweep took in male debris—clothes, shoes, newspapers and fast-food remnants, a tangle of video game controllers, a huge TV and three shiny car engines on TV trays against one wall.

Weird, but not as weird as the rest of the place, where the motif seemed to be *breasts* and the nearly naked women they belonged to. The walls held a velvet rendering of a Marilyn Monroe *Playboy* shot and posters of women in bikinis. A standing lamp featured a plaster nude and the cocktail table was a piece of glass balanced on the bright pink nipples of a woman's chest.

Calm down, Heidi, she told herself. *You've seen boobs before.* But these weren't mere boobs. These were jugs, hooters, melons, racks. And the man who owned them was living in what was supposed to be her town house.

"Nice to meet you."

She started, then realized he was holding out his hand. She shoved the candy sack under her arm and extended her hand. "Yes. Sure. Nice to meet you." She was so shaken up that she didn't notice how warm and solid his grip was until he'd let go. "So, if you're not staying, can I rent from you?" she said in a flash of wild hope.

"Oh, I'm staying." His tone and the emotion in his dark eyes suggested that was a defeat. He shot her a sympathetic smile. "Sorry."

"But all that money I gave Deirdre… What am I going to do?" In the background, she heard a car roar to life, then squeal off. Someone was in a noisy hurry. She'd hoped for a quiet neighborhood.

But this was no longer her neighborhood, unless she got Jackson McCall to move out. And she had no money to rent another place. The job at Shear Ecstasy was part-time because of school and meant only to cover living expenses.

Meanwhile, everything she owned was parked at the curb of the place inhabited by a man with a breast fetish and a pile of old nachos molding on the arm of his sofa. She turned to glance out the door. Shouldn't she be able to see her car? Maybe she'd parked farther down….

"Deirdre and your money are long gone. If you want to call Apartment Hunters or something, help yourself." He gestured further inside. "I'll make some coffee."

"No, thank you. I'll just…I have to…figure out…this." She backed toward the door, not wanting Jackson to see her freak. Her joy had snapped like a dry ficus stem and her brain seemed about to explode. She still held Deirdre's candy. Deirdre, that duplicitous… The word *bitch* formed in her mind, but that was too vicious. *That dishonest person.*

On the porch, she grabbed her tree and staggered down the porch stairs.

"Sure you don't want coffee?" Jackson called to her from the doorway. "Hell, you deserve a beer. Apartment hunting is thirsty work."

She turned to him, considering the possibility of at least taking some coffee. Then she saw his face, soft with sympathy. He felt *sorry* for her. She seemed *pitiful*. That would never do. She was on her own, for better or worse, for richer, poorer and, it seemed, homelessness. She'd made it this far. She was not about to fold at the first crisis.

"Thanks anyway." She forced a smile she didn't feel, shifted the tree to her hip and turned on her earth-shoe heel, desperate to get inside her new car where she could panic for a few moments before she figured out what to do.

Except…where was her car? The street was bare of her shiny new Outback. In fact, the block that had been busy with ballplayers was now as eerily quiet as Home Depot on Super Bowl Sunday.

Heidi's stomach dropped like the first plunge on a roller coaster and her heart flew into her throat. She spun to check both directions. No glory of chrome and steel anywhere. It was gone. Into thin air.

"Oh, my God!"

"What's wrong?" Jackson took the stairs to the sidewalk, headed her way.

"My car's gone." Could it have possibly rolled downhill as she'd feared? She set down the heavy plant, dropped the candy sack and ran a few yards down the sidewalk, peering as hard as she could toward the far intersection, desperate for a glimpse of her vehicle.

Then she remembered something awful. *She'd left the keys in the ignition.* A common habit in tiny Copper Corners, where people often left even their houses unlocked. She'd planned to zip into the garage as soon as Deirdre let her in to unload.

If only Heidi could take back those two short minutes. Get a do-over. Grab her keys like the sensible person she was.

"What kind of car?" Jackson asked, dragging her back to the terrible present.

"Subaru Outback. Silver. New. With the keys inside," she added wretchedly. "How could a car get stolen in broad daylight in two minutes?"

"No place in the city is safe enough to dangle your keys in people's faces."

"I was going to pull right into the garage." With a jolt, she realized what else she'd left in the car. Her purse. Not only did the thieves have her new car and everything she owned, they also had her driver's license, her only credit card and, worst of all, the cashier's check for every cent she owned. Yeah, it was a big check, but she was careful. Cashier's checks were stolen everyday. The clerk had warned her....

Fresh icebergs broke off into her bloodstream.

She struggled against the numbing chill. She had to figure this out and fix it. Fast. "There were guys here...playing basketball." Her gaze shot to the hoop a half block down. "They must have seen what happened." She started across the street.

"Hang on." Jackson caught her arm. "I don't know those guys, but they have a lot of late-night visitors—in and out and I don't think they're selling baseball cards. We'll call the police."

"But I'm sure they saw. They watched me arrive. I waved at them even."

"They were probably casing your car. Come on. We'll call the police." He reminded her of her brothers, jumping in to take care of things for her.

She had to act for herself, so she took her phone from her pocket and pressed 9-1-1—her first-ever emergency call and due to her own stupidity.

Standing on the sidewalk in the pounding sun, under Jackson McCall's watchful eye, Heidi explained to the dispatcher what had happened, fighting the wobble in her voice. When she revealed that the car held her purse and her money, Jackson grimaced. He thought she was an idiot.

She *was* an idiot.

The dispatcher told her to wait where she was for the detectives to arrive. She clicked off the phone and slid it in her pocket, her chest tight and her brain racing. "I'm used to a small town," she explained to mitigate Jackson's impression of her. "I expected Deirdre to let me into the garage. It would have worked fine, except that Deirdre wasn't…and you were…and I was—never mind. I'm an idiot."

"Forget it. Come inside. You have calls to make."

She did. She had to cancel her credit card and find out if she could void that cashier's check. There was no point calling about car insurance. She'd bought only the required liability policy, fibbing to her brothers that she'd paid for comprehensive because she didn't want them paying her way. She planned to increase her policy when she could afford it.

That had been shortsighted, she saw now. But maybe she'd get back the car. Maybe it was all a misunderstanding.

She felt numb, stripped of everything, even her purpose in being here. She forced herself to move, but stumbled on her first step.

Jackson caught her, supporting her with a hand against her back. His fingers pressed into the bare skin exposed by Celia's top. She should stand on her own two feet, she knew, but she was freaked and her legs weren't working so well, so she let Jackson guide her with his big hand.

He picked up the sweets sack and extended it.

"For you," she said, trying to smile. "My thank-you gift. Prickly pear candy—my town's famous for it."

"Prickly pear and beer. Sounds like lunch. Come on and I'll serve it up." He seemed to be trying to cheer her.

She wanted to respond, but reentering the boob-adorned hovel that was supposed to have been her glorious new home made her heart sink like a stone into the neighbor's grass-flecked kiddie pool.

Jackson hefted her plant effortlessly and guided her inside, pulling out a kitchen chair for her. He stuck the tree in a corner and tossed the candy on the table.

Heidi sat, noticing the clock on the wall was part of a bar ad for a German beer. "If you've got the time," was written beneath a barmaid with, of course, huge boobs. Heidi had the time, all right. It was only eleven and she'd lost everything.

She noticed a lump under her butt and extracted a pair of plaid boxer briefs.

Jackson nonchalantly tossed them into the hall. Toward the hamper? She could only hope. The man must have stripped *in the kitchen*. Did he cook in the buff? Obviously he didn't clean—dressed or naked. The sink and counters were heaped with dirty dishes. Empty cans of ravioli and Hungry-Man soup, lids bent jauntily, kept company with empty TV dinner containers on every surface. If this was his diet, she hoped Jackson took a daily vitamin.

"Beer, soda or coffee?" He opened the fridge door. The pleasant smell of ripe fruit—peaches?—was quickly swamped by rotting greens. "Whew. Something died in here." He squatted, then lifted out a plastic sack of mossy lettuce. "Looks like a Chia Pet." He carried it by finger and thumb to the overflowing under-sink trash. Beer cans and paper plates slid to the floor. He swore and shoved the cupboard door shut on the mess.

"I've disrupted your morning," she said. "Please do what you'd normally do. I'll make the calls and wait."

"Normally, I'd be sleeping, but I'm up now. I'll make us both coffee. Just make yourself at home—" He stopped abruptly, realizing what he'd said.

She'd lost her home, too, along with her car, her clothes, her computer, hundreds of dollars in beauty supplies and equipment, and all her savings.

She swallowed hard and blinked back tears, tilting her head so they'd drain inward, but it was no use. They spilled over her lids. She swiped them off her cheeks and sucked in a breath that turned into a choked noise way too close to a sob. She jumped out of her chair, thinking to head to the living room to keep Jackson from seeing her dissolve completely.

But he caught her upper arms. "You get to cry, Heidi. You got the rug yanked out from under you. It's okay." He pulled her into his arms for a hug—the kind given to a sorrowing friend.

For just a heartbeat, she let herself enjoy the sensation

of his broad chest under her cheek, his bay rum and warm man smell, his fingers splayed across her shoulder blades.

But that only delayed the inevitable. She backed away fast. "It is a shock, that's for sure. But I'll figure out what to do and where to go…and everything." Her voice faded as the enormity of her problem sank in.

"You can stay here," he said with a shrug. "Until you figure it out."

She froze. Stay here? Her first reaction was relief. That had been the plan, right? This was supposed to be her place. But she couldn't impose on Jackson, no matter how sincere his offer. "Thanks, but I'll get a hotel or something."

"With what?" He looked at her doubtfully.

Good point. She had no money and no credit cards.

"Do you know anyone in Phoenix?"

"My new boss. I'm working at a hair salon. Just part-time, since I'm a student really. Going to ASU…" With no tuition money. And she didn't exactly want her first words to Blythe to be, "Can I sleep in one of your salon chairs?"

She could call her brothers. On her first day? Three hours after her escape? She didn't even have bus fare to get home, if she were willing to give up. Which she was *not*. She swallowed across a dry throat.

If she stayed with Jackson, did that make her weak or merely practical? She needed to know before she said yes.

The doorbell rang. "That's the police," she said, delaying her decision. "Maybe they found my car." She didn't need the doubt in Jackson's dark eyes to tell her she was dreaming. She needed something to cling to. Her new life had just taken off down the road without her.

2

JACKSON WATCHED HEIDI race toward the entry hall, around the corner from the living room, the tight bounce of her backside distracting him a bit. He heard the door open and her say, "Did you find my car?" with too much hope in her voice.

He didn't catch the mumbled response, but her "oh" was so dejected he felt it in his bones. Hell, the car was chopped or halfway to Mexico by now.

She could stay with him for a few days easy. Probably she had family who would come fetch her, poor thing. Though she'd jutted that pixie chin and blinked back tears so fiercely, he figured she'd take some convincing to call them.

She led the cops to the living room where he stood and she cleared the couch for them as though she already lived here. "Were you making coffee, Jackson?" she said. She had a husky voice like that woman on *Cheers*. Kirstie Alley, wasn't that her name? It sort of locked into him like invisible hooks on a cholla cactus spine.

"Right. Sure." He'd have to talk her into staying—for her own good. He sometimes let the girls from Moons live with him when they had troubles with boyfriends or landlords. *You always have to be the hero.* That's what his ex, Kelli, said about him. *Everybody's big brother, nobody's one and only.*

What was the point in fighting his nature? If someone needed help, he helped. Period.

These days, maybe, he was the last person who should offer though. His radio station—his dream—had gone belly-up after six months, taking everything he had, everything his parents had given him. He'd thrown it out as stupidly as Heidi leaving the keys in her car. Only he'd written *Take Me* in shoe polish on the windshield.

To cut his losses and keep expenses down, he'd sold his house in Scottsdale and moved into his rental town house—supposedly investment income. Yeah, right.

But he wouldn't think about that now. Now he'd brew some java for the sprite in the living room who was about to hear the cops weren't likely to recover a hubcap.

Leaning over the coffeemaker, he got a blast of scent from his shirt, where Heidi had pressed her face. Flowers and something tropical and it made him go soft inside. She'd sort of folded into him, then stiff-armed herself away—not offended by the hug. More as if she didn't dare let herself feel better.

He pinched up some fabric and took a big sniff. Mmm. Made him think of down pillows and that lip gloss girls wore in middle school, when the first wave of testosterone had knocked him to the sand. Those middle-school girls. Batting their lashes, pursing their lips, jiggling those curves—not fully aware of their power over him and the other hapless boys under their spell.

Heidi was hot that way. With big eyes that shimmered blue—like the metallic paint on the Corvette he'd rebuilt. She had some stare on her—innocent and all-knowing both.

At least Kelli wasn't around to give him grief about taking in another stray. She'd cut out right after the station folded and her departure hadn't hurt as much as it should have. He'd been kind of distant. Still was, he guessed. Gigi had stayed here for ten days and he'd turned her down flat. That wasn't like him.

But his neutrality would make Heidi feel safe, he hoped.

How could he get her to stick around? She'd hitchhike or sleep in the bus station before she'd take charity or money, he'd bet.

Listening to the coffee hiss into the pot, he watched a fly take a lazy header into a blob of ketchup on the counter. The place was a sty lately, true. Comfortable, but messy. The kind of messy women loved to straighten out....

So she could be, like, a housekeeper. He'd trade cleaning for rent. She'd go for that, he'd bet. She seemed to have a lot of energy. And a cute little jiggle. Mmm. He felt a strange zing. As if something in him was waking up.

She's your guest, man. Or soon would be. *Shut it down.*

When the coffee was ready, he loaded the pot and some mugs onto a pizza box and carried it all out to Heidi and the cops.

Heidi stood to help, but when she caught sight of the mugs, she sucked in a breath, then swooped them up, hiding them against her chest.

"What the...?" he said.

Keeping her back to the cops, she raised one mug—a gimmee from the opening of the Toy Box sex boutique, it showed a topless girl—and frowned before she bustled off.

Like the cops would care.

He made small talk with them while she rattled around in the kitchen, finally returning with two white mugs from Moons. If the cops recognized the bar name they'd think worse thoughts than over a couple of naked chests, but the slivered moon design looked innocent enough.

They all sat and drank, while the cops took down Heidi's statement, and Jackson wondered what kind of a roommate Heidi would be. If tits on cups freaked her out, she'd hate his decor. What if she was a neat freak? Was he ready to never find his stuff where he had put it? Prepared to have the newspaper tossed out before he read it? And no hot water whatsoever? What was it with women and baths, anyway?

At least Gigi had been a slob like him.

Maybe he could get one of the girls at Moons to let Heidi stay with her. Not the best influence, though, the girls. And Heidi struck him as a babe in the woods.

The detectives finished the interview and Jackson walked them to the door. He returned to find Heidi slumped on the couch, elbows on her knees, chin in her palms, looking as though she'd just been turned down by the last foster family in town.

"Maybe you'll get some stuff back," he said to cheer her.

"Maybe." She lifted the pizza box with the coffee crap and climbed to her feet, moving as if the weight of the world rested on her shoulders. "I'll clean this up, make a few calls and get going."

"Hold on a sec," he said to stop her. "Now that you mention cleaning…I was thinking maybe you'd help me out."

"Excuse me?"

"You can see I need a housekeeper."

She looked around the room and gave a droll smile. "You think?"

"So, how about I trade you a room for cleaning? Save me calling a service."

She seemed to doubt his intentions. "Thanks, anyway, Jackson. I'll ask my boss about…options." She snatched her lip between her teeth, looked toward the sofa.

He noticed a basket of nachos on the arm. They looked pretty gross—the cheese shriveled and an unnatural orange. "If you weren't here, I might actually eat those," he said.

She turned shocked eyes on him. "You wouldn't!"

"Take the job. Save a life."

She smiled, then studied him, scrunching up her short nose and the freckles like sprinkled cinnamon that decorated it. "What were you planning to pay?"

Hell, what was the going rate? "Twenty bucks an hour?" he threw out. "Thirty?"

She frowned, ferreting out ulterior motives. "Not more than twenty. Let's see…I was going to pay Tina three-fifty a month for the room. It would take maybe six hours to clean up the first time, three after that. At twenty an hour, that's…sheesh…not even close to rent." She looked suddenly ill.

"Don't sweat the money now. Get back on your feet and we'll work it out."

She sank back to the sofa in despair, jarring the nacho basket, which landed on her lap upside down.

"Damn!" She swept the chips back into the container, leaving a grease spot and a smear of hot sauce on her tan shorts, nicely tight across her thighs. She must work out.

She scrubbed at the spots. "These are the only clothes I own." Her husky voice cracked and wobbled with the motion and she was chewing her lip raw again.

"There are some clothes in the spare room." Gigi was careless about her clothes, as well as her men, her rent and her job. "They're yours."

She looked guilty and relieved—like a person who'd screwed up her courage to make her first sky dive, but gotten a bad-weather out and taken it.

"Come on," he said, holding out a hand. "It would have been your room anyway, if Deirdre hadn't screwed up." And he hadn't gone broke and had to move into his rental property.

She held his gaze, a million thoughts behind her eyes. Doubts, hope, worry, but mostly relief. Then she gave him her hand. The contact made them both go still. A surprising jolt skimmed through him. It had hit her, too, he guessed by the color in her face and the way she blinked her big eyes at him.

Then she collected herself, gripped more firmly and yanked herself up, as if he'd boosted her onto a high step, but now she was in charge. He'd felt the heat, though. It lingered like a whisper in his ear.

He led the way to the room and she padded behind. In the doorway, he waved her forward. She looked around, a little daunted. The room was pretty jammed. He'd kept some of the station's sound equipment and shoved it in here with his own amps, bass and keyboard. There were unpacked boxes from his house—albums, CDs, books, tools, car parts and miscellaneous junk he hadn't missed in the three weeks he'd been living here. Framed posters and photographs he hadn't yet hung rested against the walls.

Even the bed was piled high—blues records he'd been sorting for a set at the bar. Though he didn't have his father's talent, he had an ear and he used it however he could.

"Wow," she said, studying the wall of equipment and CDs. She turned to him. "You're a musician?"

"I fool around. Play a little. I DJ at the bar I manage sometimes." The customers came for the girls, not the music, but what the hell. He kept up with the local music scene, too. Followed new bands, hung out at recording studios, and played back-up bass or keyboard when he could.

"You manage a bar? How interesting."

"Sure." He started to tell her about Moons, then thought better of it. "Check out the clothes." He opened the closet and picked out the first dress—fake snakeskin, pretty much a shrink-wrap job that had barely covered Gigi's substantial rack. Heidi didn't have much up top, but the dress was tight, so she could keep it in place. He held it up to her. "This'll work."

She blushed and shook her head. "I don't think so."

"You'd look hot." Every woman wanted to hear that stuff. Truth was, the thought of her wiggling into it made his throat clog. He cleared it.

"Thanks, anyway." She put the hanger firmly back in place.

"There's other stuff." He shoved through the rack of slinky, slithery, see-through, mini, micro, strapless stuff that Gigi had looked natural in. Heidi would look as though she'd dressed as a hooker for Halloween. She was the gingham and rickrack type.

"Shoes, too," he said, looking down at the floor covered with feather scarves, running shoes and colorful high heels. Definitely Gigi. "This stuff belonged to a friend of mine. Any girl junk she left in the bathroom is yours, too."

"Thanks, but—"

"If you want cash for fresh stuff, I can give you some."

"Thanks, anyway. I'll make do."

He was probably lucky she'd turned him down. He had little to spare since he'd broken his dad's number two rule: *keep plenty between you and the wolves.* That came right after *look out for the ones you love.* Which his dad had done in spades. All the way through his death. Then Jackson had flushed it right down the rat hole of his dream.

He got that tight knot in his chest, as if someone was

punching his ribs from the inside out, but he ignored it, turning to watch Heidi prowl the room. She'd zeroed in on his breast alarm clock, a gag gift from the girls at Moons for his birthday. One nipple set the alarm. The other turned it off.

"That's a joke," he said, feeling like a kid whose mother had spotted a *Playboy* in his bathroom.

"So, you're a breast man?" The question was direct, as if she'd asked what position he played in football.

"Pretty much." Yeah, he liked breasts—the way they jiggled when women walked fast in heels, how they felt like flesh pillows in his hands when a woman hung over him in sex, the way the nipples knotted when he touched them. Breasts were miracles.

She crossed her arms tight and spun away from him.

Shit. She thought he didn't like hers. *Hold on, they're fine. And nice nipples, by the way*. Breasts didn't have to be big to be great. Too late to fix her reaction, though.

She bent over, looking so good that he looked away to be polite, and picked up the framed photo of his dad and the band in 1971, before they went to New York without him.

"This has to be a relative." She tapped his dad's picture and turned the time-bleached photo to him, her gaze digging at him. "Your father maybe?"

"Yeah. He played trumpet with Tito Real—the guy beside him. Tito was percussion." In fact, the poster at her feet was the band after they'd made it big. *Wish you were here, man,* Tito had signed it. He'd still wanted Jackson's father to join them. Jackson's mother had been pregnant with Jackson when opportunity knocked, and his father turned his back. *Family tops the charts, chico,* he used to say to Jackson whenever the subject came up.

When he was young, the words and the wink that went with them had warmed Jackson like a bonfire on a crisp night. *My soul is with you and Mommy.* That was his dad's message.

But as he got older, Jackson was bothered by all his dad had given up for the family. His dad had made a living as a mechanic, but poured his heart into weekend gigs with various bands. Jackson had felt his father's disappointment like a smoke wreath circling his head, making the man's eyes water with what might have been.

"Is your family nearby?" Heidi asked.

"My parents are…gone."

"Oh. I'm sorry." She didn't seem shocked and she didn't look away. Instead, she searched out his eyes, offering support.

Which made him want to explain. "Car crash two years ago. They were driving out here from Chicago and a snowstorm blew them into a barrier. It was quick. Over like that." He snapped his finger, the sound sharp and short.

"They were coming to see you?"

"Yeah." They'd poured all their love and all their hope over him, drenched him in it. And nagged and prodded him until it made him nuts. *How about settling down with a wife? What about our grandkids?* That pain in his chest started up again, so he turned away from Heidi's gaze. "I'll clear out this junk for you."

"All I need is the bed. And just for a couple of nights. I'll pay you with housekeeping, like you suggested, if that's okay."

"Fair enough," he said and gathered a stack of records, which he moved to the shelves. She took a pile, too, and they brushed arms in the narrow space between the bed and the shelves.

"Sorry," she said, her eyes slipping away. Definite heat, which made him uneasy because she was so…sweet. Not a virgin—there definitely was a knowing glint in her eye, plus no one this hot could reach midtwenties without getting laid—but close enough to innocence to make him queasy. Naive and wide-eyed and absolutely hands-off to a guy like him. He looked down at the cleared bed, fighting the fleeting picture of her tight body curled up under the spread.

She raised her eyes to his and caught his look. Her cheeks went pink and she grew flustered. "Anyway, thanks for letting me stay."

"My pleasure." *Don't say* pleasure *like that, you ass.*

Luckily, her cell phone tinkled, changing the subject. She scrounged around in a pocket for it and put it to her ear.

"Hello?" she said. After the caller spoke, her face tightened. "Oh, yes, I'm here and everything's great." Her voice cracked with tension. She glanced at him, asking for privacy, so he left the room but remained in the hall, shamelessly eavesdropping.

"Just getting situated… I'm excited. Sure… I'm tired, that's all. I start work on Monday…. Everything's great, Mike."

Everything's great? Why was she lying? Someone back home she wanted to not worry about her.

"Tina and I will have a great time. Tell Mark…. Yes, I heard every word. I can use MapQuest as well as the next person…. What?… No. I don't need money. I saved up what I need…. What?…Oh, I forgot about the self-help books. I promised them to Celia. She's going to loan them out to the customers…. Yeah, the time will fly. It'll be Thanksgiving before you know it…. Okay, maybe I'll come for Halloween."

He grinned. She'd lied about Tina, turned down money she needed and was fighting off a visit home. There was a story there.

"Sure. Great…I know you do…. I worry about you, too." She said the last as though she was teasing the caller, but her voice shook. "Gotta go," she said brightly. "Tina wants to…um…talk. Bye. Give my love to the Lesser Worrywart…. Bye…. Bye…. I'm fine. Really."

She whispered, "God," as if to herself, so he knew she'd hung up. He slipped down the hall, not wanting her to know he'd listened in. In the kitchen, he looked for something to bring her, settling for a glass of water and the candy sack.

He found her sitting on the floor, braced against the side of the bed, legs out, staring down at her cell phone.

When she noticed him, she quickly brushed at her cheeks. Shit, she'd been crying.

"So, who was that?" he asked, pretending he hadn't noticed the tears.

"My big brothers. Worrying about me, as usual."

He sat beside her, legs parallel, and thrust the open sack at her direction.

"Thanks." She smiled, pawed around inside the bag, tickling his palm through the plastic, then pulled out two red rectangles covered in sugar crystals. "The signature jellies. Try one."

He took one from her, the brush of her skin giving him a tiny shock, like the tart fruit at the back of his throat a second later. "Good," he said as he munched, placing the sack on the floor between them.

She stared at the jelly she'd bit into.

From here, he could easily catch her perfume, mixed with the light scent of clean sweat and whatever tropical stuff she used on her hair, which was straight and thick and brushed her neck, light brown with gold streaks. The freckles made her look youthful, but he figured she was twenty-five. At least five years younger than he was. Not that it mattered how old she was….

"You tell them what happened?" he asked her.

She turned, her hair swishing back, revealing her neck and the soft pulse at her throat. "Heck, no. They'd be doing the big-brothers-in-shining-armor bit. Our parents died when I was young, but my brothers think it's their duty to carry me around piggyback as long as they can."

"They're just looking out for you." He would do the same thing in their place.

"With handcuffs," she said.

"That's love."

"That's not trusting someone with her own life, her own decisions, and mistakes and—" She stopped, then forced a smile. "I bet if someone constantly told you what to do, you wouldn't put up with it for a minute."

"Depends on what she was wearing at the time." He waggled his brow, trying to cheer her up with humor.

"Oh. Right." She blushed, then laughed, a sexy sound in her rough Kirstie Alley voice. "What a mess I've made out of my great escape." She huffed air through her bangs, which flew every which way. "If I'd just grabbed my purse I'd at least still have tuition money. The check's been cashed. Washed and written over or forged. Happens all the time, the bank manager said." She swallowed hard and pulled her feet close to her body, bracing her forehead on her knees, wrapping her arms around her shins.

"So what are you studying?" he said to keep her from sinking too low.

She turned her face to rest her cheek on her knees. "Psychology."

That explained the steady stare—part curiosity, part support. Perfect for picking people's brains apart. He shifted slightly away. "You want to be a shrink?"

"It's not contagious." She smiled slightly. "Counseling scares you?"

"Who wants to be under a microscope?"

"You'd be surprised. I was sort of the amateur therapist for the town. People got a cut, a style and free advice at Celia's Cut 'n' Curl."

"So you worked over their hair and their lives. Sounds like pure hell."

"Lots of people value neutral help sorting out their troubles."

"I'd rather have bypass surgery." Kelli had always quoted Dr. Phil or Dr. Laura or the latest pop psych book she'd inhaled. *You're repressing, blocking, deflecting*. Hell, she'd made his quietness sound like a martial art. Now here he sat with *Dr. Heidi* in the making. His roommate. And she was looking him over again, trying to figure him out. Damn.

"So what's wrong with being a hairdresser?" he said to distract her.

"Nothing. I'll be doing hair part-time still. But if I want to be a therapist, I've got to do internships, get at least a master's degree." She lifted her head from her knees and looked at him more closely, eyes narrowed. Jeez, now she was reading his mind? He tried to clear any stray horny thoughts, just in case.

Then she reached for a strand of his hair and rubbed it between her finger and thumb. "You could use a hot oil treatment."

"A what?"

Her lips had wrapped around those words like they were pure sex. She seemed to realize it. And liked it, judging by the way her fingers slowed on his hair and her next words were soft and low and deliberate. "For your hair… It's dry…. The ends are…damaged. I'd be glad to…do it…for you."

A couple of words dropped out in his head until he heard *I'd be glad to do you*. A charge shot through him like touching a live battery cable. Innocence was sexy, he realized. A million schoolgirl strip routines couldn't be wrong.

"You have such nice texture." Now her voice was huskier. She was flirting with him. Damn.

He imagined her fingers on his scalp, the snip-snip of her scissors near his ear, the tickle of hair sliding down his neck. Maybe he'd have his shirt off and it would cascade across his chest to his thighs like the brush of eyelashes. He pictured her lifting his chin, turning it to the angle she wanted, maybe with a little yank. He'd be eye level with those gentle mounds of breasts with their berry nipples that had tightened against her snug top as they talked.

"Men neglect their hair because it doesn't seem masculine," she continued, blinking her big eyes, sending waves of lust through him. "You like engines, right? Think of your hair as an engine. You want it all shiny and tuned up, don't you?"

The woman was hitting on him. Great. Heidi was the kind of woman who saw sex as a first step to forever and the last thing he wanted after a hot night was to wake up to eyes like hers demanding wedding rings and babies and 401Ks. God, no.

"So, a hair tune-up, huh?" he said to joke her away. "I'll think about it."

She blinked. "Uh. Sure." He'd made her feel foolish. He'd like to tell her she was plenty sexy, but he couldn't figure out how to do so without screwing up the moment. He was off the hook. Leave it be.

"Well, I guess I'd better start earning my keep." She shook her head, her hair swishing back and forth, a thick curtain that would feel great against his...

"Huh?"

"I'm your housekeeper, remember?" She jumped to her feet so fast he missed the chance to help her up. "You just do what you'd normally do, Jackson, and I'll turn this place spic-and-span."

She bounced out the door, a perky little cheerleader, who bobbed through life on the balls of her feet, wagging her pom-poms in everyone's faces.

That could be exhausting. How long would she be here? A couple of days probably until she worked something out with her boss. He could handle that, right? Even with the attraction?

He tried to act normal, starting in on *Gran Turismo,* his favorite racing video game, but she kept zipping in front of him like some Tasmanian devil of a virgin French maid. Then she got out the vacuum—he didn't know he even had one—and the roar got on his nerves.

Not to mention the gasps of horror whenever she found any little distasteful thing. Pork rinds didn't get good until the third day out...moisture made them chewy.

He crashed his Mazda R-X 7 for the tenth time and looked at her. She'd bent to reach under the sofa, muscles rippling across the backs of her thighs and tightening that fresh peach of a backside. He forced his eyes back to the TV screen, feeling irritable.

"This will be perfect," she said.

Out of the corner of his eye he saw her stand with a wadded cloth. She trotted away, but when he heard spraying he looked over to see her smothering his favorite T-shirt with some dusting spray—where the hell did she find that junk?

"Hey, not that shirt," he said, jumping up and grabbing the jersey out of her hands.

"Sorry," she said. "It looked worn out."

"It's barely worn *in*." He whipped off his tank top and pulled it over his head to prove his point, uneasily aware that she'd stared while he stripped.

"See?" he said.

"It's full of holes and stained."

"It's fine. It's perfect." Except the junk she'd doused it in burned his nose, so he'd have to throw it in the hamper.

He hoped to hell Heidi's boss had a spare room. Something told him the woman could mess up lots more than his favorite T-shirt.

3

HEIDI GRABBED the dish soap from among the cleaning supplies left from Tina's regime and squirted pink liquid into the rushing hot water. It was all too surreal for words.

Two hours ago, her happy new life had peeled away from the curb and now she was cleaning a stranger's town house. A handsome stranger, whose bare pecs she'd admired and with whom she'd flirted by *fondling his hair*. She was losing her mind.

How else could she explain hitting on a guy in the middle of the ruin of her life? Had to be an escape from the tension. When Jackson had whipped off his tank top, she'd stared and blinked like a kid. *Oh, what gorgeous abs you have.* He was so big and so male. Almost scary. He could crush her in an instant, except for the gentleness in him. She trusted him implicitly.

She scrubbed ketchup off a plate—the man put the red stuff on everything, it seemed—then rinsed it, fighting off what was going on in her mind…the desire to have sex with Jackson McCall.

She grabbed another plate and scrubbed it hard, pushing down the thought. It bobbed back up. No wonder. Her secret personal goal was to have wild sex with a wild man. And Jackson would be perfect.

She grabbed a *really* dirty plate and dug at it with the

Brillo pad. Sex so far had been fast and fumbling and not all that satisfying. Jackson would be slow and skilled, she'd bet.

Scrub, scrub, scrub. He had hot, knowing eyes and a smart-ass grin that made her go tight in private places. Plus, he looked a little dangerous, so big and rugged, his jaw bristling with whiskers and masculinity. She could see him as a hardboiled detective in an old movie, unfiltered cigarette dangling from a lip, shoving up the edge of his fedora with a thumb to get a load of her.

So, why not have sex with him? Talk about making lemonade from the lemons of this catastrophe. She'd been hyperaware of him sitting beside her on the floor, feeding her a jelly. *How about some candy, little lady?* Actually, it had made her tooth zing. Getting that molar looked at had been one errand she'd neglected before she left Copper Corners. After the zing passed, though, the tart taste and sweet scent had added pleasurably to the spark and sizzle of being that close to Jackson.

And then she'd wrecked it. Blurted stuff about hot oil, dry hair and shiny engines.

And Jackson had treated it like a joke. As though she was just goofing around. Unfair. She could be as sexy as the next woman, couldn't she? Well, maybe not in her cute little embroidered top.

She wasn't getting anything right.

The only good news was that she'd stuck to her plan, not crumpled when Mike called. She hadn't cried or confessed or asked for help or even sympathy. And she wouldn't. Her pride was at stake. Her determination. And her future.

At least Black Saturday was nearly over. She'd get through Blue Sunday somehow—maybe the police would find her car, her purse or even her beautician's kit.

For now, she'd get a small advance from Jackson for basic needs. On Monday, she'd go to Shear Ecstasy and talk to Blythe and at least get more hours. Maybe Blythe had a spare bedroom she could stay in? She hated to ask—it made her seem flaky—but Blythe seemed like a person who rolled with the punches.

She could ask her brothers for money. Maybe tell them Tina had moved out and she needed more for rent. But then they would doubt her judgment. Plus, if she took their money, she'd have to listen to their advice, and she was done with that.

Somehow, she'd save enough for tuition. She'd miss the first semester, but that way she'd have a few months to get oriented and make friends without being buried in her studies.

That was a relief, actually. She'd been geared up for ASU, but a little worried about how hard the classes would be. She'd agonized over the catalog and course descriptions and Googled all the professors. The result of her careful preparation was that she was a bit intimidated. So an adjustment period was good—needed, in fact. She'd go with this plan for now.

Which started with earning her rent money by cleaning Jackson's place. She'd finished the main living areas, emptying five trash bags, dusting and vacuuming, and was closing in on the kitchen. The drawers had been easy. They were mostly empty, except for paper goods, a few mismatched pieces of flatware, can and beer openers, some tools—including an entire set of weirdly shaped wrenches—and some fancy knives.

The pantry was decently stocked—obviously Tina's doing, since Jackson seemed to be a fast-food guy, judging from the six thousand packets of soy, plum and taco sauce she'd found.

Fast food and easy sex, she'd bet. She'd ruined her chance at that by suggesting she tune up his hair. Oooh, baby, so *not* sexy. Even worse, she couldn't even do what she'd offered. She had no oil treatment, no shears, not even a comb to her name.

Though her lame attempt at flirtation was not the real problem. Jackson went for chesty women who wore clothes like the ones in the closet—things so tight and short they barely covered critical anatomy. Heidi was way too small-boobed and small-town for Jackson.

She'd be his housekeeper, not his love slave.

He seemed lonely to her, she thought, wiping something gross off the counter. At loose ends. He'd gone visibly still when he talked about his parents' death. She wondered if she could help him talk through that a little. If she tiptoed very, very carefully around his gruffness. *I'd rather have bypass surgery.*

She'd bet that was true. He could sure sound fierce, but his basic tenderness showed through. Or maybe she was seeing that because he had her urges in turmoil.

In the glass-fronted cupboards, she turned the naked-women mugs so the plain sides showed, then dried the mugs she'd given to the detectives. They were plain white except for "Moons" in black script below a line drawing of two slivered moons. Heck, if you squinted, they almost looked like a drawing of a naked backside. All the nudity around here had her seeing body parts everywhere.

Her own derrière was nice, she'd been told. She considered it her best feature and worked hard to keep it in shape—running for miles and doing hours of toning videos. Just her luck that Jackson was into breasts, not butts. So much for the wild sex part of her plan.

JACKSON WALKED OUT of the gym feeling cranky. Heidi had messed up the rhythm of his Saturday. Because the gym's weight circuit was crowded on the weekends, he usually only swam laps there and worked out at home. But with Heidi bustling around, distracting him, he had needed to get out of there. She'd completely blown his video-game Zen.

The delay at the gym made him late for the recording session he wanted to listen in on. There were two studio musicians who had a great sound he thought would go well with Heather Lane, a singer/keyboard player he'd been tracking. But they'd come and gone before he arrived.

Probably too much trouble to put them together, anyway. The fiasco with the radio station had taught him his lesson—stay clear of stuff he didn't know cold.

So he climbed into the Aston Martin to head for Moons, the bar he managed and his home away from home. With the ragtop off, the car was hot, even though he'd parked in the gym's shade. He headed to the bar on a slow cruise, the breeze in his wet hair cooling him down.

At Moons, he parked by the Dumpster to keep the car from getting scratched, tugged up the ragtop and put on the canvas cover. Old-man fussy, but this was the only car he'd hung onto when he sold everything to help fund the station. He was taking prime care of his last prize—his baby.

He headed to the back door, glancing up at the smaller version of the sign out front. He liked the logo—two quarter moons you had to squint at to notice they made the perfect curve of an ass. A classy hint at the titillation inside. Come to think of it, that perky little rump looked exactly like Heidi's…or as much as he could tell through her shorts.

He wondered what kind of underwear she had on. Some sweet flowered thing. Certainly not a thong. He was sick of thongs. And those crotchless things, too. If it was that easy to get to, what was the point in going after it? There was something really hot about daisies…. *Forget it, Bucko.*

Liquor deliveries came in the afternoon, so Taylor, his bar man, was already there and the door was unlocked. Jackson pushed inside, blinking at the blue-black light flashing off the mirrors and chrome poles, getting used to the dark. He'd convinced Duke Dunmore, the owner of the bar, to add sparkling drapes and soft, upholstered chairs, which Jackson had pushed away from the stage for a classier effect. The girls said it made them feel more professional.

Professional. He shook his head, amused. Stripping was a perfectly respectable way to make a living. It was an act. If a little wiggle-jiggle brightened the dreary lives of the slobs who came in here, where was the shame in that?

But the girls insisted he call them *exotic dancers,* not *strippers.* Well, la-de-da. Still he called them what they wanted to be called.

He would love to bring live music here, but it would be expensive. Music was only background to what the customers came to see. Jackson settled for taking over the DJ booth when the regular guys needed time off or when he was in the mood.

Nevada, one of the dancers, trotted his way. She was small with long, fake blond hair and a decent boob job. Some silicon sets looked like bowling balls about to burst their bags. Felt like it, too, and cool to the touch. He preferred a nice warm human handful himself.

His thoughts flipped back to Heidi. Her breasts were

high on her chest, her nipples perky, delicious pebbles against the tongue....

What the hell was wrong with him? He wasn't that hard up, barely cared that he hadn't gotten laid in months. Something about his new roommate....

"Glad you're here," Nevada said, wiping sweat from her face with a towel. "I need fresh tunes. Will you help me, Jax?"

He got that rush he always got when someone asked him about music. "Show me."

She headed to the main stage, where she launched into some spins, splits and a pole climb worthy of a trapeze artist. Nevada didn't settle for the usual tit-waggle, ass-thrust, and her pole routines were athletic. She'd been a gymnast and danced in New York, she'd told him once.

He half closed his eyes and did a mental music sort. Right away an instrumental jazz/salsa thing his father's band had recorded popped into his head. "Got it," he called to her and headed upstairs to the DJ booth where he kept a lot of his music. He put the record on the turntable. Nevada listened, head cocked, swayed to the music, frowning, testing the sound with her new moves. Soon she shot him a thumbs-up and went at it hard, into the sound. Great. A grin split his face. Couldn't help it.

Afterward, he met her downstairs at the bar, where Taylor had already set out two seltzers. Taylor was eerily silent for a bartender, but he had a telepathic sense for when to take an order and a solid work ethic. Bartenders could be squirrelly, with all that cash passing through their hands, but Taylor was rock solid. Jackson hired no one he didn't trust.

"So, what do you think of the new routine?" Nevada asked, sucking down her drink.

"What do you think I think? You're good."

"You say that to all the girls."

"Only when it's true."

She winked at him, stirring her drink with a straw. "If I didn't play for the other team, I might consider taking you for a test drive, Jackson."

"I'll hold that thought." He winked at her.

She shot him an open smile—rare for her. She'd had a raw deal in life and seemed half braced for blows all the time. Her girlfriend—also hot—tended bar at a lesbian club across town. They had a stormy relationship, he knew from talks like these. Nevada practiced more than the other dancers—always trying new bits—so they had these leisure hours to shoot the shit.

He leaned back, bracing his elbows on the bar and looked around. He liked Moons like this—quiet and dark, just stirring for the night to come, a few folks hanging out, setting up, throwing jokes and kicking around their news.

The door opened, sending a long triangle of sunlight into the place, burning his eyes like a vampire. He'd been living the nocturnal life of the bar for six months now and it felt right. He liked the dark. Everything looked better with the details blurred.

The door closed and he saw that Jasmine, another dancer, had entered, trailed by her eight-year-old daughter. "But I don't want to read," Sabrina whined. "I'm tired of reading." Transportation snafus sometimes meant Sabrina hung around the club for a while before it opened.

"Hi, Jax," Sabrina chirped, climbing onto the stool between him and Nevada, and giving him a smile bigger than her face. She had a little crush on him. He'd dated Jasmine for a while until they both lost interest, though Sabrina didn't know this.

"I thought you were going to day camp," he said.

"Cash flow." Sabrina sounded too adult for her years.

"Horseback riding lessons are pricey," Jasmine said, coming to stand behind them, beads and bells clinking in her gypsy skirt. Her dark, slanted eyes added to the effect, except she'd dyed her hair a fake blond.

"What can I do? I'm bored," Sabrina said to her mom. "Can I try on your costumes?"

"No way."

"Why not?" she said, halfheartedly, spinning the stool.

"Because they're itchy." The real reason, Jackson knew, was Jasmine didn't want Sabrina to have anything to do with dancing.

"I'll take her to the swim club," said a voice from behind them. It was Autumn, the third of Moons' best dancers. She wore her reddish-brown hair short and had great breasts, courtesy Mother Nature. "My cousin works there and at least she'll get some exercise. She needs it. It's summer." Autumn was the most practical of the three. And the most blunt. She harped on Jasmine's bad decisions about money and mothering, but she loved her like a sister, and Sabrina like a niece.

"How 'bout I teach you to play blackjack," Jackson said to Sabrina, wanting to nix the tension. Jasmine did the best she could and Autumn could be harsh.

"Cool." Sabrina stopped spinning and beamed up at him.

"My daughter is not learning how to gamble."

"We'll play for fun, won't we, Sabrina? No money involved." He leaned back to mutter to Jasmine, "Teaches her math. All the adding up to twenty-one, remember?"

"Oh, yeah. I guess so."

"Excellent idea," Autumn said, patting his cheek.

Now that he noticed, she was Heidi's height and build—well, not counting the jugs. "Listen, you got some clothes you could spare?"

"What for? You got secret habits, Jax?"

"It's not for me. I've got this situation at home. With a woman."

"A woman at home? Oooh," Jasmine said. "I thought Gigi went back to Ohio."

"She did. This woman, see…there was a misunderstanding about my place being for rent. She got her car and her money stolen right outside the door, so I'm letting her stay for a few days."

"Letting her or making her?" Autumn said.

"What's that supposed to mean?"

"Nothing," Autumn said. "Just that you tend to be kind of…"

"Smothering, Jax," Jasmine said. "You smother people. Like a big, hairy blanket."

Somebody had to steer the girls away from trouble. Jasmine, especially. Dancers made good money, and customers offered more for favors after hours. He wasn't about to let them ruin their lives without saying a word. "Well if it weren't for me, a certain dancer I know would have paid fines up the ying-yang for late taxes."

"I'm teasing, okay. Kind of."

"And you didn't bitch about the book work I got you," he said to Autumn. She was great with numbers and he'd asked her to double-check the bar receipts, as well as the monthly financials for Duke.

"Just keeping you humble," Autumn said. "So, what's this naked vagrant's name?"

"It's…Heidi. And she's not naked." Had he said that weird? "She's about your size, except not so much in here."

He held his hands out, shaping breasts. "Maybe some shorts, jeans, shirts and slacks—something she can wear to work. She's a hairdresser."

"A hairdresser, huh?" Autumn said. "Heidi the hot hairdresser. Sounds perfect for you."

"It's not like that." He felt himself redden.

"Then why are you acting all twitchy?" Autumn asked.

"I'm not."

"You do sound weird, Jax," Sabrina said mildly, not even looking up.

"You have a thing for her," Autumn declared.

"She's from a thumb-suck town, she doesn't know what she's doing here. She was supposed to go to college, but she lost her tuition money. She's just plain lost."

"Exactly," Autumn said. "And you have to save that poor lost girl from the big, bad…hmm…who is it you're saving her from again?"

"I'm just getting her some clothes, okay? Maybe some makeup? Any of you have any extra face goo?"

"Give me a few bucks and I'll buy it," Nevada said. "I've got to snag some major pancake for this razor rash on my thigh. I look like I've got leprosy."

"The best thing is to stay out of the spotlight," Autumn said. "If you work the far stage, the lights are newer and…"

He played a few rounds of blackjack with Sabrina, while the girls kicked around technical issues, then went to check with Taylor on inventory and got busy with his routine—verifying the dancers scheduled for the night, checking in with the DJ, the waitresses, testing the lights and sound equipment, inventorying supplies. All the little things that ensured a smooth night.

Jackson hadn't really wanted this job, but Duke had begged him. They went back for years and the man had loaned Jackson the money to start his auto shop, so he had to help out, as annoying as Duke could be.

Jackson took pride in having turned the place around. Receipts were modest, but steady, and he'd hired a good crew and set new rules. Everything decent and above-board. No skimming, no hint of drugs and pure respect for the dancers.

Duke seemed under assault these days. Family stuff, Jackson had gathered. His nephew Stan, whom Jackson disliked, shadowed Duke, showing far too much interest in the nightly receipts. The kid hung with some malevolent-looking guys, more than one of whom Jackson had eighty-sixed for getting grabby with the girls.

The night flew by, business was brisk and he even spun some tunes. Got some praise from a guy from L.A.—PR flak for a record studio—on the mix of retro punk that went well with the night's dancers and their routines.

At 2:00 a.m., he locked up and headed out. He loved the drive home. Top down, middle-of-the-night quiet, warm air wicking the sweat from his skin. This time of night, he owned the streets.

He reached his place and pulled into the garage, filled with that comfortable peace he always got. He would listen to some music, then hit the sack.

Except he had company. Heidi. Yeah. He got a charge of anticipation, which he squashed flat. She was off-limits. That annoyed him and made him tense. Dammit. He needed to unwind at home, not hold his breath and tiptoe around *not* thinking about cuddling up to all that sunshine and sweetness.

At least this was only a temporary interruption of his peaceful life. He grabbed the sack of clothes from Autumn and cosmetics from Nevada and headed for the door, braced for the smell of cleanser and lemon oil, since Heidi had been cleaning like a fiend.

Instead he got the sweet aroma of something baked—fruit and pastry. By the stove light Heidi had left on for him, he saw there was a pie on the counter. Cinnamon-streaked peaches oozed from holes in the center. She'd baked him a pie?

Eager saliva flooded his mouth and he felt ravenous, with that hand-rubbing delight he used to get sliding up to his mom's holiday table. He grabbed the pie knife she'd set out—he didn't know he had one of those—cut a piece and took a huge bite, not even sitting down. Sweet peaches exploded against his palate and the crust melted like butter. It was so good he had to shut his eyes.

When he opened them, he noticed how peaceful the kitchen was, clean and gleaming even in the dim stove light. The mugs in the glass-front cupboards were in straight rows and strangely blank. Ah. She'd turn the naked ladies to the back. He smiled. Heidi was a trip.

Then he noticed a note in swirling letters sitting on a folded pair of jeans—his favorites, he realized, getting closer—which had gone missing. He thought Gigi had taken them by mistake.

> Thanks for helping me out. I'll try to make your life easier…H

The pie and the jeans were a great start, for sure. He sighed and took another bite. A roommate who cleaned house and cooked wasn't half bad. So what if she vacuumed when he was battling for number one in the virtual Indy 500? Or made him want to jump her bones when she cleaned? She could take all the hot baths she wanted, for sure. He'd need plenty of cold showers anyway.

He wrote her a note back, thanking her for the pie. He peeled the stickers from the cosmetics, so she wouldn't know he'd bought them. He almost wanted to get up early enough to see her face when she saw it all. Too stupid. He put a spare house key on top of the note. She'd need that while she was here.

Finished, he headed down the hall, tiptoeing so as not to wake her. He paused outside her room.

What was she wearing? Was she naked? Wearing her daisy panties? He pictured her lying on her side, one leg bent, her cheek in the pillow, one perky nipple making a tiny dent in the sheet, ribs swelling and subsiding with her soft breaths.

He fought the urge to push open the door—already cracked a bit—just to peek, maybe find out if she smelled as sweet in sleep as she did awake, and backed away, toward his room.

And plowed straight into hard metal—his weight bench, he figured from the clanking. What the hell was it doing there?

"Ow. Damn. Shit." He rubbed the back of his head, then the back of his thighs, which had whacked the kick bar.

"Jackson?" Heidi's voice was husky with sleep and sharp with alarm. "Are you okay?" There she stood in her doorway, softly lit by his hula-girl nightlight wearing, of all things, his torn-up Hawaiian shirt.

He didn't know which was worse—the goose egg forming on the back of his skull or the hard-on in his jeans at the sight of her in that pinned-together old shirt sagging to the middle of her thigh. Just plain begging to be ripped off. All he could say was, "Great pie."

4

"I'M GLAD YOU LIKED IT," Heidi said, fuzzy-brained from being jolted awake by Jackson's crash into the weight bench and subsequent cursing. She'd barely drifted off. Even as exhausted as she was, tension about her plight made it tough to sleep. "I moved your bench because it fit better there. I guess I should have warned you in my note." She'd never imagined he'd *back* into the room or not turn on a light. "Are you hurt?"

"You're wearing my shirt." He swallowed visibly, still rubbing the back of his head, and blinked at her. Repeatedly.

"I hope it's not a favorite." She'd found it under the dresser, buttonless and streaked with washed-out grease, so she'd been positive he'd used it as a rag. She'd washed it, along with her only clothes, in the tiny washer-dryer combo unit, figuring it would do for pajamas.

"Used to be my lucky work shirt. I had a vintage car repair shop. It's just a sweat rag now." His voice was faint, his eyes transfixed. "On you it looks new."

She blushed to her toes, hoping he couldn't see how easily she'd reddened. The only light was from a nightlight in the hall featuring a topless native woman with a hibiscus in her hair.

Jackson perused her body, top to bottom, and back

again, lingering here and there—her toes, thighs, breasts, then settling on her mouth. Something very male showed in his eyes. Maybe she hadn't blown it completely with the hot-oil-shiny-engine remark. He sure wasn't joking now.

He smelled of bay rum and car leather and cigarettes, a combination that made her think of clinking ice in smoky liquor and dangerous promises made in dark bars. Excitement coursed through her. The narrow hall felt intimate and they were very alone.

"Sorry I woke you," he said.

"Sorry I hurt you."

"Mild concussion. Couple bruises." He shrugged, still looking transfixed.

"I wasn't really asleep."

"No? Worried?"

"A little, I guess."

"So how about a nightcap? Loosen the tension." He gestured for her to accompany him. "Come on."

Come on. He'd said that to her before, just being friendly, and she'd liked the way it made her feel as though she belonged. This time there was sexual interest in the words, and she felt a thrill. Maybe something could happen after all. Right now. Tonight.

She followed him down the hall, liking the way her smaller steps echoed his big thuds. In the kitchen, he grabbed highball glasses from the cupboard and went for ice.

She noticed a heap of cosmetics beside a stack of folded clothes on the table and a key on a note. "What's this?"

"Some extra stuff from girls at the club," he said, not looking at her.

She fingered the containers. "But this is all new. You bought it for me?"

"God, not me. I'm not that kind of guy. Nevada picked it out." He grinned, but he was glossing over his thoughtfulness. "Just drugstore stuff."

"That was very sweet." She picked up the key. "And this?"

He glanced her way. "For as long as you're here."

She liked having a place until she figured out what to do, even if it reflected poorly on her self-reliance.

"You need a ride to work?" He twisted the ice tray over the glasses, his forearm muscles twining nicely.

"A bus line goes right by the salon. The stop's just on Thomas."

"I've got two vehicles. You can borrow my van, no problem."

"I'll be fine." Jackson was a generous guy. Probably in bed, too. And sex was an important step in her journey. Lemonade from lemons, right?

She watched him slide the empty ice tray back and forth under the faucet, his muscles swelling and subsiding. She imagined those arms around her body, those blunt-tipped fingers on her skin. He shoved the refilled tray back into the freezer.

"Bar's in the living room." He tilted his head toward the pass-through, grabbed the glasses, and headed that way.

She followed him to the tiki bar, pulled out a bamboo stool, which turned out to be fragile and wobbly, creaking wildly as she situated herself on its scratchy surface.

Jackson set the glasses on the bar, then reached past her to turn on the hula-girl lamp, his finger brushing the bare plaster breasts ever so lightly, a move she felt along her spine. Soon it might be her he touched so lightly…or not so lightly. She shivered.

To distract herself, she took a prickly pear jelly out of

the snifter into which she'd emptied the Cactus Confections sack during her cleanup. Slowly, she munched the tangy treat. The golden light drenching the plaster hula girl made the bar an island of warmth in the intimate dark.

Jackson ducked behind the counter and rose with a bottle of Jack Daniel's. He twisted the lid with a fist and splashed their glasses, efficient as a bartender. He managed a bar, after all. She leaned her elbows on the glass surface, which made the hula girl bobble under her lamp shade. Her painted-on eyes seemed to wink at Heidi: *You go, haole girl.*

She intended to.

"Welcome to Tiki Town," Jackson said, handing her the drink. He gave the expanse of bamboo and glass a look of possessive satisfaction. "Bought it off a roadie for Jimmy Buffett who hauled it out from Florida."

"I'm honored to be here."

Jackson clicked his glass against hers, the sound sharp in the middle-of-the-night quiet. "You look right at home, dressed like that." He looked as if he wanted to swallow her whole. She wanted him, too. This felt like their own private club and it was very, very late. They surveyed each other, energy crackling like heat lightning.

"I feel like I've been shipwrecked on an island…and now it's just you and me…all alone." She spoke over the glass, which she held close to her lips. The smoky liquor made her nose and eyes sting. How could anybody drink something this poisonous on purpose? She preferred chocolate martinis or prickly pear margaritas, something that eased the bite with sweetness.

"Aloha," he said with a wink and took a quick swallow of the booze.

She did the same, and it burned like crazy. "Mmm," she said to cover her gasp.

He burst out with a belly laugh. "You hated that."

"It was…startling, that's all."

"You don't have to drink like me, Heidi. Go ahead, scrunch up your freckles. It's nasty stuff."

She wished he hadn't mentioned freckles. They made her seem young.

He rested his elbows on the bar, leaning close enough that she could see the crinkles around his eyes, the smooth planes of his face, golden brown whiskers just emerging from his jaw.

He grabbed a jelly and handed it to her. "Wash it down."

"I can take it. Really." She leveled her gaze at him.

He came to attention and let the jelly fall into the jar.

"One of my goals in moving here was to have new…experiences."

"Experiences?" His gaze drifted to her mouth and he unconsciously licked his lips.

"Yes. Like drinking whiskey in the middle of the night with a man I hardly know in a little private bar called Tiki Town."

"I see," he said softly, pulled into her energy, despite the resistance in his posture, the wariness of his shoulders.

"Drinking whiskey…and other new things." She leaned closer, making the bar jiggle and rattling the bottles behind the bamboo. The hula girl's hips swayed wildly. Heidi's stool squealed in agony, but if she shifted back she would seem to be withdrawing. And she was pushing onward. As far as she dared.

"What did you…have in mind?" he murmured, eyes gleaming.

"Exactly what you think." The husky quality of her voice made her sound more sure than she felt, and that was good. In this quiet moment at Jackson's bar, she wanted to be a woman who went for what she wanted. Without hesitation, without waiting for him to make the first move… Would he make the first move? Hell, didn't look like it.

So she grabbed the soft fabric of his T-shirt, tugged him closer and said, "This," before she closed her eyes and pressed her lips to his.

He froze. Shocked, no doubt. He tasted of liquor and toothpaste and his lips were strong, but soft. She pushed the tip of her tongue the tiniest way out, offering it.

He didn't move, didn't reach for her, didn't meet her tongue, but she felt him start to tremble. At least that. He was holding back, so she'd show him she meant business.

She tilted her head and kissed harder, pushing up from the stool so she stood on the rung, letting him know she wanted more.

Abruptly, her lips were ripped from his and her feet slammed to the floor. The stool rung had given out beneath her heel.

Jackson grabbed her upper arms to steady her. Her stool thudded to the carpet behind her. "Those chairs are kind of rickety."

So were her legs. And her ego. Her sexy move had practically become a pratfall.

"You don't want this," he said, low. His steady gaze still held heat and at least he wasn't laughing.

"Yes, I do."

"You've been drinking."

"One swallow."

"Your life's up in the air. You're confused."

"Not about my…um…needs." Flames of mortification washed over her. The hula girl, rocking wildly, now seemed to be jeering. *You screw up big-time, haole girl.*

"You don't want me," Jackson said.

Yes, I do. She opened her mouth to say that, except her gaze caught on the picture on the wall beside his head—Marilyn Monroe in velvet with full, lovely breasts. To her left, the hula dancer's endowments jiggled. To her right, a hugely be-knockered model in a bikini smiled from a sports-car hood. Jackson was a breast man. *She* wasn't want *he* wanted. The realization stung her cheeks the way the Jack Daniel's had her throat.

"But it is late," she said, pretending to sigh. "And I'm probably overtired."

"You've been through a lot."

"True." She bent to upright the stool, then took a backward step. "Thanks for the drink." She'd left the full glass on the bar. "Good night. Sorry about the head injury." She turned and moved off, just wanting away from her humiliation.

"Can I cut you a piece of pie?" Jackson called to her, trying to make up.

"No thanks," she called over her shoulder.

Hightailing it to her room, she flopped onto the bed, glowing in the dark, she'd bet, from the embarrassment. If only she could take back the last five minutes. She could still taste the sting of the liquor in her throat, feel the burn of Jackson's turndown on her cheeks. Restless, she glanced at the clock. In the middle of a pink breast, the LED display said 3:30. Breasts to the left of her, breasts to the right of her, breasts all around her. What was the deal with breasts? She felt the urge to throw the clock against the wall, but instead she shoved the thing under the bed so it couldn't mock her.

She would use her phone as her alarm. Speaking of which, she'd have to buy a charger if she wanted to keep phone service until she'd established an address with a land line. She'd need money to pay the bill, too. Despair threatened. She'd have to ask Jackson for a cash advance.

If she could even face the man after he'd rejected her. It didn't seem possible, but somehow she'd made things worse.

As SOON AS HEIDI left the room, Jackson sagged against the bar, making the thing rock like a shack in a hurricane. He felt as though he'd just survived one—or maybe an electrical storm and his hair was still standing on end. What a mouth she had. Soft and sweet and wholesome as the peach pie she'd made him. He'd wanted to sink into that kiss, savor those lips, drag her over the bar and into his arms for hours, for all night, for night after night.

Thank God for that Popsicle stick of a bar stool. Thank God for his ability to piss women off by saying the wrong thing at the worst time.

He'd hurt her feelings, but it was all to the good.

And tomorrow he'd steer way clear. Sleep in late and zip out early—play some basketball, visit Heather, his singer friend, maybe drop by Jasmine's for more blackjack with Sabrina. No way was he hanging around the house to be tempted by the mouth he'd just tasted—those lips, slippery and fleshy, had melded with his like a missing part of his face. He wished he'd cupped her cheek, checked out the rest of her skin, pulled her close enough to run his thumbs over those nipple buds.

Forget it. He'd done the right thing. She'd given up fast, gotten hurt in a flash. Which proved how vulnerable she was. And made him certain she'd turn sex into a big, friggin' deal. He was decent at the deed, judging from his partners' reactions. He paid attention, mainly, and he knew how to hold back. Ladies first and all that. But the women he slept with were in it for the sex. Period. Heidi's heart was as tender as her lips had been, he was sure. She'd want more. Much more.

He finished his drink and took hers into the kitchen to dump. Once there, he noticed that goofy tree she'd brought. It looked a little wilted, so he poured her JD into it. Was whiskey too harsh for the roots? He dumped some water in to flush away the liquor. That damn tree was the only thing the woman owned. The last thing he wanted to do was kill it.

SHE LOOKED LIKE A HOOKER, Heidi concluded, checking herself out in the bathroom mirror on Monday morning. She wore the closest to a normal outfit she could make from the clothes in the closet and the ones Jackson had brought her—a shimmering white, see-through blouse over a red, spaghetti-strapped tank top and a pair of zebra-stripped clam diggers that almost cut off her circulation. Everything else was cropped, skin-tight or ultrashort.

The earth shoes she'd worn to drive up here were too casual, so she'd chosen a pair of sky-high platform wedges in a tiger stripe from the closet.

At the best, she looked, well, festive.

She checked her watch. Just enough time to eat breakfast before catching the bus that would get her to the salon by nine.

She hadn't seen Jackson at all on Sunday. This relieved and mortified her. He was avoiding her. What did he think she was going to do? Force her tiny breasts into his hands?

After her Sunday morning shower, she'd walked to a nearby apartment complex to check out availability and price. By the time she'd returned, Jackson had gone, leav-

ing a steamed-up shower smelling of bay rum, a cereal
bowl in the sink, and some heavy metal playing on the stereo. He'd obviously been listening for her to go and leaped
into action.

So embarrassing. All because of the Tiki Town incident.
Now she felt like an unwelcome interloper.

Living here was strangely intimate, even with Jackson
gone all the time. It was like a relationship without the
closeness. Her bathroom served as the main bath, since the
pressure was low in the master bath, so Jackson's toilet-
ries were there and she'd had to use his comb, deodorant,
shaving cream and one of his disposable razors. It was all
so very personal.

Now she ate a bowl of Jackson's corn flakes, rinsed the
dish, then watered her ficus for luck. If things went well,
she would not only have more hours at the salon, but a pos-/
sible place to stay that got her out of the awkward position of being in Jackson's debt, inconveniencing him and
lusting after him all at the same time.

The beer-maid clock told her she had just enough time
to make it to the bus stop, so she tiptoed out, locked the
door and slipped Jackson's spare key into what passed
for a purse—a leopard-spotted nightclub clutch with a
rhinestone clasp. It held a pencil and a small tablet for
notes and her phone, along with twenty dollars, including change for the bus, which Jackson had thoughtfully
left for her last night. The only things that actually belonged to her were her cell phone, her watch, the small
gold hoops in her ears, and the bra and panties she'd arrived in.

From the porch, she surveyed the house where the guys
who'd stolen her car might live. She had the urge to march
over there, bang on the door and demand info, but that

wouldn't be wise. She would call the detective in charge of her case later today to see if he had any news.

Besides, maybe it was a good thing that she was nearly naked in her new world. This would be a test of her resolve to make it on her own in the city.

Throwing back her shoulders, she took a deep breath and started down the stairs, determined to make the best of the situation. This was an adventure, a new experience. Sure, the thrill she'd felt when she pulled up on Saturday was gone, but at least she'd gotten past the horror of running up and down the sidewalk looking for her stolen car. She set off at a strong march, but the stiltlike shoes turned it into a clump-clump. Oh, well. It was the thought that counted.

The first morning of the rest of her life looked to be a warm one. Already heat burned her scalp and blasted her from the sidewalk and it was barely eight o'clock. Still, with her hopes high, the sun felt warmly encouraging, not hotly brutal, and she clumped downhill to the bus stop and her second fresh start.

Three hours later, Heidi descended from the bus and limped toward the town house, painfully aware that the return trip was an uphill climb. She paused to remove the shoe with the worst blisters on her big toe and heel. Getting off the bus, she'd twisted an ankle, which hurt, too. Damn those platforms.

The sun that had seemed warmly hopeful at eight was cruelly hot at eleven. Not to mention the fact that munching a corn nut proffered by Blythe, she'd snapped off a piece of her tender molar and now every inhalation made it twinge. She'd have to get it looked at.

But pounding sun, stinging blisters, a throbbing ankle and aching tooth weren't the worst. Not even the fact that the detective had no news for her.

The worst thing was that she hadn't even been able to work. Construction on the rest of the Mirror, Mirror Beauty Center where Shear Ecstasy was located required they turn off the water. Blythe was only doing water-free emergency dos. Even worse than that, a slow start to the business meant Blythe didn't have much for her yet. Blythe had offered her shampoo work—once the plumbing was back—but if Heidi decided to go with a bigger salon, Blythe understood completely. *Ya gotta eat, hon. Do what ya gotta do.*

Heidi's pale-faced response had alarmed Blythe, so she'd forced her into a salon chair and demanded to know whether she was pregnant, sick, broke or terrified. Heidi told the car robbery story and Blythe offered her foldout couch. The woman was already hosting her nephew and his two kids, though. *We can squeeze you in,* she'd said, waving nails made fancy by Esmeralda the nail tech, whom Heidi hadn't yet met. *What's one more mug of jo in the a.m.?*

Then she'd offered the corn nuts and Heidi had broken a tooth.

She couldn't impose on the woman. She'd stay with Jackson until she figured something else out. And got another job. Maybe at a temp agency. Her typing was decent.

She was almost home when a whistle made her turn to see two guys in backward baseball caps leaning out the window of a car loaded with buddies. "Hey, baby, how much?" one said in a tone that teased, but also meant it.

Good Lord. She couldn't give it away to Jackson and these guys thought she was selling it? "Too much for you boys' allowance," she said and kept moving with as much dignity as she could manage clip-clopping from a platform to a bare foot in the grass beside the sidewalk. How did hookers parade their stuff without breaking a leg?

The frat boys zoomed off, thank God, since she didn't have another comeback in her.

It occurred to her that maybe she should give up and go home. Maybe this was the universe telling her she wasn't ready yet. She could save for another year. There was a flicker of relief in that. *See...? You gave it a go. It didn't work out.*

No way. She wasn't folding after only three days, a few blisters and a broken tooth. Jackson had offered her a base of operations. She'd hang onto that. She tightened her fingers around the shoe strap, adjusted the position of the tiger purse on her shoulder and climbed to the porch of her temporary home.

Inside, all was silent, so she knew Jackson was still sleeping. She peeled off the other shoe and flopped onto the couch. Discouragement swelled up like the flu, making her joints ache and her stomach roil. Everywhere she turned, the answer was sorry, nothing, not yet, try again. She couldn't even get laid, dammit, she remembered, picturing Jackson's big male body in the master bed. Did he sleep in the nude or in his underwear? Those plaid boxer briefs were hot....

Why was she thinking this now? Her life was in shambles.

Actually, it helped. That little jab of sexual adrenaline goaded her into action. She should stay busy. There was more cleaning to do, for sure. The floors in the kitchen and hallway needed scrubbing and that could be cathartic. After that, she would check the paper for jobs. When Jackson got up, she would ask to borrow his computer to put together a résumé. There. A plan.

She changed into a pair of Lycra shorts and a crop top donated by Jackson's friend, filled a bucket with soapy water and lemon cleaner and got busy in the kitchen with the sponge mop.

Man, it felt good to shove that mop across the floor. She pushed down hard, really getting into it, banging the baseboards, each stroke a blow against her bad luck. Tears came and she let them run, pretending it was just perspiration. She inhaled the warm lemon of the cleanser and told herself she was making lemonade, though things seemed too sour for all the sugar in the world.

Not long after that, she was scraping madly at the wax in the corners of the kitchen, when a voice spoke. "What the hell are you doing?"

She started and stared up at a sleepy-looking Jackson. "Did I wake you? Sorry." She thought the kitchen was far enough away that her noise wouldn't reach him. "These floors are filthy." She wiped her cheeks with the back of her forearm, so he'd think she was just sweating heavily, not crying her eyes out.

"I thought the rats were bowling in the walls." He scratched himself...there.

She darted her eyes away, feeling heat in her cheeks.

Out of the corner of her eye, she saw him stop scratching. "Sorry. Not used to company."

"It's your house." She sat with her back against the cupboards, legs outstretched on the damp floor.

He sat beside her, legs parallel to hers. She kind of liked that, as if it were the two of them against the world...or her latest crisis. "I thought you were doing hair today."

"Plumbing's out at the salon. And the job's...not enough." Her traitorous lip vibrated madly. "I need a second one."

"Bummer." He studied her with sympathy.

She hated that and looked straight ahead. "I'll check

the paper. Could I borrow your computer to put together a résumé?"

"Sure. If you want."

The idea of all that preparation and interviewing and hassle exhausted her. Plus, how would she juggle it with hair work? She looked at him and had a blindingly brilliant idea. "What about your bar? Could you use another waitress?"

"My bar? We're a little shorthanded, but…"

"I need something that doesn't interfere with the salon."

"It's not your kind of place, Heidi." He shook his head.

"What does that mean? What's my kind of place?"

He assessed her. "You'd be happier in a family restaurant. The guy who owns the bar knows people in the business. I can ask him."

"For God's sake, I've been in bars before. Cocktail waitresses make better money, for sure."

"But Moons is not the kind of place—it's mostly men."

"And men tip better."

"To certain people." His gaze darted to her breasts and back up.

So it was her bust line again. Her heart sank and then her blood boiled. "So, this is like a Hooters place? You have to be big chested to get a job?"

"It helps." His eyes were twinkling at her. He thought this was so funny. Oooh, that burned her.

"What counts is serving skills, not cup size." Her voice cracked with frustration. She was tired of nothing working out. "I'm good at math, I can keep an order in my head and I can handle a cash register—"

"Calm down, would you? I'm just telling you that you won't be comfortable at Moons. Moons is a men's club and—"

"And I'm telling you I want the job." She folded her arms under her breasts, instead of over them, as she wanted to, and shot him a determined look. Then she remembered her manners. She couldn't exactly force him to hire her. "You said you're shorthanded, Jackson, and I'm glad to help out. It would mean a lot to me. I won't let you down."

He just looked at her, his eyes twinkling as if he was busting to tell a joke. "If you're sure, but I'm telling you—"

"Just because I come from a small town doesn't mean I'm small-minded." Of course, the extent of her food-service experience was one summer at the gift shop at Cactus Confections, so there'd be a learning curve. "A bar is a bar and I need the money."

"Come in with me tonight and you'll see what I mean."

"Excellent," she said. Something about the look on Jackson's face made her wonder if she was making a mistake, but there was no stopping her now, inexperience and tiny boobs be damned.

5

"LET'S GO," Jackson called to Heidi that evening, rattling his keys in his pocket, smiling to himself. The woman obviously didn't know what a men's club was. He could have explained about the strippers, but he decided she'd just accuse him of trying to scare her away.

Maybe it would be good for her to realize she wasn't quite as worldly as she thought she was. She'd meet Duke, who was coming in early tonight, so the man could recommend her for a restaurant job. She'd be a great hostess. She was organized and energetic. And so damn cute. Once she caught onto the joke, Jackson would take her home and not even say *I told you so*.

Now she bounded out of her bedroom in the most godawful outfit he'd ever seen. Very Salvation Army. She'd borrowed some cash to pick up some work shoes and must have dredged the back racks of a used clothing place for the baggy white blouse, long, shapeless skirt and cloddish brown shoes. She looked like a fifties missionary lady.

"Interesting outfit," he said.

"I thought it looked professional." She smiled smugly at him.

"Sure." For a nun in street clothes. Besides, it was better for him when she hid her tight little figure. Every minute that passed with her in his house raised his stress. It bothered him to think of her sleeping in his Hawaiian shirt, the moon through the blinds lighting her hills and dips under the sheets. Worse, in this heat, she probably shoved off the sheet—maybe the shirt, too, leaving moonlight as her only cover. Moonlight and maybe those daisy-dotted panties he'd pictured. He thought about running his fingers over her sweet nipples, tasting her soft mouth, sliding his hands over the fabric where it passed between her legs, making her moan, making her wiggle.

Stop it.

"Let's go," he said and yanked open the door to the garage for her. She stopped and stared at the van. "Tasty Cakes?" She turned to him.

"The band needed money to cut a CD, so I bought their van." The name and three futuristic Amazons in skintight space suits were airbrushed on both side panels, which made the van a good promotion for the group, who had a nice garage salsa sound. "We're taking the other car." He led her to the Aston Martin.

"Oh, how cute," she said, walking all around it.

"Cute? An Aston Martin DB6 is a powerful piece of sixties automotive engineering. It is *not* cute."

"Reminds me of James Bond."

"He drove this in *Goldfinger*. Except hard top. And with various gadgets, of course."

"Oh. Wow." She ran her fingers along the rear fender and he felt it on his skin. She looked up at him. "This is your baby, isn't it?"

"Yeah. I sold all my cars but this one. Couldn't let her go."

"So, are the engines in the living room special, too?"

"I retooled them. Eventually, I'll get something going with cars again."

She was considering his face, picking apart his meaning, making him nervous, so he opened the door for her.

She lowered herself onto the seat, her baggy skirt billowing out, not showing an inch more of flesh, but his cock jumped up at the mere chance he might see a bit more thigh or, hell, a kneecap. Ridiculous.

He climbed in beside her, started the car and pulled out of the garage.

"This is fun," she said, as he backed into the street. "I've never been in a sports car before. Or a convertible."

"So, a new experience then?" He grinned, stupidly proud to give her this first, and roared off, pushing each gear until it complained to give her a thrill. He might not give her the sex she wanted, but he could give her a ride in his car.

Her big eyes went round as hubcaps and her smile went ear to ear. She laughed into the wind, leaning her head back, letting her hair fly every which way. She managed to look sexy even dressed like a prison matron.

Neither spoke for a bit and he was just getting into the companionable silence when she turned to him. "So what happened that made you sell your car business?"

He sighed. He might as well tell the story and get it over with. She was big on questions and she'd just pick at him until he spilled. "I sold the business to buy a radio station a year ago. Except it went belly-up after a few months."

"Oh." She was quiet, waiting for more.

"The price was right and I had…money." He didn't want to say *an inheritance*. "The music business is risky." He shrugged.

"Owning the station was a dream of yours?"

Was it so obvious? "I took a stupid chance."

"Lots of businesses fail, Jackson."

"I should have known better."

"What's better than trying for something you really wanted?"

"Money in the bank. Money in the bank is better."

She shrugged. "Being completely broke myself, I see your point, but still…money's value is in what it can provide."

"My dad always kept cash between him and the wolves. That was a big thing with him. He pounded that into my head."

"Your dad had a family, so security would be important. But you're young and single." She paused, letting her words sink in and when she spoke her voice was low and serious. "I'm sure your dad would have wanted you to go for your dream."

"Maybe." Nah. He'd wanted grandkids. So had his mother. *Where's my daughter-in-law?* she'd joke in her loving way. Over and over. So much that Jackson had told them he couldn't get away for Christmas that year.

That tight ache started up in his chest. Damn. Heidi, who'd leaned her head back to enjoy the ride, was casually digging at things he preferred not to think about. These heart-to-hearts of hers were brutal. He changed the subject. "So, what about *your* dream? Becoming a shrink. How'd that come to you?"

"I've always been interested in why people do what they do. At the salon, it was natural to talk about problems. I turned out to have a knack for it. Folks would show up at the parlor the day after a haircut claiming they needed shorter bangs just to talk to me." She sighed, tilted her head, lost in thought. "One guy I'd have had to shave bald to cut his hair any more." She chuckled wistfully.

"Sounds like you miss it."

"That's to be expected, isn't it? If you love something, you miss it. But I've moved on. I've got college ahead of me."

"You don't sound so sure."

"It's a little intimidating. The courses are tough. And psychology is competitive as a field. It's hard to establish yourself."

"If you were happy where you were, why push it?"

"Because I want more."

"College isn't the only place to learn. Life's the best teacher."

He felt her study him. "It's one teacher, true."

Hell, he'd sounded defensive. "Whatever floats your boat, I guess. I picked up what I needed to know about cars from working on them. With my dad at first. Then later just on my own. Same with music."

"So, you never considered college?" she asked.

"I'm not college material." He winked at her as he parked, then climbed out and went to open her door.

But she wouldn't let it go. "Sure you are. If you want that." She looked up at him, absolutely sure of what she'd said. She had great eyes. They made him want to say, "Whatever you say. Just keep staring at me like that."

"I'm doing what I want right now." For now anyway. He gave her his hand.

She allowed him to pull her to her feet, then let go right away—that I've-got-it-no-sweat act she put on. She looked up at the bar entrance, then the Moons logo. He tried not to grin at what she was about to discover. "So, this is it…? Moons." She smiled happily.

"Yep. This is it." He hoped she'd laugh when she figured out about the bar. He took the canvas cover out of the trunk and she helped him cover the car with it, looking damned sexy in that baggy blouse in the purple dusk. The movements made her breasts jiggle like a firm mousse. He didn't hold smallness against a good breast. No, sir.

He held open the Moons back door and Heidi entered, blinking against the sudden gloom. This early, there wouldn't be any dancers, except maybe Nevada, but soon enough Heidi would catch sight of someone topless and she'd want out of there.

He spotted Duke's nephew Stan talking to Taylor about something. What angle was he working? Most of the guy's friends used drugs, Jackson was sure, though never on the premises, and he'd bet a few were connected. He trusted Taylor to keep him apprised of anything amiss.

"Very flashy," Heidi said, surveying the space. "And you have entertainment?" She nodded at the main stage.

"Oh, yeah. Lots of that." He almost laughed.

"So many stages… And there's where you play music?" She pointed at the overhanging DJ booth to the left.

"That's the place," he said. Out of the corner of his eye he saw Nevada and another dancer step out of the dressing room and head to the main stage. They were deep in conversation, evidently about Nevada's costume, since they were both plucking at its edges. It consisted of two ribbons of black fabric that barely covered her nipples and a virtually invisible thong. Nevada pulled herself up the pole, head down, still talking to the other dancer. Then she reached behind her head to untie the strings of the top and bared her breasts, demonstrating the costume, no doubt, just as Heidi looked in her direction.

"Oh, my." Heidi turned startled eyes to him. "Those women are—"

"Strippers…right, though they prefer *exotic dancers*."

"Then this is a—"

"Men's club, like I said."

"But I thought you meant rowdy or seedy…or… I didn't…" She returned her stare to the stage. "Wow." She kept watching.

"I tried to tell you that you wouldn't like it, that it wasn't your kind of place…."

"That's a difficult move."

Nevada had pulled herself high on the pole, graceful as a circus star. "Yeah. Nevada's had gymnastics training."

"She's the one who bought my makeup, right? She's very skilled." Heidi hadn't taken her eyes off the stage. "The frills on that top don't fall right for the moves she's making."

He couldn't believe how casual she sounded. "Don't worry. I'll take you home in a bit. If we wait till Duke gets here, I can ask him about restaurants for you—"

"The waitresses don't have to dance, do they?" She was still watching Nevada.

"No, but—"

"And they get big tips?"

"When they look like that." He tilted his head in the direction of Rox, who passed by wearing a strapless black leather top and silver hot pants.

Heidi evaluated the passing woman, then turned to him, a determined glint in her eye. "But there's no required uniform?"

"No, but—"

"Then I'll take the job."

"Are you out of your mind?"

"Not at all. It'll be fun." She gave him one of her brilliant smiles, the most confident he'd seen so far. "I'll start tonight."

"Tonight?" he said faintly.

"I need the money, I'm dressed for it and I'm wearing sturdy shoes." She looked down at the brown blobs on her feet.

He opened his mouth to argue, to tell her she'd made her point, but he looked into those fierce blue eyes—so bright they made his own eyes sting—and decided he'd better shut up.

If Heidi thought cleavage didn't count, she didn't know much about men, but if she wanted to try a shift, he wouldn't be the one to say uncle. "Let's get the paperwork," he said on a sigh. His joke had backfired, but he found himself smiling.

Two hours later, Heidi climbed onto a stool at a high table in the break room at Moons, exhausted and sweaty and aching all over. The clothes she'd bought at Goodwill to make a point about modesty with Jackson were an unbreathable poly blend, so she'd sweated horribly and the skirt had no kick pleat, so it not only interfered with her stride, it chafed her knees with each step.

The cheap but sensible shoes were leather and easy on her arches, but they'd given her blisters on the tops of her toes and her heels. At least the sores were in different places than the ones caused by the wedgies.

She was grateful to Jackson for sending her on break. *It's a marathon, not a sprint,* he'd said, a warm hand to her back. He was constantly helping people, she noticed, and seemed to see everything at once. One second he was taking change to a waitress, the next, fetching paper goods for the bartender, supervising the DJ, settling a bar-tab dispute, joking with the customers, making sure the dancers made their cues.

She lifted her feet from the carpet, which was a bizarre

hodgepodge of squares in sixties designs—pink-and-or-ange stripes, lime-green shag, white daisies in AstroTurf—and planted her stinging heels on the stool beside her.

She'd asked for the job partly to show Jackson she was no wimp, but she could see she could make decent money if she built her stamina. And got better. She'd transposed one order, been late with three others and forgotten one, but the customers were so transfixed by the dancers on stage and the ones doing lap dances that they hardly noticed when their brandy and sodas came late. She'd get better and faster and smile harder and her tips would grow, without her having to show any more leg or breast.

Dying of thirst, she gulped the 7-Up she'd gotten from the bartender and tried not to stare at the two bare-breasted dancers standing a few feet away doing their hair in front of makeup mirrors. She hadn't met these two. Jackson had introduced her to three dancers he'd called "Moons' stars"—Nevada, who'd bought Heidi's makeup, Autumn, who'd given her the clothes, and Jasmine, a gypsy with hair she'd bleached a blond all wrong for her skin color. She'd liked all three right off.

The break room was inside the dancers' dressing area, so there was a Coke machine, a snack dispenser and a re-frigerator, along with two rows of lighted mirrors, one with sinks. The bathroom, or what passed for one, was around the corner. It was just three toilets with low tiled barriers between them.

The walls of the huge room were Pepto-Bismol pink and Day-Glo orange and the air was dense with the smell of hairspray, cosmetics and clashing perfumes. Overhead, speakers piped in the throbbing pulse of strip music from the lounge.

She sneaked a glance at the women at the mirror. Both

sets of breasts were huge and barely quivered when the women moved their arms to work on their hair. Had to be silicon. And they both had hair extensions badly in need of repair, cheap and snarled.

Rox, the waitress training her, whipped in then, climbed a ladder behind the two dancers, opened the cupboard and removed a clear plastic sack of bar towels, which she carried back out. The dressing room was a very busy, very confusing room. It was used for storage and janitorial supplies and men and women wandered in and out while the dancers changed clothes or walked around with no tops on. Very bizarre.

Jackson entered the room and she adjusted her posture to seem calm and energetic. It hurt to fake it, but she didn't want him to think she was in over her head. She had her pride. Lately, that seemed like all she had.

"So, how are you holding up?" he asked in a tone that suggested he expected her to be suffering.

"I'm getting the hang of it. Doing great," she said cheerfully.

The two dancers tied each other's tops and bobbled past them, nodding at her and shooting Jackson flirtatious smiles. He smiled back, but didn't even glance at their bodies. Amazing. He must be used to it.

He moved to sit beside her, so she took her foot off the stool, then winced in pain.

"Feet hurt?"

"Not really. Well…maybe a little."

He looked down at them. "Look at those shoes. Sturdy doesn't necessarily mean comfortable, you know. Give them here." He gestured for her to lift her feet.

"I'm fine. Really."

Jackson leaned down and popped off both shoes.

The relief was enormous. "Oh, wow," she breathed.

Then he lifted one foot to his lap, his palm warm as a hot pad on her sole, and examined it—top, sides and heel. "Major blisters. Let me grab bandages. Scoot out of your panty hose for me." He left the stool, then headed for the cupboards.

She became vividly aware they were alone in the room. Rather than run to the restroom alcove, she stood and reached under her skirt to wiggle out of her panty hose while Jackson had his back to her. The dancers would have made this into something erotic, but she was just shoving them off, keeping herself mostly covered.

When she looked up, Jackson was staring at her, mouth agape, first-aid kit in one hand. Caught, he jolted forward to his seat.

She felt a little twinge of triumph. Sexy didn't have to be graceful, she guessed. She balled up the stockings and sat on them.

Jackson opened the blue metal box and took out adhesive strips and an antiseptic gel. She expected him to hand her the stuff, but he picked up one foot and set it on his lap. It was nice the way he was taking care of her, this big bear of a man, so gentle and solicitous. He made her feel…safe. She didn't want to think too hard about how much that meant to her right now.

The air between them warmed with intimacy. With her leg high like this, cool air reached her panties. She felt…exposed. All Jackson had to do was duck his head and he'd be able to see the place between her legs. The thought made her damp and she wanted to squirm on the stool.

She noticed that her toes were incredibly close to Jackson's zipper. She could shift her foot just a little bit and touch him *there,* where he…*bulged?* As she watched, he swelled upward. Oh, wow. He was aroused.

She lifted her gaze from the sight and snagged his. He knew she knew. Her heart leaped in her throat and her blood surged through her in thick waves. She took a raspy breath.

Jackson cleared his throat and busied himself squeezing antiseptic gel onto his finger—was his hand shaking?—which he applied to her injured spots, his touch so careful she fairly melted.

He used his teeth to tear open a Band-Aid, holding her gaze. Could something happen? Chills raced along her nerves and she held her breath while he softly pressed each pad in place.

Finished, he lifted her foot. "Nice toes," he said, running a finger over their tops, studying them. "Round and even."

She shuddered at the sensation.

"Feel good?"

She could only nod.

"I bet your arches ache." He massaged her instep with both hands, using a firm stroke.

"Oh, God, that's soo-o-o good." She had to brace herself with two hands on the backless stool so she wouldn't fall off altogether.

"Sounds like it." He had to clear his throat again. He did a lot of that around her, as if he were clearing thoughts, too—intimate ones, she hoped. He curved her sole over his knuckles and tugged downward in a fabulously skilled way.

She fought the urge to moan—it sounded too much like sexual pleasure, which this almost was.

"I do this for the dancers once in a while," he said,

moving to the ligaments in her toes and the muscles at the ball of her foot, avoiding her blisters. "They wear monster heels."

"No wonder the girls like you so much." Of course, he probably slept with some of them. Why not her, too?

"Mmm," he said, rubbing the base of her heel. He moved to her ankle and slightly up her calf with a delicious twisting motion that turned her to taffy. He kept at it, squeezing the muscles with perfect strength so that she had to gasp and wiggle in her seat. A faint moan escaped, despite her efforts to hold it in.

At her knee, he hesitated. Would he go higher? She wanted him to. Desperately.

But he released her leg with an outblown breath and picked up her other foot, rubbing its surface with his hot palm, then running his thumbs across the tops of her insteps and along the ligaments between her toes. So lovely, so relaxing, *so arousing*. The looser her feet and calves got, the tighter her sex became.

She wanted him to keep at it, keep going, slide those fingers higher, until he was touching her *there*. She wanted him so bad she was feverish with it. Did he want her as much? There was the bulge to consider. She opened her eyes.

Jackson stopped rubbing and looked at her. Oh, yeah, he wanted her. Bad. She had to take action. Her heart battered her rib cage and she could hardly breathe, but she made herself move. She extended her toes and deliberately rubbed the ball of her foot across Jackson's zipper and the solid length of him, warm under her foot.

He made a sound, his body quaked and his eyes drifted closed. When he opened them, pure fire blazed there. Pure fire and helpless desire.

JACKSON COULDN'T BELIEVE what his sweet houseguest was doing with her toes. Or that he was allowing it. And he had no intention of stopping her, either.

He'd had women caress his joint with incredible skill, but the barest brush of Heidi's foot over his zipper had blind lust pounding through him like never before. She sat there, dressed like a bag lady, arousing more than a lap dance from the hottest dancer.

God, he wanted her. He wanted to do what her eyes were asking him to do—slide higher up her leg, shove under her skirt and touch her. She breathed roughly and fingers of blush surged up her cheeks the way blood filled his parts. He knew his reaction was as plain on his face as it was under her foot.

He imagined touching her under those sensible panties, making her squeal and rock against his finger until she came.

But he couldn't do it. No matter how hot and hungry and desperate she made him. She would want more than he had in him.

Two dancers entered the dressing room, laughing together, granting him the perfect out. "Company," he said, nodding at the women, then regretfully moved her foot off his lap and to the floor. "Back to work, huh?"

"Right. Back to work." She flushed with surprise, uneasy about what had just happened, he could tell. She really was out of her depth. More proof he shouldn't let things get out of hand.

"Better soak your feet when we get home," he said. "There are salts in the bathroom."

"Salts, sure… Jackson…I…"

"Let's just move on." He smiled a reassuring smile.

Without her foot in his palm, his hand felt empty. He'd liked the weight of it there, the heft of her leg, being connected to her that way. He almost wished he had a foot fetish. Anything but what he was feeling—fresh, clean desire. Something he hadn't felt in a long, long time.

Heidi picked up the glass in front of her, the bubbles clear and round as tiny marbles, and drank, exposing her pretty throat to him. Abruptly, she set down the drink, winced and grabbed her jaw.

"What's the matter?"

"I broke a tooth this morning."

"Sounds like you need my dentist."

"I can't afford dental work right now."

"Dr. Dave takes payments. He's a friend of mine. Teeth troubles only get worse." He was always hounding the girls to get in. Some of them would happily plunk down thousands for bonding and bleaching, but ignored toothaches and bleeding gums. "The number's at home. In the meantime—" he fished a packet of Tylenol from the first-aid kit and handed it to her "—take these for the pain."

She swallowed the pills, licking moisture from her lips in a way that had him limping out of the break room as though he was the one with the blisters.

He kept an eye on her the rest of the night. She made up for her inexperience with effort, he noticed, whipping from table to table, zipping around the lap dances, as if the dancer sliding her body against the seated man—hands glued to the chair arms, since the customers weren't allowed to touch the dancers—was merely chatting about the weather. Ignoring the erotic action all around her, she slapped down cocktail napkins, took orders with a big smile and dashed off sporting her baggy costume.

He could tell she was worn out, but whenever she

caught him looking at her, she beamed, hiding it. She was…spunky. And determined. She made him smile. Perked him up. He'd thought all that energy and motion would annoy him. Instead, it made his blood kick up. He'd been sluggish, he realized, out of it. Asleep at the wheel of his life.

He could still feel her heel in his palm, her toes on his cock, and hear her moan in his head.

After the bar closed, he went about his end-of-night tasks, looking over the receipts, talking through the liquor orders, checking the dancers' schedule for the coming nights, and when he finished, he found Heidi asleep, curled in a ball in one of the round upholstered chairs. Her shoes were off and that god-awful skirt had slid high on her thigh. She looked like a child who'd collapsed with exhaustion trying to stay up past her bedtime.

He squatted so he was at eye level with her. "Heidi?"

She opened her eyes, blinked in confusion, then rubbed her face with both hands. "I dozed off. Sorry." She pushed to a sit and put her feet on the floor.

"No wonder. It's the middle of the night. I'm ready to go."

She nodded, picked up her little purse, slipped on her shoes with a grimace and pushed to her feet, ignoring his proffered hand. She started off at a quick march that instantly collapsed into a limp.

"Here." He extended an arm as if to put it around her, but she smiled foggily. "I've got it. I'll just…" She braced herself against him and peeled off her shoes with another wince. "Much better." She strode forward on feet that were bare except for a few flapping Band-Aids. She seemed determined not to show any distress. Why did she insist on making it so tough on herself?

He sighed and caught up with her. At the car, he lifted the cover on her side and opened her door.

She dropped into the seat and leaned her head back. As he rolled up the cover, he watched her. She was wiped out. She wasn't cut out for Moons. She needed an office job. Something that used her brain, not her feet.

He climbed into the car, planning to mention that she'd make more money at a temp job, so she wouldn't feel like she'd failed, when she turned to him and said brightly, "That was fun."

"Fun?"

She blinked her big eyes at him. "Intimidating at first, of course. I mean the air is heavy with sex. Women walking around bare-breasted and the lap dances are overwhelming."

"I guess." For him, the nudity was just part of the scenery. Not even particularly sexy anymore. Kind of like working in an ice-cream store. Soon enough, you had your fill of every flavor.

"And all those turned-on men," she continued. "I kept my eyes away from their laps, I'll tell you." She laughed and even in the dark, he could see she'd turned red.

"Very sensible of you." He smiled, happy to have her in his car, he realized. Happy to listen to her chatter, which she continued to do.

"Of course, with me so new, it helped that the customers were distracted. I gave a guy who'd ordered scotch-rocks a gin-tonic and he sucked the whole thing down without noticing."

"That happens."

"I figured out the secret to handling it, though. I just focused on the people—the lonely men behind the rapt stares, the struggling women behind the G-strings. Jasmine has a daughter, did you know that?"

"Huh? Yeah. Sabrina's cool."

"She seems to be a stabilizing influence. She gives Jasmine a future focus."

"A future focus?"

"Yes. This lifestyle seems to go with a lack of impulse control, an inability to delay gratification. Of course, there were probably traumatic issues during childhood and adolescence that contributed to the mindset—"

"Hold up on the Freud. It's way too late at night."

"Sorry. I guess I'm just wired. Figuring this all out." Her husky voice squeaked from exhaustion. She was amped on leftover adrenaline. He recognized it from how he felt after spinning a great set of music.

"I really liked Autumn," she said more slowly. "I was adding a tab and she did it in her head like that." She snapped her fingers. "Of course, she rolled her eyes at me for being so pokey."

"Autumn's all attitude, but she's solid. I've got her doing some bookkeeping for me."

"That's smart of you. Did you know Nevada tried out for the U.S. Olympic team? And that she danced in New York?"

"She told me something about that."

"I wonder what went so wrong that she ended up here."

"She makes good money dancing," he said, bristling on Nevada's behalf. "There's nothing wrong with stripping."

"She had different goals, Jackson. That's obvious."

He didn't like the judgment in her tone. "Things don't always work out. You move on, play the cards you're dealt, hit or stick, bust or jackpot."

She was silent, considering his words. "Maybe, but I believe there are patterns in our lives and the stories we tell ourselves about our own limits. If we understand why we made negative or limiting choices, we can shift our thinking to make better ones—be more deliberate about the direction we take with our lives, instead of passively reacting to what happens to us."

"I hope you don't plan to say that shit to the girls. They get testy when I call them strippers, so don't go poking around in their childhoods or they'll turn you into one big paper cut."

She laughed lightly and the sound filled his head. "I'm just thinking out loud, Jackson. Just talking. People usually ask for my advice. I don't force it on them." The moonlight shone in her eyes and gleamed on her cheeks.

"Good, because I have enough on my hands just keeping things running smoothly without the girls getting cranky on me."

"There is one thing I have to insist on fixing, though."

"What?" Here it came. He should have known she'd be trouble.

"Their hair. I've never seen so much damage in one place in my life. Overtreated, bad extensions, wrong styles, terrible weaves. What do you think about my offering a discount at my salon for all Moons employees?"

That wasn't so bad. "They spend *beaucoup* on their hair. If you save them money they'll love that."

"Great." She sat back with a satisfied sigh. He noticed he was pulling into the driveway without having had his usual late-night contemplation. Hmm. He pushed the garage door button and it ground upward.

"Wait a sec," Heidi said, touching his arm. "It's so pretty. Look at the moon." She tilted up her head and he looked up, too. It was almost full, and big and bright as a spotlight shining down on them. He noticed the neighbors' head-banger music was at a lower volume than usual, and the summer air was soft against his skin.

Heidi dropped her gaze from the sky and looked straight at him. "Thank you for the job, Jackson. I think I'll like it a lot. And I have another favor to ask."

"Sure," he said, groaning inside, knowing that at this moment, he'd do anything she asked, no matter the consequences. Kiss her, make love to her, take her to Disneyland.

"Can I stay here for a while? Just until I save up enough to rent another place? A month or two?"

Elation and dread crashed head-on in him. Right now, he could barely fight the urge to kiss her and if she kept blinking those big eyes at him in the moonlight, he just might do it. In two months, he could be insane from fighting his urges. But part of him was glad she was around. She woke up something in him that had been asleep a long time. "Stay as long as you like," he said. Of course.

"Thanks, Jackson." She was honing in on him, testing his sincerity, so he looked straight ahead at the open garage, where he should pull in, but he liked how the night had settled around them, comfortable and close. And he liked how she smelled. After the night's work, her skin had a glow to it and her own scent, sweet and human, swirled in the open car like an eddy of smoke from a campfire.

"It's nice how you look out for the women at the bar," she said.

"Someone has to help them."

"Don't be smug about it, please. I'm just starting to like you." Now her eyes twinkled with humor. He realized from the moment he'd met her, she'd been off-balance. Her normal self was certain and quick-witted and challenging.

"Deal," he said, adding, "I like you, too."

Her gaze shifted at his words, became deeper, sharper, hotter. "But not that way?"

He felt his jaw go slack. How could she not know? She'd had her foot on the evidence. But that wasn't enough for her, he knew. He'd turned her down twice and she doubted her own appeal. He could fix that with one kiss. Just a taste. Something more complete than that creaky contact over Tiki Town. She looked puzzled and uncertain and he could make it all go away.

A feeling swept over him, an eager hunger that made him feel surprisingly alive, and he just let it win. He pulled her into his arms and kissed her.

She moaned and wrapped herself into him, kissing back eagerly, pushing her tongue at him, which he happily took, giving her his.

Slow down, keep it short, just enough to reassure her, he kept telling himself, while he let the kiss go on and on and on. His hands itched to cup her breasts, which she was pushing at him, to reach for her ass, wiggling on the seat, to pull her onto his lap, to touch her in secret places.

She made a needy sound that threatened to push him over the edge. If they kept this up, he'd start ripping off the buttons on this goofy blouse she wore—and they were sitting in the driveway, not even in the house, the distant sound of the neighbor's music throbbing like his lust, traffic from Thomas Road a white-noise roar that made this seem like a hot dream.

Catching the tail end of his good sense before it slipped away, he pushed off her mouth and held her away by the upper arms. "That's enough."

"Not even close." Her voice trembled like her body was doing.

"It's late. We're both tired."

"I'm wide awake. And so are you."

"You need to—"

"I need to get laid!" Her eyes went wide. "I can't believe I said that." She put three fingers to her lips.

He chuckled. "Me, either." Her urgency got to him, though, made him feel…fully alive. "It's been a long day for you and a longer night. You need your sleep."

He leaned forward and pressed his lips to her forehead. It was cheating, he knew, but he wanted to touch her skin, breathe in her smell, let her hair brush his cheek, memorize her like a kid under his first female trance.

Damn, it was hard to do the right thing.

He sighed, and drove into the garage.

6

NUMB WITH SHOCK and disappointment, Heidi watched the back of the garage approach as Jackson pulled the car in. She couldn't believe it. The man who had taken her mouth in a way that had her practically passing out with lust had just kissed her on the forehead. *There. That ought to hold you.*

Part of her was pissed. The rest was alive with frustrated desire. Even the spot on her forehead where he'd touched his lips seemed to throb the way her sex was.

She'd acted too desperate and scared him off. Why couldn't she be cool and sophisticated like the woman of the world she fully intended to be? If she could just get laid, dammit, she'd be so much more *relaxed* about it all.

Jackson parked and came around to open her door and offer her a hand up. She took it automatically, but their gazes caught and held. Jackson wasn't as easy-breezy about that kiss as he'd seemed. He looked...dazed.

As soon as she got to her feet, he released her hand and rubbed his palm down the side of his jeans, as if she'd scalded him. "Don't think I don't want to take this further," he said, his dark eyes glittering almost gold with tamped-down heat. "It's just... Hell, we live together and now we work together and..." He let the words drop like a stone in a deep well between them.

She opened her mouth to say something, but her throat was tight and dry and she didn't want to blurt anything needy.

When they broke eye contact, it felt like two magnets being ripped apart and Heidi wobbled in the wave of it, glad Jackson had turned for the door by then. He held it for her and she walked through on legs wooden as bowling pins. She felt his eyes burning into her back, wanting her, but holding back.

In a few minutes, she lay in bed with her heart pounding, hoping that Jackson would appear in her doorway. Instead, she heard mournful jazz coming from his room, then a keyboard, which she knew was him playing along. She thought of those fingers and how they might move on her body….

Oh, she had a keyboard he could play….

She closed her eyes and cupped her hand over herself, imagining Jackson in her doorway, silhouetted by the light from the hula-girl nightlight, his strong hands braced in the doorway, hair tousled, saying her name as if he couldn't help himself. *Heidi, I must have you. I've never wanted a small-breasted woman before, but I want you like life itself.*

It was her fantasy, dammit. And it worked better than the tasteful erotic literature she employed from time to time when her frustration grew intense.

She would try again with Jackson. Figure out the right time and place. Not act desperate, for God's sake. He thought they couldn't sleep together if they were living and working together. Sure they could. If he didn't have a problem with it, neither did she. She was on a quest to try new things, dammit, and sex with Jackson fit the bill exactly. He was just dangerous-looking enough to be thrilling, yet gentle and protective enough to be safe. Just about perfect, dammit. Now all she had to do was convince him.

TWO DAYS LATER, Heidi wiped a trickle of drool off her numb chin and blinked against the sunlight in Dr. Dave's parking lot. The past ninety minutes had fixed her tooth, but destroyed her credit. Not really. His receptionist, Rochelle, had expressed sympathy over her financial plight and promised an easy payment plan. Still, Heidi was in the hole.

Speaking of which…she ran her tongue across the gap where her wisdom tooth used to live. Dr. Dave had declared it impacted, so while he was fixing her broken molar—which had required a root canal and would need a crown—he'd yanked that, too. Efficient, but more money. She would be paying off this dental adventure until she retired.

Dr. Dave saw lots of Jackson's girls, it turned out. In fact, he'd asked Heidi if she were a dancer. She'd blushed purple and rattled on about how working at Moons was a great way to study people and prepare her for becoming a therapist—then she'd noticed Dr. Dave and his assistant were politely poised with water squirter, suction and drill, waiting for her to stop babbling so they could get back to work. The mask, safety glasses and elaborate magnifying lenses didn't hide Dr. Dave's amusement. Maybe the laughing gas had made her chatty.

Now she patted her puffy jaw to make sure it was still there, then climbed into the van that Jackson had let her borrow. He'd been excessively polite and virtually absent since their kiss in the driveway. The morning after, she'd found Dr. Dave's refrigerator magnet in front of a fresh pot of coffee, and the bathroom steamy from Jackson's recent departure. He'd been gone this morning when she got up, too. Noon was his usual wake-up time, so she knew he was avoiding her.

She drove toward home. A honk made her turn. Two young guys shot her a cheerful hand gesture—bent-down fingers and a chest pat—heads bobbing with approval. Of the band painted on the van, not her, she knew. She was too old for the guys. She was making all kinds of wrong impressions on people—dressing like a hooker, driving a band van like a teen groupie. What the hell. She was trying on new lives right and left. She shot the kids a big grin she could tell was lopsided because of her numb jaw.

A spurt of excessive cheerfulness told her the sample pain meds Dr. Dave had given her had kicked in. She had already downed the two tablets at the water fountain outside his office when she noticed the instructions said *one* pill every four hours. So she'd feel extra cheerful for a bit. Especially because she hadn't eaten before the procedure.

When she got home, she thought she detected Jackson's bay rum scent in the air and her heart spun up like a hard drive reading a CD, but she soon discovered he'd come and gone, leaving her a note.

Gone to the grocery store with The List. Practically need the van to hold it all. J.

She'd meant to pick the things up herself, using the money she'd made last night. She wanted to contribute to the pantry, since this was her home for a few weeks. It was nice of him to shop for her, though. Complaining was his way to assert his manhood. Couldn't let a chick order him around. She smiled at his thought process. He was a teddy bear stomping around like a grizzly.

She wandered into the living room and looked around. *So this is home, sweet home.* The thought gave her that good cozy feeling. Of course the place was full of naked women and engines and she was full of happy pills. Surely, Jackson wouldn't mind if she modified the decor a bit— at least covered the nipples under the cocktail table glass with fabric? Put the engines in the garage? She would ask him…if she ever saw him again. She might have to leave a note, since he was avoiding her. She hated that she made him uncomfortable in his own home. She had to fix that somehow.

Sleep with him. Yeah.

A wave of wooziness made her plop onto the sofa. At least she was making progress. She felt a goofy, lopsided grin fill her face. She'd faced adversity and triumphed. Gotten her tooth fixed, found two jobs—three, if she counted housekeeping—and a place to live. And she hadn't run home or cried to her brothers. That was the main thing.

She'd lost a semester of school, but she'd get there eventually. In the meantime, she'd learn from real life, as Jackson had said. She felt mostly relieved. Uneasily, she realized she should be less content about her limbo, but what the hell….

The bikini-clad babe on the Corvette caught her eye, looking as though she wanted to get laid right there on the hood. So would Heidi. Right here on the couch. She felt ready. Eager. Ripe. Sex sounded so…*delicious* right now. She stretched out on the sofa, feeling her body respond to the idea, her sex tightening into an eager knot.

I'm not what you want, Jackson had said. Because she was, what, young? Not that young. Twenty-five to his thirty. She seemed naive, probably. She hadn't known a men's club was a strip club. And there was her desperation to consider. Maybe he thought she wanted to fall in love. He couldn't be more wrong. She certainly wasn't falling in love with the first man she slept with in the city. Heavens, no. She expected to have many sexual adventures before she settled down.

And she wanted them to start right now, dammit.

Jackson didn't see it, though. She must not seem confident enough. If she were a dancer, he wouldn't hesitate. She remembered that when she'd shoved off her panty hose in the Moons break room, Jackson had dropped a jaw as though the action had turned him on.

Why not go that way? Do a simple striptease. Nothing fancy. Just a little wiggle and shimmy and a slow peeling off of her clothes. Acting sexy, she would *feel* sexy. *Be* sexy.

She wouldn't have the same skill as the dancers, but she'd put more feeling into it. The strippers' expressions were cool when they performed, as if their emotions were turned inward. And no wonder. Strange men were getting aroused by the women's moves and bodies, not their personalities or characters. It was a performance, an illusion, completely impersonal.

For Heidi, this was very personal and her emotions would be fully engaged and directed at what she wanted— sex with Jackson. She'd show him all she wanted was a good time.

Her heart sped into high gear and she pushed to her feet, then had to grab the sofa arm to steady herself. She was just buzzed enough to shrug off any remaining inhibitions.

She headed for her closet to find something to take off.

The fake snakeskin halter dress would be hard to shimmy out of and the bikini top was big enough to hold three sets of her breasts. Jackson's friend had been stacked.

She settled on a spangled tube top and a pair of red spandex shorts that cut her in the crotch. She had to go without panties, since the unsexy petunia-patterned granny panties she'd bought at the drugstore—two for two-fifty— were too voluminous for the skintight, high-cut shorts. She pulled silk drawstring pants over the shorts and covered the tube top with a black gauze see-through blouse with satin ties. She could strip herself of the pants and blouse and still be covered by the tube top and shorts. She'd get to the naked part after Jackson succumbed to her erotic dance. In bed. Where she'd be more confident of her jiggly thighs and puny boobs.

The finishing touch was the pair of black stilettos from the closet. They were too big and slid off her heels, but she clenched her toes and figured she could hold them on long enough to give Jackson the general idea.

She checked herself out in the bathroom mirror. Not bad. She tilted her head, tried a sultry look, then released the ribbon ties one at a time. Decent... Now a little shimmy. Her breasts jiggled okay for their size. She'd just make sure he saw plenty of her best feature—her butt. She turned to check it out. Excellent. She pulled her hair up with a few pins so she could shake it down like in shampoo commercials. Then she redid her face—heavy on foundation and color to counteract the lopsidedness of her swollen jaw and to hide her youthful freckles. She even used lip liner and dotted a beauty mark onto her cheek for drama. Putting on mascara, she slipped and poked herself in one eye, which turned red, but she didn't care. She'd hardly felt the sting.

In the living room, she decided to use the upright post at the edge of the kitchen like one of the dancers' chrome poles. She put a sax piece with a strong rhythm on the CD player and practiced a few turns around the pole as she'd seen the dancers do. She slid up and down, performed some dancerly undulations, and peeled off the blouse, shook off the pants and tossed them around a bit. Not too athletic or dizzying, but decently seductive.

Then she waited for Jackson, her heart rattling in her chest like popcorn in a microwave bag. No way could Jackson resist what she had planned. If he could, she would just die.

JACKSON GRABBED THE GROCERIES, three plastic sacks to a hand, and hip-checked his car door shut. He'd bought every frickin' thing Heidi had written down, including twelve-grain bread, fresh spinach—bleh—and vitamins. He was pussy-whipped and he wasn't even getting any. But he wanted to make it up to her for turning her down.

He shook his head. What the hell had happened to his manhood? Jackson McCall didn't turn down sex that hot. He'd lost interest the past year or so, but with Heidi he'd been exercising restraint muscles he didn't know he had. It wasn't healthy to want a woman this much. Something could get permanently strained…or, hell, broken.

From the garage, he heard music playing inside. Sax. Loud and heavy on the downbeat. Didn't sound like Heidi to him. She was more of an easy-listening kind of girl. Not this hot, sultry beat. What was going on? He turned the key in the lock, pushed open the door and carried the bags into the town house.

"Hey, there, big guy," Heidi called to him in the voice of a woman thinking about doing *thangs*. He moved forward and saw that she'd positioned herself against the support beam between the rooms, one knee bent, foot braced on the post, and she looked downright *eager* to do thangs.

She was all covered up, but she wore Gigi's do-me heels and her face said *do-me, too.*

Good lord.

Something was wrong, though. Her hair was pinned up crooked and her right cheek sagged. Plus her lipstick didn't quite match the shape of her lips.

"Are you all right?" he asked. When uncertainty flew across her face, he corrected himself. "I mean you look…different."

"I am different," she said, smiling a slow cat smile and pushing away from the pole. She swayed and her ankles gave way a little in the spike heels. She was loaded? "Different than you think I am."

Then he remembered. "Did Dr. Dave fix your tooth?" he asked her gently.

"Yes, he did."

"And did you take something for the pain?" He tried not to smile.

She frowned, reading his meaning. "The shoes are big, that's why I'm wobbling." She strode firmly forward and her feet snapped in and out of the heels like they were flip-flops. Gigi had big feet.

He just stood there, sacks dangling, caught by the look in her eyes.

She came right up to him and put her small hands on his chest, fingers spread. She smelled so good. It made him think of spring flowers and sweet cries of pleasure. "You're exactly what I need, Jackson." Her words spun through him, her gaze tore him open and he rocked in the white-hot breeze of raw desire.

Behind her, the saxophone moaned like a beast in heat.

Heidi slid her fingers under his T-shirt and stroked his chest. "You feel good," she whispered.

He fought his reaction, noticing that her lipstick line was definitely crooked and the mole on her cheek had *smeared?* It was drawn on? Her right eye was bloodshot as hell and both lids sagged. The woman was high as a kite.

"I think you're the one who feels good," he said, his blood thudding in his ears. "Feeling-no-pain good." He dropped the groceries to the carpet, cans clunking together, and grabbed her wrists, stopping her lovely fingers mid-stroke.

"You think I'm not the kind of woman you have sex with," she said, her eyes sparking at him like an acetylene torch, "but I swear I am. Let me show you."

It was tough not to smile. Even harder not to kiss that crookedly painted mouth. "Heidi, listen—"

She shut him up with a finger to his lips. He wanted to suck it until she moaned. "Not another word. Just watch." She backed away, swaying to the music while she slowly, slowly pulled the strings of her shirt, one by one, until the sides fell away, revealing a shiny strapless deal covering her breasts.

Shit. She intended to strip for him. "Really…you don't need to. I get the point." He stepped toward her.

She held up a hand. "I practiced. Just stay there and let me do it."

So he did, groaning inside, not sure he could bear what he could tell would be alternately funny and insanely arousing.

She fixed him with a stare that made him feel like something she'd caught in a trap and intended to eat raw, then yanked her shirt off her shoulders and he wanted to offer himself up for exactly that. She let the shirt fall off her arms, then caught the edge of it so she could tease the floor. He felt the move as though it was his skin she was brushing with the flimsy fabric.

She took a quick turn around the pole, then did a sinuous slide down and back up, mimicking the strippers, but with real feeling in her face. The contact with the pole seemed to arouse her. She took a harsh breath, then bent toward him and wiggled, which made a pale crescent of one breast pop out of the top, revealed almost to the nipple. Lust thudded through him, making him sluggish, unable to hold a thought except that he wanted to touch, to hold and have her.

His reaction must have been obvious, because her face went pink and her eyes shone with triumph. She might be loaded, but she wasn't numb and she looked like a woman on a mission. Maybe she wasn't quite as innocent as he kept telling himself she was.

Or maybe his lust was taking over, making it all right to drag her into his arms and do all the things he wanted to do—take her, make her cry out in helpless pleasure.

Then she slowly slid the shirt between her legs, rubbing it against herself so that the contact registered in her eyes. She cupped herself through the fabric and rotated her palm over the mound of her sex. This wasn't the fake self-touch the strippers performed. She felt it and so did he.

A groan escaped. How could he endure this to the end?

She smiled a smile that lit her eyes, enjoying torturing him, swung the blouse over her head like a cowboy's lasso, then released it. It landed on his shoulder and he got a whiff of his own deodorant, which on her somehow smelled better, sweeter.

Then she tugged at the strings on her pants, swaying her hips to the throbbing music. Oh, God, now what? Inside, he moaned along with the sax.

The pants shivered down her legs, snagging at her knees, revealing tiny red shorts so tight they made little sausages of her trim thighs and outlined the split in her sex. This was torture. He wanted to clutch her hips, fall to his knees and kiss her through the fabric, please her with his tongue.

She stomped the pants the rest of the way down, her body jiggling firmly, then she stepped out of the silky puddle and stood there, a little uncertain, looking hot and sweet in that crooked tube top and those crotch-pinching shorts and oversize shoes. Her thigh muscles rippled as she swayed from the pain meds and nerves. He watched a continent of blush spring out above her breasts and flood the creamy ocean of her neck.

"Very nice," he said, applauding softly, his palms clammy. "Thank you."

"But I'm not done," she said, as if she'd just remembered something else. She reached into her hair, tugged, grimaced, then managed to release the pins so that her hair sank to her shoulders in haystack tangles. She shook her head to settle it, then began to dance, rocking her body in a wave that ended with soft toe kicks. Her face showed that she felt the friction of the shorts against her sex, where he wanted to be right now.

She picked up the discarded pants and rubbed them across her ass while she shimmied in a classic burlesque move. Then she dropped the pants and backed against the pole and slid slowly down to a squat, her knees angled outward, a muscular move popular with the dancers, which had the effect of pointing him to her spot, inviting him in, to touch, to taste, to enter.

He took a step forward, unable to stop himself. He longed to explore her softness, see how wet she was, and how swollen, touch her just so. He dragged his gaze upward to her face, where her eyes echoed her body's message. *Do it. Take me. Make love to me. Please.*

He wanted that, to push and thrust into all that softness, all that woman, to let her calves lock around his ass, hold him in place, make him give her all the pleasure she wanted.

Now she pushed to her feet, trembling from the strain—that move took conditioning—and spun herself around the post, leaning her head back…which made the breast slip out completely, so his eyes feasted on the small brown nipple. She spun again, evidently not noticing. "Whoa," she said, and staggered, off-balance.

He rushed to catch her.

"Thank you," she said, standing into his arms, the heels bringing her nearly to his height. The smeared lipstick made her look like a kid who'd been sloppy with a strawberry popsicle and perspiration had smeared the drawn-on mole even more. Her freckles glowed through the overdone makeup and her powder-soft scent was as innocent and fresh as a spring breeze. Her body felt good against his. Taut and firm, but also soft as fruit, pressing against him. He knew that if he reached down, her ass would be perfect against his palm, round and ripe for a taste.

"How am I doing?" she whispered, her warm breath teasing him.

"Great," he ground out roughly. "Except for…" He used his thumb to wipe away the lipstick smear.

She grasped his thumb between her teeth, gripped his hand and sucked it into her mouth.

He fought for air. "Maybe you'd better lie down," he forced out.

She released his thumb. "With you?"

Oh, yeah. His cock surged. He was about to buckle and drop.

She blinked at him, a slow flicker of lashes heavy with gunk. *Bul-ink, bul-link.* Round as a baby doll's eyes, a

Bombay Sapphire blue with a dark edge, and they sparkled with desire.

She put her arms around him, pressed herself against him, breasts to thighs, and looked up into his face. "Take me to bed."

Then she rose on tiptoe and kissed him, pushing her tongue right where he couldn't do anything but take it in. He was only human, dammit. He grabbed her and kissed her back, lost for a moment in the softness of her flesh, the overwhelming need she started up in him, like revving an engine, grinding its gears, burning out all the oil in the machinery of it.

She trembled against him, tilted her mouth to grant him better access and he tasted the soft tissue just inside her lip, felt the hard smoothness of her teeth, the heat of her eager breath.

He was really getting into it when he tasted medicinal clove and brushed the rough surface of what had to be a temporary crown. She'd been to the dentist, he reminded himself, and she was high on meds. He shouldn't be messing around in her mouth.

He broke off the kiss.

"Don't stop," she said, going for his lips.

"You need to sleep this off."

"No, I don't."

He knew what he had to do and did it. He squatted just enough to grab her by the upper thighs and haul her up over his shoulder.

She shrieked. "What are you doing?"

"Putting you to bed." *And getting the hell out.* If he'd carried her face up, he'd never be able to resist her mouth. This way, he only had to deal with her sweet behind against his cheek.

She pounded his back with her fists and kicked, catching him in the 'nads with one pointy toe.

"Ouch. Damn. Watch it."

"Serves you right, you big gorilla."

She was good and mad. At least that. He burned with the awareness that all he had to do was turn his head slightly and he could put his mouth on her butt, sticking out of the tiny shorts. His palm cupped her upper leg. If he slid his fingers upward, he could slip so easily under the fabric. The idea made him ache all over. He'd captured her like some caveman and he could hold her down and stroke her to madness.

Nope. No. No way. He closed his eyes against the curve beside his face, so firm, so close, so willing.

Though probably not now that he'd tossed her over his shoulder like a sack of shapely potatoes. In her bedroom, he whipped down the covers, bent forward and let her fall onto the bed.

"That was totally uncalled for," she said, blinking up at him, banging her heels against the mattress.

He sat beside her and had to touch her, so he settled for taking off her shoes, letting himself enjoy the smoothness of her foot, elastic with muscle, familiar from the other night. She had those great round toes he wanted to taste. One small breast was still showing and he fought to keep from staring at that rebellious little cupcake with the tempting cherry on top.

"I'm not that buzzed. Why did you stop?"

To distract them both, he massaged her instep, pressing down hard.

"Oh, that's good," she moaned. "You have great hands. I want them on me. Everywhere." The last word was a hungry whisper.

His cock surged against his zipper, wanting out, wanting in. He knew if he kept up this innocent rub, he'd soon be sliding up her calves, thighs and higher.

She pushed up on her elbows. "You think you know me, Jackson, but you don't. Maybe I'm not wildly experienced, but I'm no virgin and I won't get weird on you afterward, if that's what you're afraid of."

"Don't think this isn't hard for me."

Her eyes took on a smart-ass glint. "Is it? Is it hard for you?" She leaned forward and pressed her hand against his zipper, where he was indeed hard as a pole at Moons. Her eyes widened. "Very." She hesitated for a second, then she seemed to force herself to act and she tightened her grip on him, watching his face.

He groaned and closed his eyes while she slid her fingers around his cock, testing, exploring a gift through its wrapping.

With everything in him, he wanted to rip open his zipper, tear off his boxers and get those sweet digits doing some serious stroking.

But she wasn't herself. She hadn't even noticed one breast was hanging out. Well, not hanging—peeking. She'd feel like an idiot when she emerged from this drugged funk. He put his hands on her shoulders and gently pushed her onto the mattress. "You need sleep." He got to his feet.

"You're so…infuriating. Stop telling me what I need." But her voice was soft and her eyelids sagged. She was dozy. He watched as she stretched out her legs, pale and inviting against the midnight blue sheets. She was a delicious dish spread before him.

He pictured himself tasting her, touching her. Could he ever get his fill? He rocked on his heels, tempted to fall on her, forget all these heroic impulses and go with what his parts were yelling at him to do.

"Rest up," he choked out and got the hell out of there, his hands shaking, his cock aching. In the kitchen he threw cold water on his face, rubbed it onto his neck and took a deep steadying breath. He'd just passed up the hottest sex of his life. This better be the right thing to do.

It was. She was out of it. And for all she claimed that she just wanted sex, he didn't believe it. He couldn't bear the possibility of screwing up again. Sex was great and all, but there were more important considerations.

Right now they were damned hard to remember. He headed to his room to lock the door and lift some weights. Heavy weights and lots of them. And then a shower—a cold, cold one.

7

HEIDI WOKE TO SUNLIGHT in her eyes and the sound of the shower running. She'd slept through the night, evidently. What had happened? Her fuzzy brain chased memories until it hit the mark. Oh, yeah. The striptease, after which she'd been summarily tossed over Jackson's shoulders and put to bed like a cranky child. How frustrating. How demoralizing. She'd even grabbed him *there* and he'd stopped her hand. Was she that talentless, that unappealing, that resistible?

No. He'd stared at her, eyes gleaming with primal desire, hungry to have her. He'd thought she was high on pain meds and didn't want to take advantage of her. He'd been *heroic,* dammit.

Her jaws and thighs ached like she'd worn them out with hours of great sex. Instead, it had been dental work and a squat-thrust against the beam. She was as sexually frustrated as ever.

Now Jackson was taking a shower—again, it seemed, since she had a vague memory of waking from her post-striptease nap to the sound of water running before falling off for good. Now he was scrubbing all that muscular terrain and that impressive-feeling member. He was whistling the music she'd played for her woozy dance. Was he thinking of her?

She was perfectly sober now. What if she joined him? Ripped off this tube top and shorts and ducked under the water? A charge of adrenaline made her pop out of bed and onto her feet. She moved fast, scared she'd lose her nerve, and was soon at the slightly ajar bathroom door. She listened for a second, her heart beating fast. Jackson's whistle mixed melodically with the running water that splashed from his body to the shower floor in lush blasts.

She pushed the door more open. The small room had just enough space for the sink, toilet and shower stall, which Jackson's broad frame seemed to fill to the corners. Through the frosted glass, she made out his tan back and perfect behind, the muscles swelling and subsiding as he soaped his chest.

All she had to do was strip and offer herself to him.

Wait. Not offer herself. Take him. Touch him in a way that convinced him they both wanted the same thing. That sounded so damned assertive. So confident.

She took a half step forward, but the sight of herself in the partially fogged mirror stopped her dead. She looked horrid. Her foundation was too heavy, her eye shadow garish, the waterproof—and evidently sleep-proof—mascara had clumped and her lipstick line was crooked. The beauty mark looked like a smudge of dirt under one eye and her hair was a tousled mess. She'd slept like the dead on her back all night, but the tube top had somehow slid down, revealing a breast. She yanked it up.

She'd tried to seduce Jackson looking this way? How had he kept from laughing? She remembered how he'd wiped her lipstick as though he were cleaning up a child who'd gone wild with ice cream. All she needed was a fright wig, and two pink balloons stretching her top and she'd make a fine sexpot clown for Barnum & Bailey.

Embarrassed heat blended with the humid density of the room so that she could hardly draw a breath. She was a silly woman who'd pulled a silly stunt. She had to get out of here before Jackson caught sight of her. She backed up, but her arm caught the door. It creaked, then banged softly against the wall.

Jackson spun, then shoved open the shower door. "Heidi?"

"Sorry. I didn't realize you were in here."

That was so obviously not true, but Jackson didn't seem to care. Her goofy appearance didn't deter his stare, either, and his face lit with desire. "Did I wake you?"

She shook her head.

"Are you feeling okay?" Meaning, was she in her right mind? He looked as though he was fighting some terrific inner battle.

Again she shook her head.

"Then come here," he said, his voice rough with need, succumbing to something. He shoved the door open so hard it clunked the wall and bounced back. He blocked it with his arm and held out his hand for her. Again. He was always offering her a boost. She liked that, independence be damned.

She let him pull her closer to the shower door. Spray bounced off his body into the air between them, making a rainbow in the mist. The water hissed and splashed in a glory of white noise.

And there Jackson stood, startlingly erect. Her past sexual forays—furtive and cramped on a sofa, a car, a guy's twin bed—hadn't allowed her to really examine an aroused penis before. Here was Jackson's in full view. It wasn't beautiful—she'd never found the male member beauti- ful—but it was dramatic and promising and proud of itself and the pleasure it could give to him and his lover, who was about to be *her*.

"Come here," he growled again and tugged her into the stall. Water poured down her body, soaking her hair and clothes. Jackson's gaze poured down, too, and she shivered with a hot chill.

"You're driving me nuts," he said roughly.

A thrill coursed through her. Jackson had slept with lots of women, but she, Heidi Fields, was making him crazy. "That's what I've been trying to do."

"Then I hope you're happy." And he crushed her to him, kissing her so fiercely she could barely stay upright. She was finally getting what she'd wanted.

He tilted her chin to get at her mouth, alternating between a soft brush of his lips and a deep dip, his tongue sweeping over hers, taking it, taking her mouth. The way she took his.

They kissed and kissed, warm water rushing down in a private waterfall, until he finally broke off, still holding her tight. She was vividly aware of his erection through her shorts. "You sure you're okay?" He sounded winded and looked as dazed as she felt.

She managed a dizzy nod.

He nodded back, then stared at the silver tube top. "This has to go," he said, tugging the fabric up.

She lifted her arms so he could yank it off her body, the metal threads light scraping her skin, and toss it over the stall wall. The entire time, he kept his eyes on the prize— her breasts. Her *tiny* breasts. With the nipples tightened to knots, they looked even tinier, she knew. She had the urge to cover them with her hands and turn to show him her best feature, still encased in the circulation-compromising shorts, but Jackson looked at her as though her little offerings held the secret of eternal bliss.

He cupped them tenderly, as if they were precious and delicate and he'd worked forever to get at them. "Beautiful," he murmured.

"You exaggerate."

"Huh-uh. They're perfect for you." He ducked his head to reverently kiss the top of each one in turn.

She smiled.

Then he sucked a nipple into his mouth and she thought she might collapse from the glory of it. She moaned, heat rushing through her, feeling like pure womanhood. Instinctively, she arched her back, tightening her breasts so they tingled and ached, especially the one Jackson held in his mouth. Warm water stroked her skin, heating it, while Jackson's mouth turned her insides molten. Along with first one nipple and then the other.

They were going to have sex right here in the shower, standing up. What about protection? She had to say something before she lost her mind altogether. "I'm on the pill," she murmured. "Are there…health issues?"

He stopped what he was doing to her breast and raised his gaze. "None here."

"Good then," she said. "So we don't need condoms."

"No," he said, then lowered himself to his knees before her, his eyes following down her body until he was looking at her abdomen. "We don't need condoms." He rolled her shorts down her hips, down her thighs, until they dropped to her insteps, and she stood naked before him.

He looked up at her face, his expression full of hunger and promise, letting her see that he would have her until he was good and finished.

Lust coursed through her and her legs went from rubber to syrup. If he weren't holding her hips, she'd have landed on her best feature on the stall floor.

He returned his eyes to her stomach, bracing her bottom with spread fingers. His lips parted, his tongue emerged, signaling his intent to kiss her *there*.

She held her breath and closed her eyes, waiting for the exquisite moment. *Yes, oh, yes.* He touched her spot dead on with the tip of his tongue. A charge jolted through her, shooting everywhere, flying out her fingers and toes and bursting out the top of her head.

"Oh…Jackson…oh," she cried, breathless and happy, but nervous, too. He was going to try to make her come, she knew, and this was so sudden…so new.

He sensed her tension, because he stopped and looked up at her. "Let me make you feel good." He massaged her butt. Mmm.

His confidence melted her doubts the way his touch melted her bones. She nodded down at him, water bouncing from her hair to his face, and she gave herself over to him and his tongue and hands.

He squeezed her bottom at the same time he flattened his entire tongue against her clitoris like a hot, wet cloth that he somehow rolled over it, skimming and swirling. She began to jerk and rock uncontrollably. She reached down for his hair, something to keep her tied to earth before she flew away completely. She leaned back against the bumpy solidity of the tile wall.

For her, this act had always been hasty or clumsy or cursory, but Jackson buried his face in her, digging in as if to extract every ounce of pleasure for them both.

Then his tongue slid lower, more intimately, easing into her entrance, so that she had the warm pressure of the width of his tongue on her clit, while the pointed tip pushed inside. Meanwhile his hands massaged the area around where his mouth was working. Sparks shot off in wild directions.

She made garbled sounds and jerked convulsively, like a puppet shaken from above. She was embarrassed by the rawness of her reaction, tried to tone it down, but she could only let go, release, respond the way her body insisted. She was in his hands…and beneath his tongue…. And he was on his knees before her, worshiping at her center.

She was going to come. She realized it suddenly and it was the most natural thing in the world. She often struggled for an orgasm, inhibited by the tension, the rush and—now that she was in Jackson's deft hands, she realized—the ineptitude of previous lovers.

He seemed to sense how close she was and shifted to quick, short squeezes and licking her full length with more pressure.

Her climax hit in a huge wave, rolling through her, rippling outward from her core. Jackson held very still, while she rocked and bumped and cried out, her voice echoing against the tiles, sounding like several women at once. She felt like several women. The newly independent person who'd left home for her own life. The innocent young thing who'd just discovered what sex was all about. And the powerful sexual creature who could bring a man to his knees.

She gasped for air and sagged against the wall. They'd used up the heat so that the water cascading over her skin was tepid. Inside she burned. "That was…amazing," she breathed.

"Mmm-hmm." Jackson rose and kissed her, his erection urgent against her stomach. Reaching under her arms, he lifted her off her feet, bracing her against the tile. His turn. "I want in."

"Oh, please." She wrapped her legs around him and held onto his neck. He positioned her bottom so he was nudging her entrance with the head of his penis. She was wet and slick and he slid in easily.

"That is so…*good*." Like the greatest itch in the world had just begun to be scratched.

"Yeah." He thrust upward, filling her, the angle such that his shaft bumped her clit, tightening that marvelous muscle that was greedy for more. He moved just right—not too much pressure, not too much speed—in an even rhythm, his face tight with withheld urgency. He looked as if he'd never wanted a woman as much as he wanted her. "Am I hurting you?" he gasped.

"No. This is perfect."

"Yeah, perfect." His mouth seized hers and wouldn't let go. He'd trapped her against the wall, pinned her in place with his body. She felt powerful and helpless at the same time. No matter how she struggled, he would have her, had to have her. And she would have him.

Her nerves sang with electricity, her sex pulsed with a need that ticked higher and higher, tighter and tighter. Her skin began to prickle and she felt another orgasm on its way.

She broke off the kiss and cried out so that the sound seemed to crash from the walls into her ears again, "Jackson, oh, I'm—"

"Coming," he finished for her, his body tensing, too. She felt the throb of his climax just as her own release arrived. His body jerked, pushing up into her, giving in, giving out, giving up all he had. The thought of him succumbing to her aroused her like nothing else. She had this strong man desperate to have her.

Jackson clutched her to him, wrapping his arms around her as though she were a pillow he wanted all to himself or a child he wanted to protect, while he lifted her away from the wall. The steamy air smelled of shampoo and soap and sex. It was heaven.

They just stood there for a few seconds—suspended in the miracle of it. The perfection of what they'd done. Slowly, Jackson slid from her body and she dropped her legs to the floor. It had been so wonderful. It had been how she expected to feel with someone she loved. Of course she barely knew Jackson. This was her breakaway sex. But the feeling stayed, puzzling her. Worrying her a little, too.

"You happy?" He grinned. "Now that you've had your way with me?"

"Oh, yes." She *was* happy. And triumphant. And uncertain how to act next. Would they keep going? Do it again? Talk about it?

Jackson's face flickered with confusion. Maybe he felt the same. He reached past her to punch the faucet off. The misty atmosphere and dreamlike sound faded and the air cooled. She heard the unromantic gurgle of water down the drain.

"That'll be some water bill," Jackson said. He gave an awkward laugh.

"I feel clean enough for two days' worth," she said, staying light.

Now what? Surely they wouldn't stop doing something that felt so incredibly good. She wanted to try new positions, reciprocate with oral sex, make love in a bed, on the floor, in the kitchen. She wanted it all.

Jackson jumped out of the shower and grabbed two towels, one of which he thrust at her. Kind of brusque. As if they'd reached the end of a workout.

She just stood there, holding the towel, not sure what to say.

He stopped scrubbing himself and scrutinized her. "You okay?"

"Of course. I'm great. Just a little…"

"Woozy? Sure. All that steam and all… Plus, you had dental surgery yesterday." He took the towel she clutched and pulled it around her, tucking it tight between her breasts, as though she were a package he was wrapping for UPS, all snug and sealed. "I'm sorry if I— If that was too much."

"Don't apologize. I told you it was what I wanted."

"Good," he said, sounding relieved. "Let's get you lying down, get your blood pressure back." He swung her into his arms.

"I'm not going to faint. I'm fine." *Come with me to bed. I want more.* She couldn't quite say it.

He lowered her onto her mattress, checked her towel, then backed away like he thought she might explode. "I'll sop up the mess."

Since when did Jackson care about a little water? No, he wanted to escape. He did not want to talk about it, do it again or plan for next time. That was that. All done, mopped up and over with. She'd promised him not to act weird. Was wanting more weird? It shouldn't be. It should be as natural as breathing.

Except for that strange feeling of belonging. That surge of emotion and closeness. Hell, maybe she *was* getting weird.

Nothing in her new life was turning out as she'd planned.

JACKSON LOOKED DOWN on the scene from his DJ booth, feeling like the king of all he surveyed. He loved it up here, where he could watch the customers reacting to the dancers, feed into the energy that ebbed and flowed, depending on how the dancer grooved to the music he chose. The effect was subtle, but he swore his selections were tuned to each dancer's strengths, sometimes even their moods. For Jasmine, he went sinuous and playful. Autumn was hard-driving rock, with classic Stones. Nevada needed fast, popular riffs, along with athletic salsa.

The door to his booth opened and he turned to see Duke walk in.

"Busy night," Duke said. "Stan thinks Taylor needs some help behind the bar. I agree."

"The ad in *New Times* brought in more customers, but Taylor's handling it fine." He didn't appreciate Duke's sleazy nephew giving staffing advice. "We hired a new waitress. She'll pick up the slack." There Heidi was now, heading for a table with a tray of drinks wearing her bag-lady outfit. He got a funny feeling in his belly at the sight of her. She bent and handed out two drinks.

"She the one the girls said is living in your town house?" Duke asked him, watching her, too. Jackson didn't like the interest in Duke's face. It had nothing to do with Moons's personnel needs. He was a decent guy, but Duke liked variety in the sack.

"Heidi? Yeah."

"She seeing anybody?"

His eyes shot to Duke's.

"Just kidding." He held up his hands. "She's all yours."

"She's not mine. She's…new. Finding her way."

"And you're helping her?"

He grimaced. "I watch out for her, that's all."

"And my nephew's not in debt up to his thousand-dollar shades."

"Anyway, I've got it under control. The customer flow, I mean."

"You always do," Duke said, clapping him on the shoulder. "I'm glad I could help you out with a job." He always acted as if he'd done Jackson a favor by hiring him, when it was the other way around. Jackson didn't care. He missed working on cars some and the money here was minor, but life was good at Moons. He'd taken a couple blows lately, losing his parents and the station, so he had the right to coast a while. A year or two. Maybe longer.

"Nice music," Duke said. "What's the band?"

"A practice track from some guys I know." He could imagine Heather singing the lyrics, almost hear how perfectly they would blend. He really should put the three of them together. Autumn and the two dancers on the smaller stages were really getting into the piece. "Check it out," he said into the mic in his DJ voice. "When you groove like that, Autumn, you make grown men weep. Am I right, guys?"

Applause rose and wild whistles.

Autumn winked up at him. The girls loved it when he acted turned on for the crowd.

He noticed a cluster of young guys jostling each other near one of Heidi's tables. They were showing off and could be trouble. "Do me a favor, Duke, and tone down the frat boys at the main stage."

"You bet, boss man. You're in charge." Duke set off. He had given Jackson free rein with the place. Partly, that was laziness. Duke had a tendency to go for the short payoff, but he knew he had it good with Jackson in charge and that made his negatives okay by Jackson.

With Duke gone, Jackson was free to watch Heidi, who held a tray of drinks, waiting a discreet distance away for a lap dance to end.

When the dancer finished, she paused to talk to Heidi, leaning in, speaking intently, asking her advice, no doubt.

In only three nights, Heidi had not only developed decent skills, blisters and all, but also made friends. He was proud of her.

She set drinks in front of the three men at the table where the lap dance had taken place and they looked right through her, as if she were furniture or a maid. The idiots had no idea the incredible female form that lay beneath those baggy duds. They didn't know she was hotter and more sensual than the nearly nude woman one of them had paid twenty bucks to wave her breasts in his face.

Only Jackson knew. He'd handled that round swell of tight behind, heard that husky voice cry out as if nothing this wonderful had ever happened to her before. As if she'd just discovered sex and he, Jackson McCall, was the master of it.

At the thought, he went warm all over. His blood slowed and thickened, and he wanted more. He couldn't wait to go home with her.

Bad idea, he thought, but the urge burrowed into him, like some charming little rodent that could gnaw his struts clean through. He had to keep this under control.

It was tough. Heidi had been so different. He did his damnedest to make sure a woman crossed the finish line, but the women he'd been with, including Kelli, took sex for granted. There was no wonder in it for them. The night Gigi had hit on him, he'd sworn she was just bored. *CSI* had been a rerun.

He hadn't been bored with Heidi. He'd been wide awake and fully alive. And humbly grateful. For his fingers, his tongue, his cock. And for every inch of her. Her husky voice shouting out her pleasure in the echo chamber of the shower.

God, that had been good. It had been hours ago and he

could still feel the weight of her bottom in his hands, her tight body wrapped around him, hear her cries in his head, the water rushing over them, like a tropical waterfall. He could still feel the relief of getting in. He'd felt…new.

She'd looked a little stunned when he wrapped her up in the towel and put her to bed so that her blood pressure could bounce back. Maybe he should have said something final—put a period to the thing—but no point in overkill. She'd joked with him about using all that water, right? Completely relaxed.

He'd been reassured when, after he'd mopped up, he found her in the kitchen fixing food, calm as could be. She made a giant spinach salad and triple-decker sandwiches as complicated as a good deli's. After that, she baked peanut butter brownies and a ton of other stuff, not saying a word about what had happened.

So, everything was normal, he guessed. Life was good.

They'd had sex and it hadn't ruined a thing. And it was over. Though that gave him a major ache down below. He'd love more sex with his eager, responsive roommate.

Leave it alone. Maybe he was just coming out of his funk. And that was good. Pushing for more only meant trouble.

As if she knew he was thinking about her, Heidi looked up and gave him a little wave. He waved back, just the way she had, glad no one was around to point out how stupid he looked doing it.

8

BREAK TIME. YES. Heidi carried her 7-Up into the dressing room and sat at the table, lifting her feet on the next chair in relief. Jasmine and Autumn were at the mirrors doing hair and makeup, and she watched them work while she drank and rested her feet.

After four nights at the bar, Heidi had begun to feel more comfortable. She'd only dozed off twice in her salon chair at Shear Ecstasy today—one reason she was glad she had few clients—so she was getting used to the late hours. Her feet barely throbbed, thanks to double-wrapped blisters. Of course, she wouldn't turn down a foot massage, but Jackson wasn't offering.

He'd been friendly, but not physical, since their shower sex. No lingering looks, either. Or not when she'd noticed. He was acting as if nothing had changed. She wanted more, but refused to act needy. Mind-blowing sex was probably the norm for Jackson and she didn't want to make too big a deal out of it.

It wasn't that big a deal, really. Jackson was the first of many lovers she expected to have. And he'd started her off right. Helped her declare her Sexual Independence Day with all the roman candles and bottle rockets she could ever desire. Except she wanted more. Lots more.

The idea, however, had to come from Jackson this time.

In the meantime, whenever she thought about sex, she cooked something. The refrigerator was now jammed with deviled eggs, peanut-butter bars, brownies, chicken salad, stuffed celery, two kinds of Jell-O and a banana cream pie. Luckily, she'd lost her own appetite, so she wouldn't gain weight thanks to all this nervous cookery. She was a horny Julia Child.

Jackson's eyes went big with delight when he saw the bulging shelves and offered to pay her for her cooking, too. Lord. She wanted his body, not his money, but that seemed to be hands-off.

For now.

Rox stuck her head in the break room door, a tray full of drinks on one hand. "Autumn, grab some towels for Taylor, huh?" Autumn stopped dabbing foundation on her chin, glanced up at the cupboard where the towels were, then at Rox—opening her mouth for a retort, Heidi could tell.

"I'll get it," Heidi said and pushed to her feet.

"You're a doll," Rox said, smiling. "I'll be back after I deliver these drinks." She hurried off.

Heidi caught Autumn's stare in the mirror. Autumn was wondering about her. She watched people, Heidi had noticed. She'd bet trust was an issue in the woman's life, and her blunt remarks were a defense against hurt.

Heidi put the stepladder between Autumn and Jasmine, climbed it and stretched over the makeup lights, careful not to burn herself. She opened the cupboard and felt around the paper towels, napkins and boxes of toothpicks for a bag of bar towels. If she could just…reach…behind…oops! Three rolls of paper towels tumbled out of the cupboard, two thumping Jasmine on the head and shoulders. "Hey," she said, stepping back with the curling iron she was using, a cigarette dangling from her lip.

"Sorry." Heidi snagged the bag of towels and carried it out to Rox, then returned, grabbing the scattered paper towel rolls to carry up the ladder and put away. "I can't believe they store all this junk in your dressing room," she said to the two dancers as she rose between them.

"What can you do?" Jasmine said. "Damn. My hair." She stomped a foot and frowned in the mirror.

"We get no respect," Autumn added, stroking blush on her cheek.

Heidi climbed down and watched Jasmine try to put her hair into a ponytail. Her nails kept snagging on the over-treated curls. "Can I help with that?" Heidi asked her.

Again both women stared at her in the mirror.

"That's right," Jasmine said, nodding. "Jax said you were a hairdresser. Go for it." She held out her arms in invitation.

"You're on duty out there, aren't you?" Autumn seemed to be giving Heidi an out if she wanted it.

"I've got a few minutes of break left." She grabbed a bar stool, centered it in front of the mirror where Jasmine stood and motioned for her to sit.

She sat. "My hair won't take a curl worth a damn anymore."

Heidi ran her fingers through Jasmine's extensions, testing the texture and condition of the hair to which the false strands had been attached. "It's dry. You might want to give it some recovery time. Your natural color is nice." New hair, a rich chestnut pushed out of her scalp, contrasting with the brassy platinum she'd dyed the rest.

"No way. Blondes get bigger tips."

"I do fine," Autumn said. Her auburn hair was shiny and abundant and seemed untouched by color.

"You're just lucky Mother Nature gave you gorgeous hair and a spectacular rack," Jasmine said, pressing her own breasts together and studying them like a mother ensuring her child's face was clean. Her halter top, spacesuit silver, barely covered her nipples. "Some of us had to rework ourselves." Satisfied with her endowments, she let them drop into place.

"I say go with what you've got," Autumn said, scrubbing on mascara with hard, quick strokes.

"Your hair's a good length for your face, Autumn," Heidi observed.

She stopped, mascara wand midair, and turned to look at Heidi directly. "It's a little flat at the top, don't you think?" She scrunched her petite nose. "Not good when you're as short as I am."

"Root intensifier would give you more body. And I'd go with layers on top."

"Layers?"

"May I?" When Autumn nodded, Heidi scooped up her hair, bouncing it. "Layers would make it lighter."

"You think?" Autumn sounded eager, despite herself.

"Yeah. I'd go with…" She named a hair product and Autumn wrote it on the mirror in lip liner and thanked her for the tip.

Heidi turned back to Jasmine, then picked up the curling iron she'd been using. It was plugged into a wad of extensions at an overused outlet. "Let me give it a try, huh?"

"Be my guest," Jasmine sighed.

Heidi clicked on the iron. The overhead lights dimmed.

"One of these days we're going to set this place on fire," Autumn said.

"Seems like you should have a private dressing area," Heidi said, running a comb through Jasmine's hair, using a technique designed to protect the extensions. "A place to collect your energy, prepare to perform in peace."

"Exactly." Jasmine stamped her foot. "We're the stars, we deserve star treatment."

"Be happy Jackson fixed up the stages," Autumn said.

"But we've got mop buckets in here and cleaning supplies. The bartenders and bouncers eyeball us every shift break."

Heidi picked up the now hot iron and began to curl Jasmine's hair.

"They're on break. Give them a thrill." Autumn shrugged.

"And we could at least have real bathroom stalls."

"That's true," Autumn said thoughtfully. "You know, there's that storage room with a bunch of old furniture in the back. Why couldn't that be the break room?"

Finished with the iron, Heidi began to gently shape Jasmine's hair into an upsweep. "Maybe you should talk to Jackson," she ventured, keeping her voice casual. She knew the women would not appreciate being told what to do by a near stranger.

"We should," Autumn said. "We really should."

"Thank God for Jax," Jasmine sighed. "Did you see that preppy creep last night? He barely opened his mouth in a prick-like way and Jackson hustled him out of there."

"He can be one scary dude when he flexes and frowns," Autumn said.

"But it's all an act. He's a teddy bear." Jasmine sighed.

The idea warmed Heidi and she had to say something. "It's nice how Jackson looks out for…everyone." She'd sounded dreamy and her face heated.

Sure enough, the two women zeroed in on her. "How's that going…you living with him?" Autumn asked, watching Heidi closely.

"Good," she said, steadying her voice. "We're trading housekeeping for rent."

"I see." Autumn's mouth twitched.

"You slept with him yet?" Jasmine asked. "Ouch. Watch it."

Heidi had slipped and poked her in the cheek with the tail of the comb. "I, uh, I...well..."

"Don't be embarrassed," Jasmine said. "Jax is a blast in bed. We bounced around for a while. No big thing."

Jasmine had slept with Jackson? Had mind-blowing sex with him and considered it *no big thing.* Oh, dear. Heidi had lived a sheltered life. "Just one time," she said, trying to shrug.

"That's typical. The give-it-to-me-one-time syndrome," Autumn said. Again, she studied Heidi in the mirror. This time she seemed concerned for her. "Jackson's a good guy, but he doesn't let people in. He's wrapped up tight."

"And so bossy," Jasmine added. "Get your car tuned. Don't walk alone in the parking lot. Make sure Sabrina gets her shots. I guess it's sweet. A pain, but sweet."

"More smothering than bossy, Jaz. He's everybody's big brother...but he's a loner. Seems contradictory, but that's the deal."

"Maybe he just needs the right woman," Jasmine said.

"Loners are loners for a reason," Autumn said, but she was saying it straight to Heidi. "I never slept with him, but I know the type."

"Like I said," Heidi inserted, "it was one time."

"And it's understandable," Autumn said. "You're new in town and Jackson was handy. As long as you don't expect more."

"What more could there be?" Heidi said. Like Jackson, Autumn seemed to think Heidi was in danger of falling in love with her first good lay.

"Once you hit college, you'll meet lots of guys."

"How's that?" Heidi asked Jasmine, fluffing a last strand in front, anxious to change the subject.

"A miracle. How'd you get it to curl so well?" Jasmine turned her head a little, admiring her hair.

"Hold the heat longer on it. Tease it out very slowly."

"Oh, yeah. We know all about holding the heat and teasing it out slow, don't we, Autumn? The hotter the heat, the slower the tease, the bigger the tips."

Autumn laughed.

"You get the idea," Heidi said, pinning up the back of Jasmine's hair.

"What are you studying, anyway?" Autumn asked her. "In college?"

"Psychology."

"Ooh, you're going to be a shrink?" Jasmine said. "Practice on us maybe."

"You could use parenting lessons, that's for sure," Autumn said before Heidi could comment.

"Don't start," Jasmine snapped. "I'm not a bad mother."

"I just think some of the things you do…like bringing Sabrina here—"

"I had a transportation conflict."

"If you weren't paying for horseback riding lessons, you could hire a sitter."

"She's always judging me," Jasmine said to Heidi in the mirror. "Just like my mother."

"I'm your friend, not your mother," Autumn said.

"Then act like it." The air went crisp with tension. Anger pulsed, eyes snapped in the mirror, breaths huffed.

"It sounds like you both care about Sabrina," Heidi said softly. "You both want the best for her."

The women's gazes shot to hers, wary and waiting.

"It's hard to watch someone we care about do things we think are unwise, right, Autumn?" She pinned a coiled curl high on Jasmine's crown.

"Exactly," Autumn said, sounding vindicated.

"And when you're in a tough situation, Jasmine, it's painful when someone you respect criticizes you."

"Yeah." Jasmine shot Autumn a so-there.

Autumn rolled her eyes.

"Is there something you'd like Autumn to do differently, Jasmine?" Heidi teased a lock, while Jasmine considered the idea.

"Yeah. Stop rolling your eyes," she said.

"Then stop saying stupid things," Autumn retorted.

"You're so negative."

"I'm the only one who cares enough to tell you what you're doing wrong."

"You and my mother, who's always lecturing me how I don't appreciate all her sacrifices, I squandered my talent and my beauty and my blah, blah, blah."

"What could Autumn do that would feel positive?" Heidi gently directed their dialogue before it could descend into emotional mayhem.

"I don't know. Watch Sabrina once in a while so I can go out."

Autumn blinked, looking surprised. "But you said I'm too judgmental."

"Because you were criticizing me at the grocery store."

"Sabrina needs more vegetables. She's getting chunky."

"She hates vegetables."

"You're the mother. Make her eat them. You spoil her, Jaz—giving her every frivolous thing she wants."

"You don't get what it's like with a daughter, Autumn. I want her to have everything. I want her to do better than me, you know?" Jasmine spoke softly. "I'm scared she'll stall out. Like I did."

"There's nothing wrong with what we do," Autumn said stubbornly. "It's an art. I'm proud of my body."

Jasmine just looked at her in the mirror.

Jasmine's fear and Autumn's defiance covered shame. And Heidi wanted very much to help them both if she could without prying or offending them. "Even freely chosen, your life isn't easy. You struggle. And you have doubts."

"Yeah," Jasmine said. "I have doubts."

Autumn didn't say anything, but she didn't contradict her friend, which was as close to an admission as Autumn was likely to make.

"Despite what Sabrina says she wants or you think she needs, Jasmine, the intangibles mean more than what you buy her." Heidi continued, "Love, listening, respect, spending time with her—that's what will build her self-esteem and her confidence in her future."

"Exactly," Autumn said. "Just what I meant to say."

"Trust your love for Sabrina," Heidi added.

"Yeah…that," Autumn chimed in.

"It must be nice to be so perfect," Jasmine said to Autumn, her dark eyes crackling.

"Oh, it's glorious, believe me," Autumn said with a self-mocking smile. Her face softened into kindness. "I wish I were creative like you, Jasmine. She sews her own outfits," she said to Heidi.

"I didn't know that."

"I love that new one that's all white lace," Autumn said.

"I could make you one in black." She turned on the stool to face Autumn. "Want me to? Trade you for baby-sitting?"

"You'd do that?"

"Of course."

"Okay, then."

"All done," Heidi said, handing Jasmine the hand mirror, smiling inside at what had happened. She'd fixed Jasmine's hair and helped sort out the friends' quarrel just as she'd done at Celia's.

"It looks great," Jasmine said, turning to examine the back. "You're amazing."

"It does look better," Autumn said. "Less slutty."

"Hey," Jasmine said.

Autumn shrugged.

"I was thinking I'd offer a discount at my salon to everyone at Moons," Heidi said. "Free cut with a weave maybe? Twenty percent off on extensions?"

"Twenty percent?" Jasmine said. "That'd be great."

"I'm building my customer base."

"You need money, huh?" Autumn said. "You know, you'd make bigger tips if you'd dress sexier."

"I earn my tips doing a good job."

"That's not how men work, hon," Jasmine said. "Bigger cleavage equals bigger tips. That's math even I can do."

"Use what you have to get what you want," Autumn added.

Heidi shrugged, not wanting to offend the women, but disagreeing.

Autumn caught on and her eyes glittered with quick anger. "But you'd never stoop to what we do, right? Strip for money?"

"Don't start, Autumn," Jasmine warned. "And we're dancers, not strippers."

"I'm not ashamed. I like getting men fired up. What's wrong with that?"

"You have every right to do what you're doing," Heidi said softly. "And Moons seems like a decent place to work."

"Damn straight." But Autumn wasn't as comfortable with this as she'd sounded. There was tension in her jaw, defensiveness in her tone, bitterness in her eyes.

"It can be a drag, though, you have to admit," Jasmine said. "Some of the men are pigs and it's not like you want your fifth-grade teacher easing a folded bill into your thong."

"Everybody sells themselves, one way or another," Autumn said. "Plus, name a job where you take home a grand a night. College degree or not."

Prostitution, of course, but that wasn't the point. "That's definitely a lot of money," Heidi conceded, leaving a silent *but* hanging in the air.

"You're damn right it is," Autumn said, a muscle in her jaw ticking.

"But it goes so fast it might as well be pennies." Jasmine sighed.

"That's because you spend it on stupid things."

"There she goes again. Being negative. Attacking me."

"Okay, okay," Autumn said. "I'm just saying, think before you spend. Isn't that right, Heidi?"

Heidi remembered that Autumn was good with math and got an idea. "Maybe you could help Jasmine write a budget."

"So she can tell me I'm an idiot when I blow it?" Jasmine said. "No way."

"If you'd just make an effort," Autumn said.

"Do you think you'd value a budget, Jasmine?"

"Sometimes…maybe."

"Are you willing to help her, Autumn, without expecting perfection? Or rolling your eyes?"

"If you want that, I guess." Autumn almost looked shy.

"If you promise not to get all sarcastic and snotty on me. Don't laugh, but I'd like to start a college fund for Sabrina. Can you help me with that?"

"No sweat."

"I'm not giving up her riding lessons. She meets quality people."

"You have to cut back and prioritize…."

The dancers talked it through with Heidi gently guiding the discussion, losing herself in the moment and the success.

When Rox stuck her head into the room, Heidi was completely startled. "What are you doing, girl? Get out here. You've been on break forever."

"Sorry, sorry." She'd slipped into her Cut 'n' Curl self and felt better than she had since she'd come to town, forgetting completely that she had drinks to deliver, money to make.

And Jackson to forget. Jackson, who was everybody's big brother, a closed-off loner and a one-time lover. She'd heard it straight from the mouths of women who knew him well—had slept with him even. They'd taken her advice and she'd be wise to take theirs.

9

A WEEK LATER, Heidi sat at the kitchen table doing the math on her life. And it wasn't adding up. Ten days at two jobs—three, counting housekeeping—and she'd saved barely two hundred dollars. She'd had to repay Blythe for borrowed product, gone in on an ad with her to build business and paid her own cell phone bill. Two hundred dollars wasn't a month's rent, let alone a deposit, and, at this rate, college tuition would be months and months and months away.

To make matters worse, the plumbing was down at Shear Ecstasy again today, hence her return home and her reality check. If it weren't for Jackson letting her live here free, she'd be dead in the water. Juggling day and night jobs and spending so much time on her feet, she'd let the housework slip lately, too.

If an affair with Jackson had even been a possibility, she was too tired to have one. She wasn't sure there was any sexual tension left, since Jackson had effectively dodged her, keeping to his room or scooting out of the house just as she arrived. He kept his distance at work, though from time to time she thought she felt his eyes on her from the DJ booth.

She heard the mail truck outside, so she padded out to collect the mail. Her cheerful hello startled the carrier, who probably wasn't used to talking to his customers. Big-city anonymity. She wasn't fond of that. She missed the familiarity and friendliness of Copper Corners. And the fact that she didn't have to fear strange neighbors who might rob her. She'd taken Copper Corners for granted.

Among Jackson's bills, advertising circulars and a car magazine, she found a big, fat Town-of-Copper-Corners envelope for her. Michael had packaged up her mail and forwarded it from town hall. She carried everything inside and dug into the envelope.

Right on top was her ASU catalog. "Thought you might need this next week," he'd written on a yellow sticky with a big smiley face. Guilt speared her. She'd pored through this book, highlighting courses, circling professor names, peppering the pages with exclamation marks. It seemed so far away now. With her finances as they were, she might not be able to take second semester, either. Frustration brought tears to her eyes.

She blinked them away, set aside the catalog, then found a blue greeting-card envelope with her name on it in Mike's handwriting. She opened it and a check drifted to the kitchen table. It lodged in a blob of ketchup and she caught sight of the number on it. One thousand dollars. All those zeroes, big and bold. The line at the bottom said, *for incidentals*.

Incidentals? Good lord. It would take her three months to save this amount of money and Mike had handed it over as a p.s. to a greeting card.

We miss you, he'd written. *Hope the city is treating you right. We're proud of you. Even if we think you're crazy. Call us. The Greater and Lesser Worrywarts.*

Love and homesickness swamped her. She missed her brothers, who were *proud* of her. She'd lost the car they'd given her, along with all her money, and now lived with a strange man and worked in a strip joint.

Oh, dear.

Under the card from her brothers were notes and cards from her friends and hair clients. And beneath that was a gift from Celia—capris she'd cross-stitched to match the crop top Heidi had cheerfully worn on her big drive to Phoenix a little over two weeks ago, when she'd been bursting with hope and determination.

Everyone misses you, Celia wrote in the note she'd pinned to the pants. *The new girl is slow and silent as church… Those books you sent are all checked out, but they aren't as good as the real deal. Everyone wants you back. Come back, girl.*

Heidi's heart ached at the words. She read through the other notes from customers, all with news. Tim Thompson, eighth grade, was getting better marks since his mom had signed him up for basketball. Madge Miller's husband got a new job. Raymond Bristow had admitted he had a problem and was going to AA. Betsy's message was especially heartwarming.

Thank you, Heidi. You helped us turn the page. You get that degree and get back here where you belong. Love, Betsy Brigham.

She missed Betsy and Celia. She missed the Cut 'n' Curl and her clients and all her friends. She missed feeling safe and secure and needed and successful.

What was she doing here? She was in over her head.

A big tear dropped onto the hand-stitched Capris, smearing like a Rorschach blot. Maybe she hadn't been ready to leave home. Maybe she'd rushed her departure, like a kid so desperate for independence she dropped out of school. Why else would she feel so discouraged, so miserable, so homesick looking at a pair of cross-stitched pants, a few notes and a college catalog?

Maybe she should go back, swallow her pride. What had Jackson said? *If you were happy where you were, why push it?* He had a point.

The doorbell rang. Wiping her tears, she opened the door to the UPS guy, who had several huge boxes for her. All from her brothers, it turned out. She kneeled on the floor and checked out each one. There was a microwave oven, a portable TV, an elaborate coffeemaker, a bread maker and a fancy leather backpack with all kinds of compartments.

She sat back on her haunches, overwhelmed.

Her brothers were trying to make her new life easier. Her heart squeezed with gratitude. And guilt. She'd let them down and they didn't even know it. Again her eyes watered and spilled over. She didn't know which choice made her feel worse—giving up or struggling onward.

The sound of the garage door grinding open made her scrub her eyes. Damn. Jackson was home. She turned her body so her back faced where he would enter, and rose on her knees to put the foam padding back on top of the microwave.

Jackson walked in whistling from the kitchen, then stopped midnote. "Wow. Early Christmas?"

Still facing away, she put a smile on her face. "My crazy brothers sent me all this. Can you believe it?" She turned to glance at him, then resumed closing the cardboard flap of the box.

But Jackson came to her and kneeled, facing her. "What's wrong, Heidi?"

"Nothing. I'm just…confused."

She made the mistake of looking into his eyes, which held on tight.

"About what?" He spoke so gently she wanted to tell him.

"About being here. About my brothers giving me all this junk. They wrote me a thousand-dollar check for incidentals. Can you believe that? They have no idea how foolish I've been. I lost the car they gave me. I lost everything. And I'm making hardly any money. I work at a strip club, for God's sake. I just…I can't fix it." Her chest heaved as she fought for air and the room seemed to close in on her.

"But you are fixing it," he said. "You've got three jobs. Jeez, what more could you do?"

"Maybe I should just…go home. Start over, you know? Save up again?" Her voice rose like a child's and she hated it. "Or just stay there. Do what I'm good at. Like you said, I was perfectly happy at Celia's Cut 'n' Curl learning from real life."

Jackson just folded her into his arms.

She wanted to resist, but she felt so bad, she sank into the comfort he offered.

"Getting robbed was a bad break. Anyone would be messed up by that."

"I should never have let that happen. I was so stupid."

"What did you tell me about making the best choices I could at the time?"

"Yeah, but…"

"All you did was lose an SUV and some tuition money. Drop in the bucket. I flushed tens of thousands of dollars down the toilet when my station folded. I'm the one who's stupid."

"I guess when you put it that way…" She was trying to joke, but it hurt.

"That's my girl. Kick me when I'm down." He leaned back to look at her. "How were you supposed to know the guys across the street were jackals? Hell, your brothers would understand that."

"But I had a plan and I'm nowhere close to fulfilling it."

"You can't give up now. Look at all you're doing. Hell, I thought Jasmine and Autumn were fighting the other day, but it turned out Jaz was asking Autumn's advice about a budget. A *budget*. I thought I was hallucinating. Those two don't listen to anybody, but they listened to you."

"I just started them talking…"

"Don't give up your dream, Heidi. Just don't." His dark eyes sparked with heat. "You can make it. I know you can."

His confidence in her felt good, lifted her spirits. Maybe he was right. She took a deep breath. "I guess I can stick it out a little longer," she said, not looking at him. "It's only been a couple of weeks."

"Exactly." He sounded so relieved she had to smile. Jackson wanted her to stay. That thought touched her. Maybe too much.

"Let me help you, Heidi," he said. "I can front you the tuition money. Pay me back when you catch up."

"Stop, Jackson. You've already given me so much—a place to stay, a job—two jobs, counting housekeeping." Which she'd neglected lately.

"I want to help you," he said doggedly. "Let me give you something."

"What I want from you isn't money," she said levelly, surprised by the boldness of her words, even as they reverberated inside her with tremendous power. She was staying, dammit. And she wanted what she wanted from Jackson.

"No?" he said hoarsely. Desire flared in his eyes and it made the same desire burst hotly in her. Good. She welcomed lust over doubt any day. She focused on it, let it build, let it wash over her.

"What I want from you is *this*." She grabbed his face, his cheeks rough with stubble against her palms, and kissed him. He tasted familiar and fabulous. It was a relief to be sure of one thing.

Jackson broke off the kiss. "But, Heidi, I'm—"

"Don't say you're not what I want. You're exactly what I want. We're good in bed. We have a blast. And that's what I want—to have a blast. To try everything. And we can still work together and live together without ruining that."

He closed his eyes, fighting his desire, she could tell, and she couldn't let him win that battle. She reached for his zipper.

"Heidi…" But he didn't try to stop her and she opened his pants and took his hard length out of his boxers. He felt good in her palm and right.

"If you keep that up—" he said, almost groaning.

"You won't be able to stop me? Good." Still holding him in one hand, she used her other hand to push him onto the floor, then slid herself down so she could take him in her mouth. It was her turn this time.

Jackson moaned and his body trembled beneath her, giving her a rush of power. Holding his shaft, she slowly ran her tongue around the top of his penis, the flesh smooth and velvet under the pressure of her tongue. The incoherent way Jackson choked out her name sent a rush of confidence through her.

She took him fully into her mouth and slid her lips

down, then up, again and again, each time taking him deeper. She tightened her lips and let her tongue trace his shape, reveled in the texture, the way he pushed into her mouth.

She liked the taste of him, flesh and man. He felt good in her mouth and she quickened her pace, keeping one hand on his shaft and holding her lips tight against him. He held her head with both hands, as if to maintain contact with her.

She was making love to him with her mouth and she felt powerful and sexy and so turned on. After a few seconds, he tensed and she knew he was about to come. She wanted that, but she also wanted him inside her, so she could feel his release, maybe join him with her own, which was close now. Her body was tight with need.

As if he'd read her mind, he stopped her. "I want inside you."

She lifted her mouth from his body and sat up to take off her shorts. This was great. She was having wild, unstoppable sex right here, right now, right on the living room floor.

"Not here. In a bed." Jackson stopped her hand.

"Here is perfect."

"You deserve better." He stood, yanked her to her feet and swung her into his arms, his eyes burning for her. Okay. She'd take Rhett Butler sweeping her up the stairs. So much better than being tossed over his shoulders and thrown down for a child's nap.

He carried her to her bed and laid down with her. He started on her blouse buttons, but he was shaking so badly, she had to take over. She undid her blouse and unclipped her bra, while he yanked his T-shirt over his head. They paused, looking at each other's naked chests for a second, then, both at once, they shoved off shorts and pants. They couldn't wait to be naked together.

Once they were, they stretched out, bare bodies pressed together, and kissed desperately for a while, telling each other how much they'd missed this, missed each other. Jackson broke off and rose over her, ready to enter her. That would be great, but she'd liked pushing him to the floor, having him in her sexual power, and she wanted to keep that feeling. "I want to do it this way," she said and rolled over, forcing him onto his back.

She rose to her knees, straddled him, looking down at his muscular body and burning eyes, which said, *I want in.*

With a shaking hand, she guided his velvet shaft to her entrance. He slid in, inch by exquisite inch, filling her, warming her, fitting her perfectly. Soon the base of his shaft bumped her clit. She loved the thick fullness of him within her. She felt dizzy, aroused and triumphant.

He looked up at her, his eyes hot and hungry, as though he'd been starving and had suddenly been offered a feast. He gripped her hips, guiding her up and down on his cock. "You feel good." He seemed so caught up in the sensation that his eyes closed.

"We're good together." She leaned forward so that his shaft rubbed her spot, and sped her movements. He squeezed her hips, holding back a little, she could tell, so as not to cause her pain.

Her orgasm arrived abruptly. As if he sensed it, his eyes flew open and he held her gaze, safe and silent, suspended in intimacy. *Go for it, sweetheart.* The message was clear in his eyes and she felt it in her heart just as they rocketed off together.

When the waves subsided, Heidi collapsed on Jackson's chest, grateful, relieved and proud of herself. She'd taken charge of the moment and it had been great. Better than great. Fabulous.

She listened to Jackson's heart beat against her ear, rode his chest up and down with his ragged breaths. She knew she had to say something, not let Jackson's silence rule this time—

"You're right," he said, surprising her, his voice hoarse. "We are good together."

She smiled, lifted her head to rest her chin on her fist. "We can do this, Jackson."

"You think?" The hope in his face delighted her.

"Yes, we can." The glory of what had happened seemed to give her back her courage. "Just like I'm not giving up my new life yet." She'd save her money a little longer. Maybe work a few more hours at the salon, give herself a chance.

"I have faith in you."

Jackson believed in her. Hell, he'd loan her money if she got desperate. That made her feel entirely too relieved, but she focused on how much better she felt. She cuddled into Jackson and he hugged her tight. They breathed together for a few seconds, hearts slowly relaxing into a steady rhythm.

"So what all did your brothers send you, anyway?" Jackson mused. "I saw a microwave and a TV and wasn't that a bread maker?"

She thought of their note. *We're proud of you. Even if we think you're crazy.* Her worrywart brothers wanted her to make it on her own. She couldn't let them down, either. She pushed up to look at Jackson again, his eyes soft and full of affection. "Yep, but I'm sending it all back, along with the check."

"You're sending it back? Jeez. That was good stuff."

"You already have a TV and a microwave, Jackson."

"But the microwave's old and dinky," he wheedled.

"I can't keep it. It comes with strings."

"Seems to me it comes with love."

"Loving strings are still strings. I'll keep the backpack as a reasonable gift. They can get store credit on the rest or donate it to the Unitarian Church's holiday bazaar."

"Won't they be hurt? Your brothers?"

"They know me. They'll expect this."

"Keep the check, Heidi. You could use it for tuition."

"If I kept it, they'd know something was wrong. I bet when you left home, you didn't take money from your parents."

Jackson's entire body stilled and emotions flew across his face. "As it turned out, I took every cent they had." His self-mocking smile was full of pain.

"What do you mean?"

"It was my inheritance I spent on the station. Every cent my father had saved over a lifetime for my mother and me. 'Keep something between you and the wolves,' remember? And I blew it all." His face was pale with guilt.

"So that made losing the station so much worse?"

"Yeah, but like you said—I made the best decision at the time."

But he didn't believe that. The agony in his face was as fresh as if it had happened yesterday. His parents had been gone two years, she remembered, and she'd bet the station failure had brought back the sorrow in full measure. "You feel like you let your father down?"

"At least he wasn't alive to see it."

"He wanted you to have the money, Jackson. And your dreams. You know he wanted that."

"What he wanted was for me to get married and give him grandkids. They were always bugging me about that." He rolled away from her and stared up at the ceiling. "That was why I didn't go to Chicago for Christmas. I didn't want the speech and the hassle and the arguing." He sounded so beaten.

She waited for a second to see if he'd continue, feeling the ache in his words. Then she realized what he was telling her, the secret he'd left between the lines. "So they came to see you..." she said, pausing.

"And died on the way," he finished roughly.

He blamed himself for their death. Losing their money had compounded his shame. No wonder Jackson seemed so hunkered down, so turned inward. He was weighed down by guilt and regret and grief, always grief. Her heart surged with sympathy, wanting to help somehow.

"But that was a long time ago," he said.

"Not long when you've lost people you love, Jackson. Your parents." She wanted to look at him, but she knew it would be too much for him. "Your parents' death wasn't your fault. You didn't blame them for driving into a storm, did you? Why would they blame you?"

"Because I was an ungrateful jerk," he snapped. "I didn't appreciate them. Or all they did for me." He sat up and put his feet over the side of the bed.

"I don't believe that for one minute. I know better. Your parents did, too."

Jackson was silent. She sat up, too, but didn't speak, not wanting to disturb his thoughts.

"Hey," he whispered finally, looking at her over his shoulder. "Next thing, you'll be asking to be paid for being my shrink, too." He patted her hand, looking straight ahead and away from her, though there was gratitude in his touch.

"That was on the house," she said, hoping her words had given him some peace. "You can pay me back by helping me haul all those boxes back to UPS."

"*All* the boxes?" Recovered from his emotions, he leaned back onto the bed, and rolled over her, giving her a wicked look. "How about you hang onto the bread maker?" He kissed her promisingly. "I'd kill for a nice thick slice of homemade bread to go with some peach jam." He shifted to her neck, moving his tongue exquisitely along the muscles there. "Could you make that maybe?" He kissed her throat next, then the top of her breast, shifting his body so he could keep going down.

"Mmm, when you put it that way...I guess the bread maker stays."

He kissed the middle of her stomach, blowing hot air until she quivered. "What about that crappy microwave?" More kisses, more downward shifting until he reached her *there*.

"Oo-o-okay...the microwa-aa-ave, too. You happy?"

"Very." He rubbed his face into her sex, giving her a delicious thrill. "In fact, I'm in heaven."

"Me, too," she said, feeling lifted off the bed with pure pleasure. At last something was working out right.

10

THE NEXT MORNING, Jackson sat on the floor in the living room, his back against the couch playing *Gran Turismo,* while Heidi cleaned house.

He was trying to act normal, but he kept watching her, letting his car crash into the other racers, the restraining wall, even the spectators, because he couldn't stop wanting her for a few seconds.

Heidi was amazing. She wanted to try all the positions. They were well on their way, too, and he was plain worn out. She seemed to treat this as a personal quest. *I want to get good at this,* she'd said, blinking those big eyes at him, her lips bruised from all the kissing.

You are good, sweetheart. He'd never had sex this good in his life.

Now she was bustling here and there, bending and stretching, like that first day, jiggling around with a dust rag, then running the vacuum. He'd never thought housework was sexy before.

She kneeled on the sofa and lifted a cushion so she could suck up nuts and nachos and lint. She was bent over, her butt wiggling enticingly, teasing him, until his erection could not be ignored. They hadn't done it from behind on their knees yet.

His car crashed into the wall with a tremendous sound

and the announcer complained on his behalf. Heidi stopped vacuuming and turned to him, glancing at the TV. "You lost again, Jackson."

"I can't help it when you're doing that."

"Is it the noise?"

"No." He clicked off the machine. "It's just you. I want to take you right there."

"You do?" she said, heat instantly sizzling in her eyes, her pale face going pink with excitement. "Oh, I would like that." She fairly quivered. "That makes me hot."

"Does it now?"

"Tell me what you want to do to me," she said, blushing. This embarrassed her, but it was part of her drive to do it all.

He climbed onto the sofa on his knees behind her and gently turned her so her stomach pressed the sofa. "I want to take you like this." He moved so she could feel his erection between the cheeks of her bottom.

"Mmm." She leaned back.

"Yeah." He ran his finger down the crack of her ass and she trembled at the contact.

"Tell me what you want to do, Jackson. Explain it."

"I want to pump into you until we both explode."

"And is this the position you want me in?" She thrust her peach-shaped ass, encased in those red spandex shorts, harder against his cock. "So you can just take me?" She looked over her shoulder at him. "Force your way into me?"

"Yeah." He'd never use force, but it was her fantasy, so he wouldn't argue. He ran his hands over the firm curves, then teased the space between her cheeks.

She whimpered and pushed at him. "Do it, Jackson. I want you to put yourself inside me deep and don't stop until I come. Make me come." She was gasping now, deeply aroused.

Now he wanted her bare, so he tore down her shorts, hungry for that wet, secret place that made her squirm. He touched her and she gasped and rubbed herself against his fingers.

He was so aroused and so happy. He had this amazing woman bent over, presenting her sex to him, completely trusting him to take care of her, to give her all she wanted. He grasped her hips and pushed slowly in, reaching around to touch her warm, swollen clit with his finger.

"Oh, yes. Do that. Yes. Screw me. Do it hard," she cried, rocking against him, desperate and fast. "Make me feel it."

He pulled out and pushed in deep, the soft roundness of her ass slapping his thighs.

"Harder, harder," she begged.

He jammed into her again and again, doing what she wanted, taking care not to use too much force. He didn't want her enthusiasm to push them to the point of pain. She moaned and panted, rocking with him. They climaxed together, both crying out. He said her name so roughly it hurt his throat.

They rested for a few seconds before he slid from her body. Then she turned to him. "That was so…amazing. I can't believe I said what I said." Her eyes were wide.

"I can't believe you did, either." He kissed her mouth. "You're one big surprise." He pulled her down onto the couch with him and held her in his arms, burying his nose in her neck. The smell of sex came off them in waves and when he felt her sweet breath on his chest something in him just plain gave way.

TWO NIGHTS LATER, from his DJ booth, Jackson watched the three star dancers huddle with Heidi, heads leaned in, hands waving to emphasize points. As he looked on, one after the other turned and stared up at him—Autumn, Jasmine, Nevada and his sweet lover. Uh-oh. Whatever they were cooking up had to do with him. He'd bet Heidi was the instigator. She stirred everybody up, one way or another.

That ridiculous sack of a blouse and skirt she wore looked as sexy as a barely there French maid uniform. They'd gone at it at the last minute tonight, against the door to the garage. He'd ripped down those goofy dime-store panties she had—posies or something, not daisies—and took her standing up, in the god-awful outfit. Fishnets and stilettos were boring compared to Heidi with those girlish undies wrapped around her ankles.

Are you happy? she'd asked him the afternoon he'd come home to her crying over the packages and she'd convinced him they could keep having sex. She'd meant was he happy about keeping the bread maker and the microwave, which was how he'd answered her. But the truth was that he *was* happy. Happier than he'd been in forever. He'd let himself take Heidi to bed and, worse, spilled his guts about being the reason his folks had died, but he felt…better.

You didn't blame your parents for driving into a storm, did you? Why would they blame you? The idea tipped his thoughts about that horrible time on end. But having Heidi around turned lots of things on end. The house felt…full. Not crowded, but like home.

Maybe it was the sex and the urge that followed to hook in where it was warm and just stick. He'd gotten in. And he wanted to stay for a while. That's how it was with men, right?

He couldn't wait to get home for more. She wanted sex

everywhere, in every room. On the floor, even, as if that proved how sexual she was. She was all the sensual he could handle and then some. She was like an erotic Goldilocks, trying out all the beds, all the positions, looking for *just right*. It was all just right to him.

She said they could screw each other's brains out and nothing would change. So far, that seemed to be true. He hoped to God it was, because he liked everything the way it was.

Except for this, he thought uneasily, as the three dancers headed his way, a curvy conga line of trouble. Heidi stayed put. She'd sent them on some mission. She looked up at him and waggled her fingers. His heart lifted and he smiled a smile so big it hurt. *Tone it down,* he told himself, but he waved back anyway.

Then he realized he'd been so distracted he'd failed to announce the next dancer. He corrected that and put on her music. Meanwhile, the trio tromped in, Autumn in the lead. He turned on his stool to face them, folding his arms, braced for the story. "What's up, ladies?"

"We need to talk about some improvements to our working conditions," Autumn said.

"Like what?"

"Like a real dressing room, for one thing, with some privacy. Stalls in the bathroom, bulbs in all the makeup lights. *All* the lights."

"We need new electrical," Nevada added. "So we're not blowing fuses and risking a fire."

"And a childcare allowance," Jasmine blurted.

The other two stared at her.

"Well? It's an employee benefit."

"The point is, Jax, we're the talent," Autumn said. "We're why the people come. We need some consideration."

"Consideration?"

"Serenity to revive our creative juices," Jasmine threw in.

"Your creative…what?" What the hell was Heidi doing to him?

"She means get the cleaning supplies out of our dressing room," Autumn said. "You can use that room with broken chairs for the break room and for storage. Give us the dressing room. Dancers only."

She had a point, he guessed, and at least that was a practical suggestion.

"Plus, we should be paid to practice," Nevada tossed in. "Real dancers get that."

"You have your routines down. You want to add a little something, you come in early. What's the big deal?"

"The big deal is that Nevada's working up some new choreography," Autumn said, "and we'll need a costume allowance. Jasmine will make the outfits, but we need cash for fabric, trim and accent pieces."

"It's the New Burlesque," Nevada said. "It's telling a story, not just grinding away on the pole and waving T and A. Heidi saw a news piece."

"There's nothing wrong with T and A. Customers like the basics."

"Customers *settle* for the basics. They don't know any better. They'll *love* the new stuff." Autumn's eyes flamed at him and her chin shot up. She was a dog with a bone when she got an idea in her head. *Dammit, Heidi.*

"I'll talk to Duke," he said to appease them.

"Jax."

"Okay, okay. Jeez. Tell Taylor to give you a couple hundred from the bar for the costumes. But show me these new routines before you get too far."

"What about the other stuff? The dressing room and the brownouts?"

"I'll see what I can do."

"We can circulate a petition with the other dancers if we have to. There are other clubs, you know...."

"I'll work on it," he said, shaking his head.

"We'll count on you then," Autumn said gravely.

"Oooh, I'm up next," Nevada said, spinning and heading for the door.

"Me, too," Jasmine said, heading off after her. She paused to blow him a kiss. "Power to the people. Ciao."

Hell.

Autumn remained standing with him.

"This whole idea come from Heidi?" he asked her. "The working conditions and the act?"

"She got us talking."

He turned on his stool to look out at the woman in question, who was staring anxiously in his direction. When their eyes met, her smile broadened. He should be pissed, but he couldn't even work up irritation when she looked at him that way.

He felt Autumn beside him. "Hey..." Her stare felt like a stab in the side of his face.

He dragged his eyes from Heidi to her. "What?"

"You were looking at Heidi like she's what's for dinner."

He shrugged.

"And she's looking up at you like *come and get it*. What did you do, Jackson?"

"Nothing. I—"

"You slept with that poor girl again, didn't you? She said it was just once."

"She told you we slept together?" That surprised him.

"We dragged it out of her, but it sounded like a one-time thing."

"It was. And then…it wasn't. But it's under control."

"You'll break her heart, you big, dumb lug," she said.

He cringed internally, a little worried. "She knows what she wants, believe me." Especially with sex. She'd spelled it out with moans and whispers and touches and cries.

"She's a baby, Jax, with a shiny new heart that's never been cracked. I know the signs." Autumn had a track record with fast-talking guys who made promises they never delivered on.

"She says it's just sex."

Heidi looked up again and waved at him as eagerly as a cheerleader in a parade. His mouth went dry.

"She's flippin' enchanted," Autumn said with exasperation.

He gave a faint wave. She did look a little stunned and the sort of happy that hurt like hell when it disappeared. He kind of felt that way, too.

"You have to break it off. Look at her."

Maybe Autumn was right. Just because sex was enough for him, didn't mean it was enough for her, even if she thought it was. *Look at her.*

Damn. He really wanted to fall asleep with her tonight. Listening to her breathing drop into sleep after sex melted off the tension of the bar better than anything he'd known. What reason could he give? *You'll get hurt?* She'd smack him for that.

"Hello?" Autumn ran her hand before his eyes.

"What? Yeah. Okay. I'll end it, all right? Quit hassling me."

"She's heading up here, so you can tell her now."

"You know, you keep it up, I'll buy your whips and leather myself."

"Sounds fun. For now, play that song from your musician friends. The first cut. My favorite."

He nodded and she kissed him on the cheek. "It'll be okay, Jax. It's for the best. And talk to Duke for us."

"Yeah, yeah," he said, his heart heavy. He turned to his CD rack and searched out the music Autumn wanted, dreading Heidi's arrival.

"Hey, you." Her husky voice made his heart sing.

"Hey, yourself." He wanted to wrap her up tight in his arms, somehow prepare her for the letdown, but he knew that if he touched her, he wouldn't be able to go through with it. He turned on his stool to look at his laptop.

"I like this song," she said, made shy by the hesitation she must have seen in his face.

"It's a couple of studio guys I like. There's a singer who would do great with them."

"Why don't you put them together?"

"It's a hassle. The musicians are laid back and the singer's Type A. They'd need a manager to really make it work."

"So be the manager. Sounds like you've already figured out what has to happen."

"That takes time. I work nights."

"There's a lot you could handle during the day. Taylor would cover if you had to take some time off."

He shrugged, not wanting to get into this with all they had to discuss hanging like a fat, ugly rain cloud in the air.

"Are you afraid it won't work out? Like the radio station?"

"Stop throwing me on your couch again," he said, trying to sound lighthearted. She was close to questions he didn't want to answer.

"Don't get grouchy, you big bear. I'm just trying to

help." She gave his forearm a playful squeeze. Which gave him a killer erection. He was so easy when it came to her.

But she was vulnerable, as Autumn had said. The more time that passed, the more her hopes would rise. He had to look out for her. Close off the hurt early, cauterize it while it was small. Hell, he'd made what they shared sound like a bloody wound.

She gave him that slow, big-eyed blink and made him feel even worse. So he did the only thing he could think of.

He picked a fight.

"And what the hell are you doing agitating the girls for, anyway?"

"They're women, not girls, and I made a few suggestions."

"Jasmine wants paid childcare, for God's sake." He deliberately sounded grouchier than he felt. "That is ridiculous."

"There's nothing ridiculous about an employer providing benefits to his employees." An edge came into her voice.

"They get paid very, very well. That's their benefit. Duke's going bare bones until this place makes more money. I had to push to get the curtains and better chairs as it is."

"Happy employees make for happy customers, Jackson."

"The girls were plenty happy until you started making trouble."

"Making trouble? The lack of outlets in the dressing rooms is a safety code violation at the least, not to mention the lack of privacy. And just because the dancers weren't saying anything doesn't mean they were happy.

The fact they're taking action is a sign they're more aware of their personal power."

"They've got men groveling at their feet, throwing money at them seven nights a week. That's personal power."

"I'm talking about dignity and self-esteem."

He groaned. "Can't you just leave well enough alone?"

"Not when something should be better. And I would think you'd be happy to help them. You're the guy they go to when they have problems."

"This is different." She had a point, but so what? "Just because your own life isn't working out, don't be turning everyone else's upside down."

"What's the matter with you, Jackson?" She took a step backward, wounded, her eyes big with hurt.

Damn it to hell.

"I just don't like you meddling in things you don't understand."

"Is it us? Is that what's wrong?"

Hell, yes. But he looked into her eyes, sparkling with alarm, poised for pain, and he just couldn't say it. "Forget it. I told the girls I'd talk to Duke, so just drop it."

"We should talk about what's really going on."

"You got what you wanted. Let it go."

"Don't talk to me like that," she snapped.

Hell. He'd have to tell her the truth now. He couldn't stand her thinking he was an asshole.

"Can I interrupt a sec?" The voice made them both turn. Rox stood in the doorway. Man, he was popular tonight. Though the interruption was a relief.

"No problem," he said. "Come on in."

Heidi smiled uncertainly at Rox, then said to him, "We'll talk later." Her departing look lingered, half-wounded, half-worried and a little pissed.

He dreaded the conversation. How the hell could he explain the situation so that it didn't hurt her pride? Or hurt her at all?

"So, hey, I'm really liking this song…" Rox said, getting close and giving him her ooh-baby smile. She was looking to get laid, he knew from Taylor, since she'd dumped her boyfriend. Tag, he was it, Jackson guessed. For tonight anyway.

"Yeah. It's good."

"How do you find your music, Jackson?" she said, moving close enough to look over his shoulder at the laptop where he matched his MP3s with the upcoming list of dancers. She just wanted to give him a shot of her chest, he was sure. Double D and Nature's own, though he observed that fact without the rush of lust he'd expect from the old Jackson.

"How do you decide?" she asked breathily.

"I follow new sounds. I have friends in the business. And what I play depends on my mood and who's dancing." He looked her over. Great body, pretty face and smart. Taking business classes somewhere. Phoenix College? Probably just what he needed to get his mind off Heidi, who would no doubt grill him about his crankiness all the way home.

"So, what do you do on your days off, Jax?"

"Depends on the day," he said, trying to get more worked up by the possibility she offered him.

"And what you feel like?" She smiled, playfully licking her lips.

He nodded slowly.

"So, maybe we could see what we feel like together?" She ran a nail down the side of the equalizer, near his arm, still looking at him.

If he spent time with Rox, even just hanging out, it would clear some space with Heidi. Remind her they were a casual thing. The idea had the appeal of all-you-can-eat hot wings after a Thanksgiving feed, but he opened his mouth to say "sure." Instead, he heard himself say, "My life's complicated right now." And he was pretty sure it was about to get worse.

FROM THE BOTTOM of the stairs to the DJ booth, Heidi watched Rox hit on Jackson. It was like running her tongue over the rough temporary Dr. Dave had covered her tooth with until he'd cemented the porcelain crown in place. It had made her tongue raw, but she hadn't been able to leave it alone.

She knew what this was about. She'd been in on the conversation where Rox had declared herself so horny that she'd settle for anyone with a penis and a pulse. Jackson was far more than that, dammit, so why did she have to pick him? Why not Taylor or one of the other cute guys? There was a darling bouncer who seemed perfect for Rox.

Heidi watched Jackson smile at Rox with the same smart-ass grin he gave her. Her heart felt pinched, like a finger in a car door. She was in trouble. Sex with Jackson wasn't just a new experience, a *blast,* or breakaway sex. She was like a cocky first-time gambler who'd swaggered into the back room for a hundred-dollar game. Except she was about to lose her heart instead of her shirt.

She wasn't due for a break, but she needed one, so she hurried out back, breathing in the muggy summer air, trying to settle herself. Her uniform held in the heat, so she didn't feel cooler, but the golden sliver of moon overhead was so pretty, and just being outside in the dark calmed her. She heard Jackson's music leaking out of the bar, accompanied by the hiss of nearby cars. She took in the scent of a mesquite grill from the restaurant down the block and tried to calm down.

Would Jackson invite Rox home to moan and writhe and make the mattress creak tonight? Or wait until his day off? Either way, her mouth filled with the taste of metal and she felt faint.

The terrible truth was that she wanted Jackson all to herself. She'd been kidding herself. She cared. Too much. So, standing in the golden glow of the parking lot lights, her heart tight, her breathing shallow, her nerves taut as rubber bands, she made a decision: *Get out now. Before you get hurt—worse.*

She'd had a lovely time, set herself free of sexual inhibition, developed confidence. She'd gotten what she wanted, right? Any more would be greedy. How could she fall for the first hot guy she'd slept with? It was embarrassing and so small town. Besides, Jackson and she were on entirely different life paths. He was an ex-mechanic bar manager with a music hobby. She was a therapist in training, headed to college, where she'd meet more men, as Autumn had said. When she was ready, she'd find a man to spend her life with, a man with similar interests. Her heart was getting ahead of her good sense.

What's more, Jackson had sensed it and picked a fight to push her away. He'd read her behavior as clinginess. Maybe he had a point, though it irked her that he couldn't just say it, instead of quarreling over nothing. They should stop now, before they got hateful to each other.

She looked up at the golden sliver of the moon…it looked like half the Moons logo, as if offering a seal of approval to the place. Her heart lifted. What if she and Jackson could be together? He was a good man. He'd limited his life, but he could do more. She could help him figure out what he wanted—something with the music he loved.

But that was his life, not hers. She was sliding off course, getting distracted by Jackson. Leaning on him emotionally, too. She closed her eyes against the magic curve of moon and steadied herself. She'd gotten carried away from her own life, her own goals. She should look into taking an online psychology class. That would give her a leg up and ease the intimidation she felt about ASU. And distract her from Jackson and his amazing hands and tremendous mouth and remarkable…everything.

With a last sigh, she headed back to beer orders and tip garnering. She'd talk to Jackson on the way home. End it simply, stay friendly. Suck up the pain and count herself lucky for catching it in time. Maybe she'd wait until they got home and she'd be certain not to cry.

JACKSON FOUND HEIDI waiting for him in the Aston Martin when he finished the last hassle of the night. She'd put away the car cover and sat very still and upright in her seat. There was a quiet sadness about her that hurt to watch.

What was she thinking? She was harder to read than the women he'd known, though his relationships tended to be short-lived and based on sex.

"Sorry I'm late," he said. "The soda dispenser went wonky."

"You have a job to do," she said. He hated how blue she sounded. Maybe she was just tired.

"Listen, why don't you borrow the van in the morning so you can sleep in a little? Catch up on your rest."

She turned to him. "I can get to work on my own." He didn't like the crisp snap in her words. *Mind your own business.*

"Just an offer."

When she didn't respond, he started the car and headed home. Out of the corner of his eye, he watched her. She held her hair away from her face and didn't lean back to let the breeze blow it as usual. She was definitely upset.

Just wait until he told her they were through. She'd probably cry. The idea made his stomach churn, as if he'd gulped down too many eye-watering enchiladas at *Los Dos Molinos*.

All the way home, he tried to figure out what to say and when he pulled into the driveway, he realized he hadn't enjoyed one minute of the night drive he usually loved. The empty streets, the moonlight, the breeze lifting the hairs on his arm, the sense that he owned the night and the city. All that was gone, thanks to the complicated woman beside him. Damn.

He had to get this over with, get back to the calm, quiet life he'd enjoyed before she'd had her Outback stolen from his curb. He pulled into the driveway and threw the car into Park. "Look, I'm sorry I got pissed about the girls' demands."

"They're women, not girls. And you were picking a fight to put distance between us. I get that."

"I was what?" He didn't like the you-pathetic-little-man tone in her voice. The voice he liked to hear gasp his name when she came. "Hang on just a minute there. That's not what I—"

She braked him with an upraised hand. "It's okay. We should stop."

"What?" He darted a look at her. *She* wanted it to be over?

"It's passive-aggressive of you to deflect the real issue."

"Passive-aggressive? Deflect? It's three o'clock in the

morning, Heidi. Save the psych mumbo jumbo for daylight hours."

"Come on. Quit pretending to be this simple, salt-of-the-earth guy. You're smart and you know people. All I'm saying is to be direct and say what you mean."

"Okay, we should stop the sex. Direct enough for you?"

"Perfectly," she snapped. "Good."

"Good," he snapped back. He'd meant to be gentle, but she got him going with that superior tone. He looked up at the sky and wanted to howl in frustration at the shred of moon he could see.

He pushed the garage door button and it growled up. He drove in and braked too hard. She was out the door and letting herself into the house before he even turned off the car. *Okay, be that way.*

He went straight to his room, not even stopping in the kitchen for a taste of something great she'd made. He was especially fond of her cinnamon bread. In his room, he put heavy metal on his stereo so he could lift weights. That's what he did when he was frustrated, and she'd just have to put up with the noise.

For a few minutes anyway.

The woman was messing with his head, making him feel guilty about how he treated the dancers, how he ran his own life. Lying on the bench, he ripped off some butterflies, pushing hard, working fast, hurting himself. He'd gotten soft eating all that crap she cooked. He had to get down to fighting weight again. Though what the hell was he fighting?

What did he want with Heidi anyway? She'd never be happy with him. She'd be harping on him all the time, digging into his head about his feelings, his *motivation,* his *soul.*

Screw that.

He heard her go in the bathroom, followed by the sound of rushing water. She was taking a shower. A shower. Heidi in the shower, naked and beautiful, going pink from the heat, steam making her look like something from a dream. He let the weights clunk to the floor.

They'd had great sex in the shower. No new moves he could think of in water, but with Heidi every time seemed new.

He could slip into the stall right now and make love to her without a word. They deserved a farewell go. A beautiful end to a damn fine time, right?

She's a baby, Jax, with a shiny new heart that's never been cracked. Autumn was right. And he could hurt her with no effort at all. Just by being himself. He went for overhead presses, loading on extra weight to distract himself with pain.

He was driving himself into muscle-tearing extra reps when he got a whiff of her flowery scent and his arms almost buckled.

"Jackson?" His name sounded so good in her husky voice.

He barely got the over-weighted bar onto the upright, his vision gray from the strain. He sat up.

She stood in his doorway, backlit by the nightlight in the hall. He could clearly see the outline of her breasts and the curve of her hips through his old Hawaiian shirt. God, she was gorgeous. He leaned forward to turn down the music…and hide his hard-on.

"I'm sorry I was snotty," she said, folding up her attitude like the Aston Martin's ragtop. "The point is, you were right. Sex can be complicated when you live and work with someone."

"It can? I mean, yeah, it can." Damn, because just then all he could think of was pulling her onto this bench and making love to her fresh-washed, shower-warm body, burying his face in the curtain of her hair and cupping the small mounds of her breasts until she gasped for more.

"And, also…" He watched her pretty throat work over a swallow before she continued. "You should feel free to bring Rox here. This is your house, after all."

Even in the dimness, he could see that was the last thing she wanted him to do. Seeing her face like this, pained, but being brave, gave him a charley horse in the chest and made him want to comfort her and protect her and promise things he had no business promising.

"I wouldn't sleep with Rox if she came to me naked with a gun," he said, his voice rougher than he'd intended.

"You wouldn't? Really?"

"No, I wouldn't. She's not…" *You.* The word bubbled up, wanted out. He opened and closed his mouth like a desperate bass in a net.

"She's not what?" Her eyes searched his face, looking for the very thing he had to hold back at all costs.

"I'm just not interested in her, okay?" A strange ache swamped him, so strong he wanted to groan, so he blurted something sure to piss her off. "I'm glad you see this my way."

"Your way?" She looked irritated, then her face took on a wicked light. "Anyway, now we'll both be able to bring a lover home without the other person getting weird."

"Both?" He sounded like a dope.

The possibility of Heidi bringing a guy here trickled through him like acid from a cracked battery, melting the insulation from all his wiring. She would make love to the guy. Moan his name, wiggle and twist and practically pass out from pleasure. Damn. Damn. Damn.

She spun on her heels and left, but not before he caught a gleam of triumph, like welding sparks in the dark. Somehow she'd won this little battle. And he wasn't in the mood to lose.

And just who did she have in mind to screw? Taylor? He wasn't good enough for her. Nice guy and all, but he was a bartender. Surely not someone else at Moons. One of the customers who saw through her tacky clothes to the hot woman underneath? A sleazebag checking out strippers? Surely she wouldn't stoop to that. She should wait until she got to college and found some appropriate guy and she'd better get proof of a blood test first.

Jackson might not be the right man for her, but he sure wasn't letting her get in trouble while she was under his roof. He'd talk to her about it. When he could do it without pissing her off. *You smother us, Jax.* Jasmine was always telling him that and Heidi had declared him smug. He was who he was, dammit, and that wouldn't change.

Except, he was different, he realized, rolling his shoulders back to ease the tension that idea caused. In little, inside ways. Heidi had started something rolling through him, adjusted his gearing so he ran…well, different.

He had the uneasy feeling he'd never be the same again.

11

HEIDI PULLED her peace offering for Jackson out of the oven to let it cool before she frosted it. Cinnamon bread—his favorite. Living together these past two days since their decision to stop having sex had been rocky. They'd been testy and moody and just plain cranky. They both had hurt feelings, she knew, and she missed his big bear of a body in her bed. And not having sex was definitely making her grouchy.

It was time to fix it. For both their sakes. She needed his help with the dancers' new act and she had an idea that would help him, too. He'd never agree to it as long as this tension was in the air.

Hence the peace offering, which included the hot oil treatment she'd offered him the day she arrived and a haircut, which he needed. His shaggy hair made him look a bit too ferocious. He was due back from the gym soon and she'd set out a stool, towels, her scissors and the hot oil mix she'd made herself with dried rosemary leaves and olive oil.

She started coffee and set out two Moons mugs, since she wasn't up for watching Jackson bring bare breasts to his lips, and gave her ficus some water. The tree seemed to be suffering, which was odd, since she watered it regularly. Maybe more light. She shifted it closer to the window, stood back and sighed. It looked the way she felt—wilted and lost.

She'd just finished frosting the bread and the last of the water had sizzled into the decanter, when the garage door opened, signaling Jackson's return. Her heart pounded with anticipation and she fought to keep her smile from spreading beyond a reasonable greeting. She still had it bad.

He walked in, a plastic shopping bag hanging from one hand, and sniffed. "Cinnamon bread?" He sounded eager as a child.

"All for you. To apologize for how I've been acting."

"And I got this for you." He held out the sack, emblazoned with the burgundy and gold logo of ASU. Inside, she found three psychology textbooks marked *used*. "From the bookstore. Assigned by the psych professors. These three looked interesting." He seemed almost shy. "So you can get a head start."

"Jackson. That's so sweet of you…" Her throat tightened with emotion, so she bent her head to flip through the pages of the first book. "I can't wait to dig in." What a good man he was, supporting her dream, when she'd barely realized she'd been neglecting it herself. Here he was, backing her play.

She looked into his beaming face. "I have something else for you. I thought I would do…your hair."

"Do my what?" Heat spiked in his eyes.

"Your h-hair." She stumbled over the words, caught off guard by the sexual reminder. "Give you the treatment I promised the first day, remember? Hot oil?"

"Oh, I remember."

"To keep your hair tuned up?" She smiled, trying to make a joke when she was feeling the same heat she saw in his face.

"I don't know, Heidi…."

"I'm all set up." She gestured toward the sink where the stool waited and the countertop with her equipment. "And I'll give you a haircut afterward."

"A haircut…?" He swallowed hard. "That would be…nice." He sounded as though he longed for it, and dreaded it, too. "Where do you want me?"

How about the table? Shove that cinnamon bread out of the way. Except maybe the frosting would be fun… They'd forgotten to try sex with food. "Right here," she said, patting the stool by the sink with a shaky hand. "Shampoo first so the oil will absorb better."

He sat on the stool and she unfolded a towel for his shoulders to keep his shirt dry.

Instead, he crossed his arms at the hem and whipped it up and off. There was his naked chest, muscles shivering as he tossed the shirt to the floor. She went rubbery at the sight, just like that first day when she'd polished his best shirt.

"Sure…why not? We can do it that way," she mumbled, rolling the towel into a pad for his neck, avoiding the luscious sight.

He leaned back on the towel and she reached past his head to turn on the water, aware that her breasts were inches from his face. She could feel him staring at them, wanting them. Doing his hair had sounded simple and thoughtful when she'd decided to do it, but now she saw it would be torture. All she could think of was his lips moving the millimeters necessary to take her nipple through her top.

After dreadful seconds, the water was hot and she turned the sprayer onto Jackson's dry hair, running her fingers through the thick strands.

"Mmm," he said.

She risked a glance and saw that his eyes were closed, his face soft with the pleasure of the warm water on his scalp.

She relaxed a little, applied shampoo, scrubbing deep with her nails, then massaging his scalp with her finger pads.

"Nice," he murmured, then opened his eyes, catching her gaze. "No one's ever washed my hair before."

That fact touched her, but she strove to sound sensible. "That's too bad. It's so good for you. It stimulates…the roots."

"You bet it does." But he meant something else and her breath hitched and her fingers trembled. She pushed on, scrubbed harder, settling herself.

"Ow…easy there."

"Sorry." She slowed down before she scraped off his scalp altogether and focused on what she wanted from Jackson. "I have an idea you can help with."

"Yeah?"

"The new numbers the girls are working on require great music, you know." She felt him shift gears.

"I'll put some pieces together. No problem."

"I'm thinking live music would be better—more theatrical—and the girls agree."

"Live music?"

"Yes." She rinsed his hair, using the spray nozzle.

"Mmm." He released a deep sigh of pleasure. He'd never be more vulnerable than right now. This was the perfect opportunity for Jackson to do what he really wanted to do. She'd just give him a little push.

"So, I thought, why not get your studio guys together…with the singer, too?"

"You want me to…?" Obviously sluggish from what she was doing to his hair, it took him a second to figure out what she was asking. "Huh? You mean get Heather at Moons? She'd never go for that."

"If she sees the routines, she might." She worked the water through, shampoo swirling down the drain. "It's not stripping so much. It's more of a revue, really. The idea is to bring in couples, not just men. And live music is just the edge we need."

"I haven't talked to Heather about working with the guys, let alone about singing in a topless club."

"So, now you have a reason to talk to her. It would mean so much to the girls…."

She felt him ponder the idea, struggling against the soothing water and her fingers on his skull. She kept the water going a little longer, maintaining the trance, she hoped.

Eventually she had to ask him to sit up. She wrapped a towel around his head and went to warm the measuring cup of oil in the microwave, holding her breath for his next words.

"Heather *is* between gigs," he mused. "I do know that."

She brought the oil to where he sat, set it on the counter and stepped between his legs to pat the excess moisture from his hair with the towel. "Sounds perfect."

Water trickled down his chest, tempting her to lick it off. How had they missed sex in the kitchen? Kitchens were sexy places. Of course, with Jackson, every room was sexy. She sighed, fighting to focus on her purpose. "Nevada's choreography is amazing. She'll like that."

"The guys will, too, no doubt."

She drizzled the thick liquid onto the top of his head, spreading it with her fingers, inhaling the soothing rosemary scent.

"Oh, God." He closed his eyes.

His voice made her melt like the oil. She imagined trickling it onto his chest and arms, whipping off her top and rubbing herself all over him. Why, oh why, hadn't she thought of oil or massage even? They'd missed so many options.

And now, here she stood between his legs, hands covered in oil, unable to do anything about it. Jackson's hands rested on his knees. He could grab her hips in an instant and yank her close. *Come here,* he would say in a hoarse voice....

What he did say was, "Are you about done there?"

"Just about," she said, gratified that he felt the same tension she struggled with.

She fetched plastic wrap and approached, tearing it off as she came.

"What's that for?" He raised his brows in wicked query.

"To keep the heat in while the oil soaks."

"You're wrapping my head in plastic?"

"To make your hair healthy and lush. Trust me."

"I do. You're the only person who could talk me into this." His voice held wonder and confusion. "And just about anything else you want."

She moved between his legs again and began covering his head, trying not to shake too badly.

He gripped her hips to steady her and she almost gave up and dropped into his lap. Instead, she asked, "So you'll do it?"

"Oh, yeah, I'll do it," he breathed, lifting his gaze to her mouth. *I'll do anything you want.*

She felt dizzy and unsteady on her feet, so she forced herself to focus on the plan. "That's great, Jackson. The girls will be thrilled. And I'm sure Heather will see what good exposure this will mean. I think we can do media and everything…" She babbled on about the possibilities as the heat between them slowly dissipated.

"You've had your way with me again, haven't you?" Jackson said finally, giving her a weak version of his smart-ass grin.

"Not quite," she said, "but it will have to do." Beyond Jackson, she noticed the books he'd bought her. A reminder of her real goal, her purpose for being here. Stick to the plan. "While this soaks, how about some coffee and cinnamon bread?"

"You had me at the first whiff," he said.

She sliced bread and poured coffee and they talked about the new routines and the music the dancers needed. The scene was unnervingly domestic, intellectually stimulating and sexually tense, all at the same time. Her brain felt tied in knots. To calm herself, she sipped slowly, focused closely on the musky taste, the warm moisture, the mug against her fingers.

Jackson stared at Heidi while she sucked coffee with those luscious lips, groaning inside. The woman was killing him. All the while she was running her fingers over his scalp, pouring hot oil in his hair, he'd become so dazed she had him starting a band, getting a singer—drummer, too—and, while he was at it, maybe writing some music.

He watched her lick frosting from the tip of her finger, wiggling in her chair, and went soft inside. She was saying something about contacting the entertainment reviewers and writing news releases, but he could only watch her running her pink tongue around her finger and fight the urge to lunge across the table and grab her. He had to get out of here. He realized she'd asked a question. "Huh?"

"I said, don't you think an ad would help?" She leaned

closer, which squeezed her breasts onto her forearms. Did she have any idea what she was doing to him?

"Duke will never agree to a new ad," he said, but he had to clear his throat to get the words out.

She blinked those big eyes at him. "Too bad."

"Maybe we add copy to the regular one," he choked out. "I could talk Duke into that."

"That's great," she breathed, pushing to her feet and moving to the sink. "Let's rinse out and do the cut."

He moved to the stool again.

"Lie back for me," she said softly.

Oh, yeah. Lie back, sit up, go down, roll over. He'd get in any position she wanted him. And there were her fingers on him again and warm water and her nipples inches away. Jeez. There seemed to be some direct wiring from the top of his head to his cock and it was shooting off electricity in hot bursts. He could only hope she wouldn't ask him for anything else—the Aston Martin, his last dime, his first born—or he'd give it to her and then some. Bad enough he'd promised her a band, for chrissake.

A band he hadn't even put together.

He closed his eyes and fought hot desire, keeping his hands on his knees, like the men at Moons getting a lap dance. No touching. Absolutely no touching.

He made it through the washing and rinsing, but then it was the haircut, his fantasy come to life. Her fingers felt so good on his scalp. And she ran the comb through his hair while he stared at her nipples through the flowery top she'd worn the day they met. He wanted to taste them.

Scritch, scritch. The scissors snipped the hair near his ear and bits of hair slid down his body like her eyelashes when she went down on him.

Stop it. Think baseball. Think two strikes, three balls.

Make that blue balls.

She smelled so damn good this close. And her breath was sweet on his face. She stood between his legs again. He could close his thighs on her and she'd sit on his lap and he would touch her and she would squeal…and there was more of that hot oil over there. Man. Ripping off her little top, smearing the hot stuff so she was slick and slippery, sliding over him, sliding into her body where she was slick from a whole other kind of liquid. Too bad he hadn't thought of oil when they were still doing it. He hadn't cared about anything fancy when he was with her. He just wanted her.

He still did. He liked having her here. Baking him bread, sitting at the table talking things over. That could be nice. Or maybe it was just the sex. *It's over, you big, dumb lug.* That's how Autumn would put it.

Snip, snip, tickle, tickle. She wiggled in front of him, her fingers flicking, comb flying, bits of hair fluttering down his chest. She leaned forward and her thigh brushed his erection.

She froze, scissors poised and her eyes hooked his in that way they always had, like invisible cholla spines. "This is hard," she murmured. She looked right at his lap and he got harder. "I miss…"

Sex. She meant *sex.* "Yeah. Me, too." But it was a dead end. A problem. And she had to move on.

To someone else. Another guy. The thought zapped his hard-on like a bucket of ice in his lap. He had to make sure she'd be safe. "You will be careful, right?"

"Huh?" She stopped midsnip and looked at him. "Careful about what?"

"Make sure he's a decent guy, I mean?"

"Excuse me?"

"Any guy would be happy to be with you—believe me—but don't just—"

"Screw the first guy I meet? Like I did with you? Is that what you're saying?" She sounded pissed and amused at the same time.

"You know what I mean. You're not the kind of woman who sleeps around. You need a solid citizen. A guy with a regular nine-to-five and a future."

"I know what I want, Jackson. I can pick my own lovers, thank you."

Something about that bothered him, so he said something stupid. "I just don't want you getting into trouble on my watch."

"On your…what?" She dropped the hank of hair she'd been trimming and it fell in his eyes. "I've already got two worrywart brothers. I don't need a third." She yanked up the comb full of hair, jerking his head up.

"Ow."

"Sorry." Snip, snip, whack, yank. No more slow tugs or sexy *snnnnick, snnnnicks*. Now she was doing a time trial of a haircut. She was pissed.

He'd done it again—said the wrong thing.

In the nick of time.

FIVE DAYS LATER, Heidi sat with Jackson and watched Jasmine, Nevada and Autumn work through the new routines for "Let Us Entertain You," which was what they'd named their revue. Duke was due in a couple of hours to "check out this burlesque business," so the girls were desperate to put on a good performance.

They were doing a seven-veils dance, using practice scarves until Jasmine finished the actual costumes, and Heidi thought the moves were genius—erotic, athletic and dreamlike. "This is so much better than the usual routines," she said to Jackson. "It's sexy, not vulgar. Women customers will love it." They hadn't stopped talking about the project since the hot-oil treatment, cinnamon-bread incident.

Jackson just grinned.

The band was improvising a Middle Eastern sound with a heavy calypso rhythm. "And the music is incredible. You really came through, Jax." Heather sang scat, high and haunting. "And Heather's amazing."

"I still can't believe her reaction to singing in a strip club. She thinks it's *trippy,* can you believe that?" He shook his head, still smiling.

"The drummer's great. I know you had to do some fast talking to get him."

"He's pretty laid-back, but we'll see how it works out."

"They sound great together, Jackson."

"Yeah." He sighed contentedly. He'd been livelier and chattier than she'd ever seen him, making her even more proud she'd pushed him to do this.

"Hold it!" Nevada barked at Autumn and Jasmine, who stopped, grateful it seemed for a breather, since Nevada had been working them hard. "*Legato* on the keyboard," Nevada said to the musicians, "but keep the drums big. More bells, too." She sounded so sure of what she was saying that no one questioned her, not even the exhausted dancers.

"You go, girl," Heidi whispered.

Jackson snorted. "I've never seen Nevada this…"

"Alive? Driven?"

"No. Bitchy. She'll hit her stride, I hope. Right now she's fired up and freaked."

"This is what she always wanted to do, so of course she's enthusiastic."

"I'm surprised that Jasmine and Autumn are taking it without backtalk. They're never this—"

"Responsible? Dedicated?"

"No. Wimpy. But that, too." He gave another happy sigh.

"You know what we are, Jackson, you and me? Impresarios."

"Is it contagious? Or illegal?"

"We're entertainment producers. I'm proud of us."

"It's all you, Heidi. You started this. And it's all good."

His smile lit his eyes with pride. Working on the project together had been fun. She felt surprisingly close to him and they hadn't slipped and had sex once. Darn it. "Duke won't shut them down, will he?" she asked, her next worry.

"Not if we present it right. Relax." He patted her knee. The simple gesture of assurance warmed her entire leg.

She was slow to look away and he was slow to notice.

The dancers moved on to the next number, "Dance of the Phoenix," based on the myth of the bird rising from the ashes. All three had fairly complex moves, including cartwheels and splits and a three-person flip.

They were deep into the song when the outside door opened. Sunlight flared, turning the velvet illusion of the bar into a sad gray until the door closed again.

"Shit. Duke's early," Jackson said, and they watched him head their way carrying stapled papers. He didn't look happy.

Heidi's stomach knotted.

"Let me do the talking," Jackson said, leaning close to her ear, almost overriding her nervousness with the pleasure of his nearness.

Duke sat in the chair to Jackson's left and shoved the papers across the table at him. "What's with all the cash to Wilson Construction?"

"Minor stuff. Stalls for the johns, new electrical. Gotta be done. For safety reasons."

"I approve all expenditures." Duke's jaw tensed.

"Right. And I hire all staff," Jackson said, not backing down. "What's with the new bartender?"

"Dupree's a friend of my nephew's. Stan vouches for him."

"I won't manage a place with people I don't trust."

"Dupree's got experience."

"I'll bet."

"He'll be no problem and Taylor could use the help."

"We'll see."

"I'm serious about okaying expenditures," Duke said.

"Then I guess I should tell you I hired a crew to haul out the furniture from the back room and sell it."

"You did what?"

"Relax," Jackson said in a low voice that seemed to soothe Duke. "We get a percentage. Should be enough to cover the cupboards I want to build."

"You want to build cupboards? Hang on now—"

"For storage. We'll use the space as a break room and for supplies. The girls need a dressing room to themselves."

"What are you doing, Jax?"

"The right thing. Selling the furniture should cover the prefab stuff I'll buy. So no net expense."

The two men eyed each other, while Duke's ruffled feathers settled. She admired Jackson for sticking to his guns and presenting the girls' demands so matter-of-factly, like a done deal, despite his own doubts about them.

"I know what you want," Jackson soothed. "It's all fine."

Duke held his gaze for a second, then seemed to slump into the chair, as if arguing was too much trouble. "Everybody knows what I want these days. Stan thinks I should open a combo bar-Laundromat. Suds and Duds, something stupid like that. He thinks I'm made of money and his friends scare the hell out of me." He turned to the stage, taking in the dancers. "So why are they prancing around with clothes on?"

"They'll have costumes for the show," Heidi said, irritated by his dismissive tone. "This is just a rehearsal—a taste of what's to come."

"Costumes? Who's paying for that? And nobody said anything about live music." He eyed the band, frowning.

"Jasmine's making the costumes," Jackson said in his calm-down voice, "and the band's working free. If the show flies, we give 'em a percentage of the door."

"Looks to me like you've got the inmates running the asylum."

"The inmates?" Heidi said. She opened her mouth, prepared to object, but Jackson grabbed her knee, stilling her.

"What Duke means is why mess with success?"

Duke nodded. "Men come here to see women as naked as we can get 'em. If they want a show, they go to Vegas." He seemed caught by the dancers' moves, though. Impressed in spite of himself.

"That's the idea," Heidi said. "This will be a taste of Vegas right here in Phoenix. We'll draw new customers. Couples, not just men. More liquor sales, more cover charges."

"Yeah?" He turned to her, half-smiling, as if he were amused by her interest.

"Especially if we advertise. Tell him, Jackson."

"I thought we'd use the *New Times* ad to promote the show."

"I'm not throwing money at this."

"The ad's already in the budget," Jackson said. "We just

use a photo of the revue, add a couple lines of copy. Heidi will work up some publicity to go with it."

"To reinforce the impact," Heidi added.

Duke looked at her, then at Jackson, putting something together in his mind. He looked back at Jackson. "I don't get this, but we go back a ways, Jax. So, one week's ad, one weekend trial. If receipts drop, we're done." He winked at Heidi, then pushed wearily to his feet. "No outlay on the cupboards."

"No problem."

Shaking his head, Duke headed to the bar, papers in hand.

Jackson watched him go, then turned back to her, a wry smile on his face. "Duke thinks you've got me twisted around your little finger."

"He does?"

"Don't look so innocent. You know you do."

That gave her a shiver of pleasure and a rush of power. "You mean I can have my way with you?" she teased.

"Be careful…I'm only human." There was the familiar sizzle.

"I know….Me, too." She'd never had to exercise this much self-restraint in her life. It was worth it, though, she was pretty sure. Because now they were working together for the dancers' sake. And it was helping Jackson, too. She was delighted to see his enthusiasm build, his energy return, focused on the music he loved, his dream. It wasn't a radio station, but it was close.

For herself, she loved the sense of accomplishment she'd begun to feel. The dancers consulted with her on which dances to include in the revue, how long they should be, what order they should be in. She'd helped them work out a few personality snarls along the way, too.

At first, Nevada had been too rigid a taskmaster, Jasmine had been late to practice and brought Sabrina with her, and Autumn had been reluctant to invest extra time in something that might not pan out. Heidi had talked them through it. She'd babysat Sabrina, showed Autumn the math on the income and eased Nevada back a bit.

She'd worked up the ad, too, drafted news releases and now she would talk up the show with entertainment reporters. She'd consulted with Jackson through it all, coordinating practice sessions with his band. They were a good team. He calmed her when she got nervous and she boosted him when he had doubts.

Sometimes she wished they'd never slept together, so she wouldn't have this terrible tension in her chest—and in her sex—whenever they were together. Other times she thought if they could just have sex again, they'd have everything either of them ever wanted. Which, of course, was completely crazy.

A WEEK LATER, Heidi sat in her salon chair waiting for the three dancers to arrive. Autumn was coming in for a haircut, Nevada for a touch-up to her extensions—though Heidi planned to talk her into a more elegant cut—and Jasmine was having her nails done. A second purpose was to show her their newly finished costumes.

Heidi tapped her fingers on the arms of the chair, catching the attention of Esmeralda, the nail technician, who frowned and rolled her chair close enough to capture Heidi's hand. She studied her nails, then shook her head. "Dear Goddess of Light, look at these blobs of keratin. You are a disgrace to the beauty business."

"Sorry," she said. Tension had her chewing her cuticles lately and she kept her nails short for convenience.

"How about a free manicure? As a thank-you for all the new clients. I've never done so many specialty nails in my life." Heidi had passed out Esmeralda's cards at Moons and the dancers and waitresses were trickling into the shop.

"Nails get in my way and polish chips too easy."

"Then let me read your palm." Not only did Esmeralda do nails, but she also read fortunes. Her slogan was "Esmeralda knows hands…inside out."

"I've got clients coming in now." Heidi didn't want to learn her life would be sad, her career goals unmet, her love life a web of mistakes. Even if she didn't believe her future was etched into her palm, she didn't want to take a chance on hearing bad news. Luckily, the bell jangled, signaling the dancers' arrival.

Jasmine, Nevada and Autumn waltzed in, dressed in tight, short clothes and hooker heels, costumes in plastic over their arms. Everyone in the salon stared—Blythe's client under the dryer, the one in the waiting area and the woman she was giving a weave. Even Blythe, serene in any storm and impossible to shock, stared, a foil square poised in her uplifted fingers.

"Costumes, Heidi!" Jasmine squealed, rushing forward. "Wait'll you see."

"You can change in there." Heidi pointed toward the rest room, but the dancers tossed the plastic-shrouded items onto spare dryer chairs and began whipping off clothes.

In seconds, each had donned a different costume. Autumn wore a white see-through, boa-trimmed robe over a transparent orange blouse and thin, flame-colored skirt. Jasmine had on a harem outfit with numerous glittering veils and Nevada wore a body stocking with small, white balloons representing bubbles from a bubble bath.

"Wow," Heidi said. "How perfect."

"And they fit the choreography to a T," Autumn said. "Show her, Nevada."

Nevada leaned down and snatched a veil from the hip of Jasmine's harem costume with her teeth.

"Easy to remove with teeth or toes." Autumn demonstrated, flexing her big toe at Jasmine's navel to whip away another veil. She spun, did a backbend and bit off another veil.

The watching customers exclaimed in delight. "Oh, sugar, do that again," the woman under the dryer said.

Heidi's cell phone rang as the dancers repeated the move. Frowning, she answered it.

"Heidi? It's Mike."

"Mike? Oh, hi!" She'd had only fleeting conversations with her brothers since she'd sent back the money and some of their gifts. There was so much her brothers didn't know about her life she hardly knew what to talk about. Plus, she'd been so busy helping with the show, she hadn't had much time. "Can I call you back? I've got clients right now."

"How are you, bunny? Really?"

"I'm fine. Really."

"Are you still getting along with your roommate?"

"Absolutely." *If only we hadn't had sex.* But Mike meant Tina, of course, not Jackson. Sheesh.

"She travels so much. Aren't you lonely?"

"Not a bit." Which was true.

Autumn spun, whipping off her Phoenix bird skirt with a rip of Velcro, revealing a feathered G-string. "Too much crotch?" she asked the women.

"Too much what?" her brother asked.

"Too much…off," Heidi improvised. "Some friends are showing me their shopping bargains."

"I'm glad you're making friends." He'd die if he knew they were strippers. Her brothers would think Shear Ecstasy odd, too, since it was located in a beauty boutique that centered around a boudoir photography studio. Entering the building, you were immediately presented with soft-focus bedroom shots, which also lined the walls of the salon. Heidi's world was filled with sexy stuff—here and Moons and home.

"Don't sound so worried," she said. "It's like you expect the worst."

"No news feels like bad news. You should call us more. Did you get all the classes you wanted?"

They didn't even know she wasn't going to school. Maybe now would be the time to start with the truth. Ease into it. She swallowed, watching Autumn toss scarves through the air to land in the spectators' laps. "Actually, Mike, I've decided not to register until next semester."

"You what? You're not going to school?"

The women applauded loudly. The one under the dryer managed a wolf whistle. "Take it *off,*" she yelled.

"What's going on there?" Mike asked crossly.

"Ninety percent *off.* I need to get more established at the salon."

"But we thought you were in such a rush to move so you could make the fall semester."

She'd been in a rush because she was scared to lose her nerve.

"Is it money? Why did you send back the check?"

"It's my decision. It'll be fine. I know what I'm doing."

"Take it all off!" The woman under the dryer was really getting into it.

"Who *is* that?" Michael asked.

"We're, um, stripping…color. *All* the color. Look, give my love to Mark. I'll call you later. Bye. Love you. I'm fine. Bye."

She clicked off the phone, her ears burning, her face hot with guilt. At least she'd delivered some of the bad news. Eventually, when she had things under control, she could laugh with her brothers about her little start-up troubles.

"So, what do you think, Heidi?" Jasmine asked. The other dancers looked equally eager for her opinion.

"The costumes are fabulous. You did great, Jasmine."

"She did, didn't she?" Autumn said. "Pure genius."

Jasmine beamed at Autumn, who'd been noticeably more positive with Jasmine since that counseling session in the dressing room and a couple of follow-up discussions. Jasmine kept checking with Autumn about possible purchases, too, which helped Autumn's attitude about her friend's maturity. Hardly an eyeroll passed between them these days.

"Full rehearsal today before work," Nevada said. She'd told Heidi she had a history of quitting when things got hard, but she was sticking to the revue like the balloons Velcroed to her bodysuit.

"Yes, O, Queen of Pain," Autumn said, but she was smiling.

The dancers changed back into their street clothes and handed each customer a small stack of flyers to distribute, urging them to bring a crowd.

Heidi got started washing Autumn's hair and Jasmine sat at Esmeralda's station to get her nails done. Nevada parked in Heidi's salon chair with a magazine to wait her turn.

"Who was that on the phone?" Autumn asked, her voice echoing in the sink. "You looked nervous."

"One of my brothers worrying about me." She lifted Autumn's head and scrubbed the hair at the back.

"He should worry. You work in a strip club, hon."

"There are tons worse jobs than that," Nevada said.

"At least your brothers care," Autumn said quietly, while Heidi rinsed. "My brothers don't give a damn about me until they need money. And they always need money."

"They mean well, I know," Heidi said, applying cream rinse.

"Family can be a pain," Jasmine said from the nail station. "When I go to my mom for sympathy—when I'm desperately down—what does she do? Jump all over me about my bad decisions."

"She should get Little Miss Positive lessons from Heidi," Autumn said, sitting up so Heidi could cover her hair with a towel. "Look how they helped me." She put a finger to her cheek and twisted it, wearing a supersweet smile.

"You've got a ways to go."

"Come on. I'm giving you one-third fewer eye rolls, at least."

"My point is that my mom kicks me when I'm down, right? But, get this, when I told her about the new routine she made her usual disgusted face, but I didn't even feel it. 'Come see the show, Mom,' I told her. 'Just come see.'"

"Not bad," Autumn said.

"I was like Teflon. Her bad vibes hit me and bounced off."

"You felt confident," Heidi said, leading Autumn to her chair for the cut. "So her criticism doesn't wound you."

"Your brothers must have freaked about you working at Moons," Autumn said. "What did they say about you living with Jackson?"

"They don't know yet," she said, running a comb through Autumn's hair. Not willing to share her uncertainty with the girls, she didn't explain all the other things they didn't know about her life. Like everything.

"What's the big deal?" Jasmine said. "Lots of men and women are roommates."

"If you want, you can move in with me," Esmeralda threw in. She'd posted a notice on the salon bulletin board, wanting someone to help with utilities.

"Thanks," Heidi said, wondering, as she had when she first saw the posting, if that might not be a smart thing to do.

"Wait a minute," Jasmine said slowly. "Are you sleeping with Jax still?"

All eyes honed in on her.

"No. Not anymore. No."

"Good," Autumn said. "Jackson is Jackson. Don't think you can change him. People don't change. Especially men."

"I don't buy it," Jasmine said. "No man on earth doesn't need a little redo. I wouldn't take one as is. No way. What's the point of getting involved?"

"And there's your problem," Autumn said.

"And yours is that you hook up with guys who are all talk. Jackson's not like that. Jackson has honor. He's one of the good guys."

"But limited," Autumn said, holding Heidi's gaze in the mirror. "And not the kind of guy Heidi wants. She's just getting out there, mixing it up with college guys, am I right?"

"Sure," she said, feeling hollow inside. She pictured Jackson's expression when he looked at her sometimes—as though he needed her to fix what was wrong, fill what was empty. Sometimes she thought he might be what she needed, too—a safe place to be—a haven, a comfort, an outstretched hand when she needed a boost.

"Damn," Autumn said softly.

Heidi's attention jerked to the mirror and Autumn's stare. "What?"

"He got to you, didn't he?" she whispered.

"No. I don't know. I just…ache…you know."

"You have to be strong," Autumn said.

"Hey, who's studying to be the psychologist here?" She laughed, trying to lighten the mood.

"Everybody's an expert at something," Autumn said. "I know bad relationships like the back of my hand."

"And I have a master's degree in bad mothering," Jasmine said with a sigh.

"You do your best," Autumn said, which made Jasmine blink in surprise.

"I'm a world-class quitter," Nevada said with a pained laugh.

"Oh, for those days," Autumn said. "Now you never stop. You're driving us into the ground, Nevada."

"We have a show coming up."

"You're all doing remarkable," Heidi said. "The show, of course, but look how you stood up for yourselves at Moons."

"We did good, didn't we?" Jasmine said, beaming.

"You did great," Heidi agreed.

Autumn leaned forward to grab the stack of college course schedules Heidi had left next to the comb jar. Jackson had made the rounds to all the junior colleges in the Valley for her, even snagging the new ASU pamphlet. "What's with all this?" Autumn asked.

This might be the perfect time to mention school to Autumn. "Just looking at options. You live on the west side, right? Check out ASU West. Might be an accounting class you'd like. My brother hired a woman to do bookkeeping for Copper Corners with just a two-year associate's degree."

Autumn leveled her a look in the mirror. *Don't push me.*

"Only if you're interested." She shrugged and busied herself with the blow dryer and round brush.

Autumn flipped through the pages, feigning nonchalance. She kept at it though, through the rest of the style, and carried the catalogs with her to the other chair, where she switched places with Nevada, who wanted an extension touch-up.

Heidi was explaining how a shorter, feathered cut would add appeal to Nevada's small, round face, when she noticed that all three women were looking at each other in the mirror, smiling.

"Tell you what," Nevada said. "I'll let you whack off my hair if you'll let us fix your look."

"Excuse me?"

Now three sets of eyes trapped her in the mirror.

"The three of us have been talking about how we could pay you back and the obvious way is to improve your look. First of all, you've got the prettiest eyes, but they get lost because your lashes are stubby. I have some sable spikes that will really make your eyes pop."

"And your foundation is too pale for your coloring," Autumn added. "I have the same problem, being a redhead."

"And that prison outfit you wear at Moons has got to go," Nevada said.

"We know you're broke," Autumn said, "so we'll chip in on something decent. Just come shopping with us."

She looked into their eager faces. They'd planned this all out. So, what could she do but say yes and hope she wouldn't end up looking like she belonged on stage, too, in a feathered G-string and see-through bikini?

12

ON THE NIGHT of the premiere, Heidi tugged at the scooped neck of the leotard the dancers had bought for her. She'd agreed to a minimal makeover and the most modest choice they'd offered was this black leotard with a short red-silk wraparound skirt that played peekaboo with her thighs. She felt a little too exposed. On her feet, she wore kitten heels with delicate straps, a compromise from the stacked stilettos the women had urged on her.

She smoothed the flyer attached to the hostess stand that proclaimed the first performance of "Let Us Entertain You" would begin in an hour. The photo showed the three dancers in their "Phoenix Rising" costumes, complete with the elaborate headdresses that Jackson had paid for and Jasmine had gotten Moons employees to assemble during breaks. Bartenders, waitresses and dancers had glued feathers until the room reeked of adhesive, and feather shreds floated like spidery snowflakes in the air.

Now Heidi chewed nervously on her index finger. Esmeralda would yank it from her mouth. *Good Goddess of Light, if you won't let me fix 'em, at least stop torturing the poor things.*

That made her smile, which relieved her tension like a rubber band abruptly released. Her heart had been doing push-ups off her diaphragm for the last hour.

Tonight had to go well for the girls' sake. And Jackson's, too, since success with the band would propel him onward with managing. People had to pile in soon or opening night would also be closing night. The early regulars were already complaining about the extra five-buck cover charge.

She felt movement behind her and turned to find Jackson standing beside her. His gaze skimmed appreciatively over her body. Her heart stopped its push-ups and ricocheted against her ribs.

"I like the new look," he said softly.

She hadn't been sorry to say goodbye to the bag lady uniform. She'd made her point with Jackson and she enjoyed looking sexy as much as the next woman. "This breathes better than polyester."

"It breathes, huh? Well, it's making me pant."

She smiled, flattered as always by his praise, remembering when he'd held up that ridiculous snakeskin dress and told her she'd look hot in it. *He talks like that to all the women in his life, remember?* He was an emotional island. Warm and welcoming, but an island all the same, with all that implied about self-containment. He'd offered her a brief vacation there and that ought to be enough. She had to stop wanting more.

"A watched parking lot never fills," he said softly, placing a hand on her back. Heat radiated from his touch, soothing her as it had from that first hug the day of the robbery. Of course, his touch was more than comforting. Arousal hummed to life like a sturdy furnace in winter, promising no signs of slowing down at all.

"I can't help it." She turned to him and found herself practically in his arms. "A lot is riding on tonight for the girls."

"They're women, remember?"

"Right." Trust him to use her arguments against her. "But this is a breakthrough. Autumn's considering college. Jasmine's more sure of herself and Nevada's so determined she makes a drill sergeant look like a pussycat. If this doesn't go well, I'm afraid it will sink their spirits." She wouldn't mention her hopes for him. He'd scored a midweek gig for the band at a Scottsdale resort and had auditions lined up at a few clubs. Last night, he'd left Taylor in charge of the bar for a couple of hours so he could be there for the first one. She'd convinced him Moons' employees would all survive without him for a few hours here and there.

Jackson smiled a slow smile. "Don't they teach you in shrink school you're not responsible for other people's lives?"

"You're pretty savvy for a guy who claims to have only bars and tunes and maybe sports cars on his mind."

"I'd rather surprise people than disappoint them." He frowned at his confession, which explained a lot about him.

"Who did you disappoint?" His parents, she guessed, but she didn't want to put him on the spot. "I mean, you're always helping people, from what I see. Look at all you've done for the girls. Like buying those headdresses."

He shrugged. "The girls had their hearts set on the stupid things."

"Plus, didn't I hear you intervene with Duke so Rox could do a school internship and still stay on part-time here?"

He shrugged. "You got me. So we're both do-gooders."

When they'd first met, she'd thought they were practically separate species, but they certainly shared this characteristic. Jackson had underestimated himself. He had so much potential. She could help him grow.

Don't think you can change him, Autumn had warned. But hadn't Jackson changed over the past weeks? Gone from being content to float from video game to weight bench to Moons, locked in orbit like a lonely asteroid, to building a band, arranging gigs, putting himself out there, all the while serving as solid support to her and the dancers?

What if they could be together? What if she had fallen in love with the first guy she met outside of Copper Corners?

Jackson was studying her face so closely she felt herself blush. "What's wrong with your eyes?" he asked.

She lifted her fingers to her face, then realized what he meant. "Jasmine talked me into fake eyelashes." She laughed.

"They look like furry caterpillars riding your lids."

"They feel like it, too, but I promised Jasmine I'd try them out." She reached up and tugged at one. It hung on, though, and the pain made her eyes sting. She blinked quickly.

"Let me do it." He cupped her cheek with one hand and gently pried off the lashes, his fingers gentle on her face. He dropped the strips into her upturned palm. Then he tilted her face to examine her eyes. "Much better. You have great eyes just plain. And a terrific blink."

"You're complimenting my blink?"

"Oh, yeah. It's very…promising."

She blinked again. And again, reflexively, unable to stop herself, now that he'd drawn attention to the gesture.

"You're really working me over, huh? Testing your sexual powers?"

"Sorry. Can't help it." But her body warmed at his words.

"You're something else, you know that?" Jackson looked at her with the urgent desire she remembered so well. He ran his thumb along her jaw, lingering on her skin. He wanted to kiss her, she could tell, and she wanted that, too.

But she watched him gather himself, tone down the light in his eyes until all that remained was a mischievous twinkle. "When you finally get that diploma, your clients won't know what hit 'em."

"You make me sound dangerous."

"Oh, you are. To me." But he seemed to regret saying so and he changed the subject. "You enjoying the books I bought you?"

"I've started them." She'd been too distracted, really. And exhausted. Working with the dancers every spare minute, fighting her desire for Jackson at night in bed when she could hear him clanking around with his weights or playing his keyboard, she couldn't concentrate on serious things like other people's personality disorders.

"That's good. Get you geared up for school. You'll knock your professors dead."

"Sometimes it's daunting. That's a lot of heavy content."

"Are you nuts? You could write those books. You know that stuff cold from real life. You've got the dancers eating out of your hand. And I bet you've got hair clients naming their children after you."

"Oh, stop." But she loved it. She felt more confident after his words. She looked into his eyes and saw affection, admiration, support. Love? Was there love?

There was lust. Plenty of that. She wanted to melt into

it, go with it. Where was the harm? How could something that felt so good be bad for her?

"It's nice having you around, Heidi," he said, making her turmoil even worse. "Even when you polish the bathroom floor so I just about break my neck."

"Sorry." She cringed. "I read a tip about using car interior polish and—"

"I was too wrapped up in myself," he said, cutting her off, almost in confession. "You opened my eyes. Thanks."

"Thanks for taking me in. And…everything." A feeling rose in her heart, the sense that something important had happened to her because of Jackson that wasn't part of her plan but was nevertheless right. "I really—"

"Not much of a crowd." Duke's voice was sharp beside them. They both jumped a little. Duke eyed the nearly empty lounge and shot Jackson a pointed look. His nephew Stan, the jerk, mimicked his expression, then headed for the bar.

"It's early." Jackson shrugged.

Duke just looked at him, then followed his nephew.

"If a crowd doesn't show, Duke will pull the plug," Heidi said.

"If tonight's slow, we have tomorrow. Then we'll see."

She was startled when he took her hand, laced his fingers with hers and squeezed. *We're in this together, partner.* It felt so good that her knees buckled a little. She squeezed back.

They stared out at the parking lot together. Then Jackson spoke, his words soft and slow, heavy with meaning. "I never would have pulled the band together if you hadn't hounded me. I haven't felt this good about anything in a long time."

She was so touched she could hardly speak. "You just needed a nudge."

"You think that's all you were…a nudge?" He turned to her. "How about relentless and unstoppable and undeniable and—"

She put a finger to his lips. "Don't ruin it." She tried to tease, but the finger on his mouth was too intimate and he didn't smile. Instead, he looked at her in a way that shot fire through her. She let her finger drop away.

"—and irresistible," he finished and then he kissed her. Softly, holding back, as if taking a sip of something very fine he intended to savor.

Stunned by the kiss—this was the first time he'd started an embrace—she stilled, wanting more, but not daring to go for it.

Jackson broke off the kiss as quickly as he'd begun it and turned her toward the street, pointing at several cars nosing into the parking lot. The first was a Mercedes from which two well-dressed couples emerged. After that came a Corvette with two young guys, followed by a Hummer with a half-dozen corporate types.

Jackson grinned at her and squeezed her hand. As they watched, more cars arrived…a Jaguar with an older couple, a BMW station wagon with two couples, a Cadillac with three women. The first group entered the bar, happily forking over the cover, asking about the revue, which was why they'd come. All new customers and mostly couples.

"We did it," she breathed to him.

He winked. "We sure did."

"As long as they like the show."

"What's not to like?"

"True." Through the hands they gripped tight, they exchanged excitement and pride, standing a little longer to savor the moment. She could still taste his kiss on her lips.

"I'd better go to work," she said finally, letting go. She

looked up at him and his expression stopped her heart. *I never want you to leave*.

What if she never went?

After that, Heidi was so busy she didn't have time to even think about Jackson, let alone catch his eye to see if he still had that look on his face. She told herself she'd read too much into the kiss, the look. The halo effect of working together, the triumph and shared pride, had masked the impossibility of their relationship. Right?

The revue went remarkably well for a first night. The sound system went out briefly, Jasmine missed a cue on the bubble dance, and the band skipped an interlude on the seven-veils song, but no one minded. The feathers had been so ineptly applied to the headdresses they melted free under the hot lights, but the girls tossed them into the audience and soon everyone sported a white feather over an ear, tucked into a lock of hair or poked into a button-hole, adding to the festive atmosphere.

The bar was insane with liquor sales and the applause at the end of the show was wild.

After closing, Duke called the employees together for a congratulatory glass of cheap champagne, crowing about the show as if it had been his idea all along. Everyone stayed a little longer than usual, the dancers kicking around ideas for new numbers, the band fired up about the fact that an entertainment reviewer had inquired about where else they played. Heidi ached with exhaustion, but it was a happy weariness from good work for a good cause.

Finally, everyone was gone and Jackson was walking the band out. When he returned, they would lock up and head home like any other night. Except…what about that look? The new feeling she'd had standing with him?

She wanted to go home and make love, but she didn't dare. It would just be a waste of time.

Move out. The words popped in her head. Esmeralda wanted a roommate. It would slow down Heidi's savings, but it would eliminate the nightly temptation of being in Jackson's house. Maybe now was the time to go. She'd keep doing housekeeping for him and she'd see him at work.

That would be smart. She'd talk to Esmeralda on Monday, then tell Jackson. The idea made her feel so sad, but it was for the best.

All alone in the bar for the moment, she walked onto the empty main stage and looked out at the audience. What would it be like to perform for strangers? It was intimidating just standing there with clothes on. Imagine doing it nearly naked. She walked around the three-foot mirrored cube that rested in the center of the stage. She turned toward the back wall—which was a floor-to-ceiling mirror—and was surprised how dramatic she looked under the overhead spot. The push-up bra the girls had foisted on her gave her decent cleavage in the low-necked leotard. Her wraparound skirt parted to reveal most of her right thigh. In the white light, her hair shone bronze. She straightened her spine, threw her shoulders back so her breasts stuck out. Pretty damn sexy, if she did say so herself.

Then she noticed Jackson behind her in the mirror and watched him move from the darkness of the audience area into the lights of the stage, his gaze on her.

She spun, embarrassed that she'd been admiring herself.

"Don't stop. You look great," he said softly, reassuring her. "Reminds me of that striptease."

"Right. On pain meds? Pretty ridiculous."

"Not at all. It was charming and sexy and very you." He

stepped closer so the light struck his face and turned his black Moons T-shirt and jeans a soft gray. He looked so good to her. Dangerous and wild, but also safe. Emotion shone in his eyes. "You had me so hot I could hardly see."

"You threw me over your shoulder like a child."

"So I wouldn't take advantage of you."

"I wasn't that loaded."

He reached for the switchbox against the wall. She thought he was going to shut off the light, but instead he pushed a button that started the disco ball spinning, sending white circles of light everywhere, turning the stage into a magical snow globe. "Why don't you dance for me?"

"Dance? I can't…I'm not—"

"Sure you are. You're very good."

"You make me feel that way."

"You don't need me for that. But I've been glad to be along for the ride."

The ride. It had been wild and wonderful. Like roaring through the city in his exotic sports car. Maybe Jackson was saying goodbye, too.

"Dance for me. The stage is all yours. And this time you won't get dizzy."

"If you'll pick out my music."

"Hear the music in your head." He stepped onto the stage, keeping his eyes on her the entire time, making her feel like the sexiest woman alive.

When the mirrored cube was the only thing between them, he sat on it, legs apart, palms on his knees, braced to watch. "Just dance, Heidi."

She began to sway, slowly at first, intimidated by the dark seats beyond the stage. They were empty, but she could picture men staring, expecting erotic moves, splits, spins, pole work.

"Look at me, Heidi. I'm the only one here. Dance for me."

So she did. Staring into his fathomless eyes, her only mirror, she performed an instinctive undulation, a wave of motion from the top of her head to a little kick of her toes in her kitten heels.

"Nice," Jackson breathed, warm light reflecting in his eyes like candle flames in each pupil. She was turning him on.

More confident now, she went on tiptoe and spun—these shoes didn't slip off her heels as Gigi's oversize ones had. She went to the pole, leaned her head back and did a slow turn. Jackson smiled.

She wanted more hunger in his eyes, so she tugged the leotard off both shoulders, revealing the tops of her breasts. He inhaled sharply, so she slowly removed her arms from the long sleeves of the leotard, pushed it down to her waist and stood for him in the black-lace bra.

"You are so beautiful," Jackson said, the heat from his gaze hotter on her body than the light burning down on her. She felt free, standing there, all woman, and sexy as hell.

She danced backward to the pole and slid slowly down, her thighs aching. She kept her knees apart as the dancers did, deliberately showing the space between her legs, covered by her leotard, but she felt wanton and raw all the same. Could he tell how aroused she was?

"Maybe this wasn't such a good idea," Jackson ground out, wanting her in a way that sent fire through her.

A fire she had to have put out. And there was only one way. This dance would become something more. A lap dance and then sex. One last, lovely time. Right here on this stage. Something she would remember forever.

She pushed to her feet. "I can't stop yet, Jax. I haven't showed you all my moves." She danced over to him, un-

tying her skirt as she went. She whipped it off her body
and draped it over his shoulder. She didn't need codeine
to loosen her inhibitions because she had the confidence
of all the great sex they'd had together.

"What are you doing?" She watched a shudder roll
through him.

"What you want me to do," she said, moving closer. All
that covered her now was her bra and the bottom half of
her leotard. Her legs were bare in the low heels. Under the
leotard, she wore a black-lace thong the girls had talked
her into. She hadn't liked the feel of fabric between her
cheeks, but now she was glad. A thong was much sexier
than her flowered granny panties, though Jackson claimed
they turned him on.

"Heidi," he said, hungry to touch her, she could tell from
his tone. She'd missed that sound in his voice these last
weeks. He seemed to hardly breathe.

Still swaying, she pushed the leotard the rest of the way
off her body, kicking it up to land in Jackson's lap. He
made no move to catch it, his eyes glued to her body, and
it slid to the floor of the stage. She stood before him in her
tiny thong and bra and shoes, staying brave, feeling sexy.

"You have to stop," Jackson said very low.

"But you wanted me to dance," she teased. "To move
however I feel. This is how I feel." She ran her hands
across her stomach and then up to cup her breasts. His rapt
expression convinced her she was as sexy as she felt.

"If you keep that up…" Jackson held very still, his hands
on his knees, not moving, only taking her in with his eyes,
but he wanted to take her, she could tell by the way his
breaths came ragged and rough and his eyes burned into her.

She was so excited she could hardly stand. She'd never
felt more desired in her life. She closed the inches between

them until she stood between his parted thighs and took off her bra. "If I keep this up," she said slowly, teasing her nipples with her fingers, "what will you do?"

In answer, Jackson grabbed her shoulders and pulled her onto his lap, crushing her mouth to his.

She kissed him back, her heart thudding in her chest, her pulse pounding in her ears, adjusting herself so she sat on his lap, legs on either side, feet on the floor. His jeans scraped against her panties, his erection a solid bulge against her sex.

Jackson tore his lips away. "I can't stop wanting you." He grabbed her bottom, his fingers digging in, straining her sex, his palms warm, owning her. He seemed so desperate and lost. He wanted more than sex and she welcomed it. She wanted more, too.

"Let's keep on," she said. "We're good together."

"Are you sure?" he asked, his eyes begging her to be.

In answer, she tugged his T-shirt out of his jeans and yanked it up and off and tossed it to the stage. Now they were both naked to the waist.

Jackson ran his thumbs over her nipples, giving her a delicious rush. She caught sight of herself in the mirror to the side. Jackson's fingers on her breasts in the white-hot cone of light looked so erotic, and she liked how small and pale her hands appeared on his broad, strong back.

As she watched, he took her nipple into his mouth, sucking hard. She arched her back, the sight thrillingly erotic in the mirror. They were half naked and making love on stage, exposed to the room, the sparkling lights turning it into a performance. She pictured people watching them, admiring their incredible passion, envying their desire for each other.

She looked like a woman who knew what she wanted and was certain to get it right now with this man.

Jackson lifted his mouth from her breast to take her lips, kissing her deeply. She wanted more and rubbed herself against his zipper. "Touch me," she whimpered into his mouth.

Obeying her, he slid his fingers up her legs, skimmed her inner thighs and stroked her with his thumb. The thong gave him easy access. "It's been killing me not to touch you like this."

She trembled helplessly, electrified by the delicious pressure of his thumb on her clit. He rubbed her up and down, slow and even strokes, knowing exactly what she liked.

How she'd missed this.

She reached down, going for his zipper, but he stroked her even more deliberately. "I want to watch you come."

She was helpless to stop him and writhed against his thumb.

"Is this how you like it? Tell me."

"Yes," she breathed. "Farther inside, too."

He pushed a finger inside her, hooking a spot that sent up a throbbing rhythm of urgency, while his thumb circled her clitoris, brushed it, then went away, then repeated the move, nudging her closer and closer to orgasm.

Jackson bent his head to lick a nipple, the tip of his tongue curling, pressing tight against it, intensifying her response more and more.

"Oh, oh…Jackson."

"That's right. Come for me."

The wave hit and she closed her eyes, flying off, twining and twisting on Jackson's fingers, which held her in place, while the rest of her spun through the circles of white light in this snow-globe of a stage.

Gradually, her movements slowed and she fell forward so Jackson could hold her against his warm chest. She felt his pounding heart against her own and heard his labored breathing in her ears.

She wanted him to feel this kind of pleasure and she wanted him inside her. She went at his zipper, pushing to her feet so he could raise up enough to shove his pants off. He gripped her bottom, gasping for breath and she lowered herself slowly, letting him fill her up and make her ache all over again.

Now they faced each other, joined at the groin. They'd had sex in this position on a bed, but never with both sets of feet flat on the floor so they could push with maximum power. She half stood, then sat, then did it again, feeling each inch of him on the way up and back down again.

"You feel so…good." Jackson's voice was strangled. She loved the power she had over him, loved the way his need built as she rode him faster and faster. He was ready to come….

"I don't know what I'm doing," he said on a gasp. "I'm lost in you." He released himself and she joined him with her own climax.

They held each other as the waves slowly passed. Heidi watched them recover in the mirrored wall, holding each other, encircled by each other's arms, their bodies swaying from the force of what they'd shared. "I can't believe we did that right here in Moons."

"With you, I believe it," he said, looking mystified. "I've never felt like this before."

"Me, either." She was lost in Jackson, too. He made her feel safe and sure of herself, not anxious or scared. With Jackson, she could rest. She refused to think beyond that.

They helped each other dress, then Jackson surprised her by lifting her into his arms. The first night at Moons, when she'd had blisters, he'd tried to help her out of the bar, but she'd refused. Why had she fought so hard? Why not enjoy the relief? Tonight, she let him carry her. She could be independent and self-sufficient tomorrow.

Jackson carried her around the bar turning off lights and checking locks as they went. Soon, only the soft security lights lit their way to the back door. Outside, Jackson's feet crunched on the gravel as Heidi rocked gently against his chest. He carried her to the van, which he'd driven instead of the sports car to hold the band's equipment. The ridiculous women airbrushed on the side of the vehicle seemed charming to her now.

Jackson lowered her gently to the seat, then leaned in to kiss her with a warm, all-encompassing embrace, lips and tongue and arms and chest, holding her close. This was how it felt to be the one woman in Jackson's life—the center of his universe, the home of his hope, the hope in his heart.

Jackson climbed into the driver's seat and started the car, pausing to squeeze her knee. "You okay?"

"I'm great. You?"

"Never better."

She smiled so big her cheeks hurt. They talked, mostly about the show—Nevada's determination, Jasmine's new focus, Autumn's enthusiasm, the band's possibilities—eventually falling silent under a blanket of intimacy like the lightest, warmest fleece.

"I kind of wish my parents could have seen that," Jackson said. "The strippers would have shocked Mom at first, but she'd be cool. She always loved my dad's music. When she watched him play, she used to get this…I don't know…glow."

"I bet your father courted her with music."

"Probably."

"He'd be proud you started the band."

"When I was a kid, I wanted talent like him, but didn't have it. I think it disappointed him, but he never showed it. Mostly, we worked on engines together." The light went green, but Jackson didn't accelerate. There was no one behind them at 4:00 a.m. He sighed. "Yeah. I wish he could have seen that tonight." His voice shook a little.

"Maybe he did," she said, her heart aching for him. "Maybe your parents were sitting right there in the audience, clapping and cheering and proud as hell of what you've begun."

He turned grateful eyes to her. "Sounds like wishful thinking to me, but I'll take it." He gave her a long, quiet kiss full of tenderness and connection. The light turned red and green again before Jackson drove them across the intersection.

When they pulled into the townhouse driveway, Heidi got such a rush of familiar joy she could hardly breathe. She'd felt this way about Copper Corners. And now she felt it about this tiny town house in this grungy neighborhood. Even the ratty sofa on the neighbors' porch seemed welcoming. Heidi was home. She hadn't even met the neighbors—she'd been too wrapped up in Moons and Shear Ecstasy and Jackson. She'd have to take over a batch of brownies and say hi. She'd get to know them since she'd be staying.

They made love once more and it was wordless and sweet and intimate. They'd slid from having sex to making love as easily as breathing. That meant something, didn't it? It had to, because it changed everything.

13

I CAN'T LET HER GET AWAY. That was Jackson's first thought in the morning.

"I have to get ready for work." Heidi's soft voice in his ear was full of laughter.

He came to and realized he'd locked her body in a wrestling hold, legs scissored tight. "Not yet," he murmured, pulling her on top of him, pretending it was just sex he wanted, when it was really her. He wanted to take care of her, help her, protect her, have her all to himself.

"I'd love to stay, Jax, believe me, but I'll miss my bus."

"So miss it. Drive the van. No, you'll look better in the DB6. Take it."

"Really?" She slid off his body onto her side to look down at him. Her face looked so soft from sleep he had to reach up and cup her cheek. "But that's your baby."

"So are you," he said, pretty sure he shouldn't have said that, but too groggy to hold back. Besides, she smiled the biggest smile he'd ever seen on her face.

Then she kissed him and he wrapped his arms around her tight, slid his legs between hers so they were twined together like positive-negative wire leads, and just held on.

After a bit, they made love, slow and relaxed, and he couldn't remember ever feeling this great—comfortable, easy and alive. He craved her sweet body, those slow-blinking eyes, that creative little tongue of hers. She practically purred under his touch, wanting more and more, wanting all he had to give. She was so eager, so fresh, he just wanted to bury himself in her as deep as he could go.

This was fine. This was that love thing. That bond you felt. Something itched in him, some worry, some warning. But he pushed it away. She needed his help. He'd gotten her work and a home and he'd helped her bounce back from the robbery, so why couldn't he go on doing it? He'd never hurt her. He was in love with her.

"What are you up to today?" she called to him from the shower, a few minutes later. She'd banished him from the shower stall, claiming she'd never make it to work, so he sat on the hamper just watching her gorgeous body move.

"Practice with the band. We're kicking around names." Last night, they'd sworn it would be something with "Moon" in it.

He followed Heidi to the garage to watch her leave like some lonely puppy. So what? He didn't even care when she rabbit-hopped off in the DB6, didn't even grimace at the gears she was stripping. She looked damn fine in it. Freshly laid and cheerful, wiggling her pretty fingers in a wave. He wanted to run after her down the hill just to keep her in sight till the last second.

This wasn't like him, he knew—this moon-eyed kid thing he had going on. But then he'd never been in love before.

And he felt good. Better than he had in years.

Maybe your parents were sitting right there in the audience, clapping and cheering and proud as hell of what you've begun. Her words about his parents played in his head, making him feel downright peaceful. And damn positive. That was good.

He pushed aside that niggling doubt, that sense that he was missing something important about all this and just rode the wave.

EARLY MONDAY MORNING, Jackson cuddled Heidi on the couch. They'd just made love. He'd been minding his own business, working on a calendar for MoonDanz—as the band had named itself—while Heidi cleaned, but the way she dusted turned him on and they'd gone at it again.

"This is taking over our lives," she said, laughing, cozying into him.

"So what?" Maybe it wasn't natural to want to be in bed with her 24/7, but he didn't care. The good feeling had stayed. Being with Heidi had started a shift in him. He thought he knew why.

Losing his parents, then losing their money had sent him low. Made him sluggish and grumpy…dead inside. Heidi woke him like an espresso right out of bed. Life surged through him and he was wide, wide awake. He didn't even mind her questions so much. It was as if she'd shoved him out of a dark cave into the sunshine with her small, strong hands.

"It's crazy, don't you think?" She squeezed him tight. "But I love it."

And I love you. The words were on his tongue to say. She probably already knew it. Where was the harm in putting them out there in the warm air they were breathing together?

Something. Something made him hold back. There was a dreamlike quality to what was going on that made him feel as if he were holding his breath, waiting for the other shoe to drop.

Ri-i-ing. Or the doorbell to chime. "You expecting anyone?"

"No. You?"

"Nope, but I'll get it. You get dressed."

She grabbed her clothes and hightailed it down the hall. He zipped himself up, stepped into his flip-flops and headed to the door. Through the peephole he saw two earnest-looking, clean-cut guys. All they needed were white shirts and name badges to be missionaries. But they wore golf shirts. Salesmen, maybe? He opened the door, braced for a pitch. He was in such a good mood, he just might buy. Brushes, time shares, Tupperware, he didn't care.

The men looked startled to see him. "Sorry, um, we're looking for Heidi Fields?"

"You're in the right place." He froze for a second, something making him hesitate. "And you would be?"

"Mike and Mark Fields…her brothers."

Her brothers? The guys who wanted to carry her piggyback through life? The guys who thought she was living with Tina instead of him?

"May we come in?" the lead brother said impatiently.

He realized he'd been staring blankly at them. "Sure. Come in, come in." This was no time to introduce himself as her roommate, let alone her boyfriend. Hell, he hadn't even thought of himself that way yet. What reason could he have to be in her place this early on a Monday? "I'm Jackson McCall…Heidi's landlord." The crescent wrench on the entry table, which he'd been using to tighten the screws on a mic stand, caught his eye. He lunged forward and grabbed it. "Plumbing troubles."

"Who is it?" Heidi stopped dead in the entrance to the hall. "Mike and Mark?" Her eyebrows shot up.

"I was just telling your brothers that your bathroom sink is leaking and I'm fixing it." He signaled her with his eyes. "Being your ever helpful landlord and all."

She looked puzzled by his words, opened her mouth as if she wanted to correct him, then faltered. "Right. My ever…landlord…right."

"So, I'll get on that now." He waved the wrench in the air, then headed down the hall, hoping he hadn't overdone it.

Once in the bathroom, he turned the water off and on, then banged on the faucet. Hell, it did leak. He put his ear against the door to listen, clunking the U-joint now and then to sound busy.

He couldn't make out the words, just Heidi's husky voice high with nervous cheer, then low responses from her brothers. At least no one was yelling. Yet.

Was there evidence of their lovemaking in the house? Heidi had been cleaning, so probably not. On the other hand, why was he sneaking around like a criminal? He should just walk out there and tell them, "Look, I love your sister. You don't have to worry because I'm taking care of her."

But standing there under the alarmed stare of her earnest brothers, he'd felt like some creep who'd corrupted their sweet little sister and couldn't have said a word if his life depended on it.

HEIDI'S FACE FLAMED as she watched her brothers take in the living room decor. Twin sets of eyes roved from the Marilyn Monroe velvet painting to the bimbo poster, the nude in the pole lamp, the hula girl on the tiki bar and the pièce de résistance, the pink-nippled cocktail table.

"Interesting," Mark said, staring at it.

She'd meant to ask Jackson if she could tone down the nudes, but she'd grown used to the campy art.

Mike's gaze shifted from the row of engines to her face. "So…is this Tina's stuff?"

"Jackson's. We, uh, let him leave it here and he takes a bit off the rent. Plus, I kind of like the look. It's…different."

The brothers looked at each, then at her, puzzled, not quite believing her.

Why had she lied exactly? And why hadn't she corrected Jackson, told her brothers that he was her boyfriend? Or at least her roommate?

Because Jackson would seem like a liar? Partly. But mostly because, seen through her brothers' eyes, the arrangement would seem tawdry, hasty, out of character, downright bizarre.

There was so much about her life she had to explain to her brothers before she could discuss her relationship with Jackson. Hell, she wasn't ready to discuss it with Jackson yet. And now the poor man was banging around in the bathroom pretending to fix the plumbing.

She had to buy herself some time to figure out what to say. "How come you just popped by, anyway?"

"I mentioned the Arizona mayors conference, didn't I? On water quality?"

"Maybe…" She had a vague memory of a comment.

"And I decided to do some networking," Mark added. "There's some interest in developing Copper Corners as a retirement community, so I just thought I'd come along."

"To check on me, right?" They were both acting too sheepish for it to be as simple as they pretended.

"We miss you, Bunny." Mike's eyes warmed. Mark's, too, as he nodded. They stepped forward to hug her, one after the other. She was swamped with homesickness. She loved her brothers, missed their solid selves.

"I miss you, too," she said, forcing her words to come

out lightly. "And I'll be coming down in a couple of months. Thanksgiving, remember?"

"You said Halloween," Mark said. "I promised you'd judge the pumpkin carving contest."

"You have sounded strange over the phone," Mike said, "Nervous and jumpy and right now your eyes are darting all over the place. What's the matter, Heidi?"

Everything. Getting caught. Jackson hiding. Seeing them again. The startling homesickness she felt. "You just surprised me. If I'd known you were coming, I'd have—" *Not been making love on the sofa with my landlord.* The thought of what her brothers had almost interrupted mortified her completely. She hardly recognized herself. "Let me make you some breakfast."

"We ate on the road. Coffee would be good. We thought we'd take you out to dinner tonight, if you're free."

She was working tonight. At Moons. A strip club. The last place she wanted her brothers to know about. "I, um, have plans. How about brunch tomorrow?"

"Plans? With Tina?" Mark asked hopefully.

"Tina's in California." Which was true.

"Is the woman ever in town?"

"I like being on my own."

"So, you have a date tonight? Is it someone special?" Mike probed.

"What's with the third degree? Come into the kitchen and I'll make some coffee. I have cinnamon bread."

"Mmm." Mark rubbed his hands together. "Sounds great. We really miss your cooking."

She laughed and led them to the kitchen, where she busied herself putting the filter in the coffeemaker, her hands shaking, her mind racing. It was cowardly to keep lying to them. Should she just tell the truth? *Jackson's not just my landlord, guys. He's also my roommate, my boss and my lover. It all started when the Outback got stolen.*

Yeah. Right.

She would sound hopelessly unstable. She wanted her life all straightened out before she broke the news. From her brothers' respectable viewpoint, she'd been living like a self-destructive runaway.

She hadn't thought past the moment in weeks. Doubt poured hotly through her. If they knew the truth, they'd never stop hassling her.

She sliced hunks of cinnamon bread, slathered them with butter and popped the plate into the microwave, feeling her brothers' eyes on her back, their worry heavy in the air.

"So, how's the salon?" Mark asked with false cheer. "You getting lots of new clients?"

"Slowly, but surely," she said, taking the bread from the microwave. Most of her work came from Moons and the discount she'd so readily offered was costing her a fortune in hair color, mousse, extension wax and other products.

"And you're starting school next semester?" He spoke too urgently.

"That's the plan." She put the plate on the table. Though with all that was going on at Moons and with Jackson, she hadn't thought much about it lately. "I have some textbooks to get a head start." Which she'd barely cracked. Right now, *Basic Psychology* was propping a wobbly leg in the break room. "Everything is completely under control."

A horrible hissing sound made her turn. Coffee grounds and water slopped over the sides of the angrily steaming machine. She hadn't gotten the filter fully in place. "For Pete's sake." She jumped up to fix it, rescuing enough coffee for two half mugs. She picked them up, then noticed the naked women on the sides, so she fished out two plain Moons mugs and transferred the drinks, hiding the bawdy ones in the sink. She carried the mugs to the table.

Mark and Michael took big sips. "Mmm," they said, then tried to hide the fact they had to pick coffee grounds off their tongues and lips.

"Try the bread," she said. "I made it with the bread maker you gave me."

"I picked that out for you." Mark beamed.

"The microwave was my idea." Mike nodded at it.

"I told him the TV was overkill," Mark added. "Mmm. Bread's great. Make some of this when you come down."

"We already had a TV set, but I appreciated all the gifts," she said, not wanting to give the pair ammo for the who-knows-best brotherly competition.

"And some pie, too?" Mike added. "Pumpkin for Thanksgiving?"

"And peach," Mark threw in. "Your peach is the best."

"Sure. Pumpkin, peach. Mincemeat if you want." Her heart swelled with love. Her brothers were pretending it was baked goods they missed. "How's Celia doing?" she asked.

"She's swamped," Mark said.

"But she wrote me about the new hairdresser."

"She's good, but she's not you," Mike said with an indulgent smile. "That's Celia's real complaint. She misses you."

"Everybody does," Mark added. "Every time I walk by the Cut 'n' Curl someone pops out to ask when you'll be back. For a visit, of course." But he clearly hoped she'd return home.

Her heart ached at how he was trying to hide it. It was

nice to feel irreplaceable, but she'd established herself here. She was moving ahead, wasn't she? She put a palm to her sternum to ease the cramp that seemed to close off her lungs.

While her brothers ate her homemade bread and strained coffee grounds through their teeth, Heidi asked about everyone in town, listening to the stories with an odd melancholy.

Her brothers seemed to be visiting from a faraway world, while she'd gotten trapped in a strange limbo, nowhere near where she'd intended to be. In college, on her own.

Footsteps made her look up to find Jackson standing in the archway holding that ridiculous wrench, his Moons T-shirt splotched with water. "Got that all handled for you, Heidi," he said in a big, fake voice. "Hope I didn't disrupt your visit."

"We're grateful to you for keeping things in repair," Mike said, holding out his hand to shake Jackson's. "I'm Mike."

"Pleased to meet you, Mike. You can count on me," Jackson said soberly. "Your sister needs anything, I'm there."

"We appreciate that," Mark said, shaking his hand, too. "We sure don't want to have to worry about whether Heidi's got hot water for the shower or decent air-conditioning."

She bristled, listening to them talk about her as if she were an unaccompanied minor being handed off to a flight attendant. "Guys, I'm fine. Really." She tried to laugh.

"Would you like some coffee?" Mark asked Jackson. "Or some bread. Heidi does the best baking."

"I know—" He caught himself. "Uh, she lets me sample her…stuff."

An idea too racy to contemplate explaining. "Help yourself," she said to him.

He grabbed a slice of bread and she felt him start to sit, then catch himself. "I'd better get going." He lifted the wrench. "Drips await. Nice meeting you both." He didn't even look at her, just hustled off.

"Friendly guy," Mark said, leaving the words hanging in the air. *Did he hit on you? Do we need to put him in his place?*

She sighed, so confused about what she wanted to say, should say, and what her brothers could handle. "Jackson is a great landlord," she said finally. "A nice guy who helps everyone he knows." He'd been helping her like crazy. With a place to live, a job, another job, with sex—lots of that—and now with her brothers.

Tell them the story. Tell them about Jackson. But what exactly was there to tell? Was this love? Could it last? And why had Jackson lied in the first place? Maybe he was as uncertain as she was. She had to talk to him before she talked to her brothers. Maybe at brunch she'd spill it all. Or maybe she'd hold off. By Halloween she'd have more to report. Or maybe this would all be over and done with.

JACKSON TOOK OFF, wrench in hand, completely shaken. Meeting Heidi's brothers, seeing how concerned they were about her had flipped him out. Had he taken advantage of her innocence, exploited her curiosity? Been the big, bad wolf Autumn had hinted he was being?

He loved her. He wanted her to stay. But that didn't mean he was good for her. Seeing her through her brothers' eyes made him wonder. He should talk to her about this…soon.

Or let it drop and hope it all went away, along with her

brothers. He had practice and Heidi was due at the salon. He called her cell a couple of times, and was almost relieved when she didn't answer. Which wasn't a good sign. He didn't want anything to rock this boat they were gently floating in. He didn't want to answer any of the big questions.

Practice required every ounce of his attention, since Heather was moody and expected to be catered to, his two friends kept saying *whatever* instead of declaring what they wanted, and the drummer had to be cajoled to stick it out the entire session.

For three hours, Jackson tiptoed around personalities, guessed at interests and cobbled moods and motivation together. Focusing on the music helped and somehow they worked up a strong playlist for the gigs Jackson hoped to score this week. The sound was hot, the vibe good, and he saw big possibilities if he handled things right.

Brain-dead from the effort, he returned to the town house, dread in his heart. What was he going to say to Heidi? If only they could forget about her brothers' visit. He needed her opinion about how he'd handled the touchy aspects of practice, but she'd probably want to hash out what had happened with her brothers and what it meant. He was relieved she wasn't home yet.

When he finally heard her key in the lock it was almost time to head to work at Moons.

She entered and plopped the backpack her brothers had given her heavily on the table. "I was studying," she said, but she didn't sound happy about it. "Or at least trying to. I'm in over my head. Out of the study mindset." She looked up at him. "How are you? How was practice?"

"Okay. Complicated. But we still have a band."

They looked at each other, not saying a million things. Finally they spoke at once.

"Did your brothers—?"

"Why did you lie—?"

"You go ahead," he insisted.

"Why did you lie to my brothers at the door?" she asked, blinking up at him. "Tell them you were just my land-lord?"

"Because it was awkward. We were just…you know… doing it."

"Yeah," she said, not blaming him at all. "But why didn't I just say that we live together, that we…that you and I…that we're…seeing each other?" She looked troubled and confused.

Because you were ashamed. The thought rolled through him like a bowling ball, knocking down all his pins. Hell, he'd been ashamed *for* her. "Because you were in shock," he said.

She frowned, nodding slowly. "It's that they don't know anything about my life. And it just seemed like so much to tell. At once, right?" She was trying to convince herself.

"Sure," he said.

"They're taking me to brunch tomorrow. Maybe I'll tell them then."

"Or you could wait," he said abruptly. "Why upset them? Before everything's straightened out…in your life, I mean."

"No. I should tell them. We're together, right? Aren't we, Jackson?" She stepped toward him, moved into his arms and he buried his nose in her sweet hair.

"Yeah," he said, never wanting to let her go. "We're to-gether. Want me to come with you? Talk to them for you?"

She leaned back and looked up at him. "No. It's up to

me. Maybe I'll tell them about the Outback being stolen, too." She chewed on her lip, nervous as hell. She looked exactly like the uncertain girl who'd stood on his doorstep expecting to move into his town house a month ago.

"If you want me to come, too, just let me know."

"It's my problem. I'll handle it."

But what exactly would she tell them about him? He wasn't sure he wanted to know.

Heidi rushed to change for work and they set off like usual, except for an odd tension in the air—like a note held too long and too high.

They talked about the MoonDanz practice—she had suggestions for smoothing the rough edges on the band's personalities—and about the night ahead. Taylor was going to cover for Jackson for a couple hours while he accompanied the band to an audition.

It could have been the jabber of any other night, but there was a whole separate conversation going on. *What are we doing? Are we really together?* God, he hoped so. When he thought about not being with Heidi, the old gloom whistled through him like a leaky window in winter.

When they got to Moons, he noticed Stan was deep in conversation with Dupree and a couple of his shady buddies, which raised the hair on the back of Jackson's neck. Something fishy going on there. He'd look into it after he got back from the audition later tonight.

By opening time, Jackson was standing at the hostess stand, supposedly greeting customers, but really keeping an eye on Heidi as she flew by. She wore her new clothes— the sexy leotard and rip-away skirt she'd stripped out of for him—but he had fond feelings for the homeless outfit.

She was such a wonder to him. And she made him so

happy. He wanted her in his life. Determination rose, building heat like an engine testing high idle. They needed more time. He'd grab her on her break, take her out back and tell her he loved her, that he wanted to make it work with her. Sure.

"Jackson? Is that you?" The puzzled male voice made him turn toward the entrance, where he saw, to his horror, Heidi's brother Mark, standing with Mike among a group of men wearing name tags. They were huddled around the hostess stand. His heart slammed into his chest and nausea rose. What the hell were they doing here?

"Hey," he said, forcing a smile, "Mike and Mark, right? What's up?"

"We were all headed for dinner—a bunch of us from the mayors' conference—and I recognized the sign from your shirt." He pointed at Jackson's Moons T-shirt. "We figured if you liked the place enough to buy a shirt, it must be good."

"Ah, well, this is a bar, not a restaurant. And I'm the manager." He had to get them away from here before they realized where they were or caught sight of Heidi. "There's a great Thai place up the street. And, let's see, good Greek food on Seventh Avenue. Not to mention pasta to die for at—"

"Wow." Mark's eyes went wide.

Jackson turned to see a dancer stroll by in a tiger-striped leotard.

"Hey, is this a—a—?" Mark started.

"A strip club!" said a third man, one of their group, evidently, since he wore the same name tag. "You guys are pretty dialed in for being from out of town," he said to Mike, who just stared, wide-eyed.

"This is a strip club?" Mark asked Jackson.

"Yeah, so, uh, you probably don't want to come in."

"No, we don't." Mike turned for the door.

"Hell, we'll eat after. This is great," said the third guy. "There's even a show." He slapped down the cover, the rest of the party lining up behind him.

"I think we'll pass," Mike said to the guy.

"Come on. Be a man, not a mayor. Two more." He plunked down cover for the Fields brothers. They looked at each other, Mark shrugged, and they let themselves be swept inside on the wave of social pressure and testosterone.

Jackson led them to tables far in the back, out of sight of Heidi's section.

"This isn't our thing, you know," Mike said to Jackson, obviously embarrassed. "For God's sake, don't tell Heidi."

He grimaced, unable to say a word.

"So...you manage this place?" Mark asked, seeming more intrigued than his brother. "Must be interesting." He looked around, red-faced, trying to act cool, but clearly shocked.

"It pays the bills," Jackson said.

Mark brought his gaze back to Jackson's face. "Listen, I'm actually glad to run into you without Heidi around. We'd appreciate if you'd let us know if she has any problems with the rent or with her roommate, who seems to be AWOL most of the time. She's so stubborn about asking for help." He reached into his jacket pocket and handed him a card. "If something comes up, call. Anytime. Anything."

"Sure," he said, feeling sick. "Heidi's a smart woman, though. She knows what she's doing." His throat felt dry.

"Even smart women get into trouble," Mike said, moving in.

"We don't get why she's putting off school," Mark said. He seemed to be the gentler brother.

"We're afraid she's losing her way, wasting time."

"Sure." With a dead-end job at a strip club and a guy like him? They had a point.

"She's more insecure than she lets on," Mark added.

Beyond the brothers and across the stage, he could see Heidi serving beer to a customer, who leaned forward, as if to hear her better, but really to get a shot of cleavage. The guy put a hand at her waist, just acting friendly, but Jackson tensed, wanting to tear the guy apart.

Heidi slid easily away, smiled an "I'm flattered, but hands off" smile, and kept working. Normally, that classy move would have impressed him. But standing beside her gray-faced brothers, he felt like a class-A prick for putting her in a place where such a maneuver was required.

He noticed Rox at a nearby table and motioned her over. "Get these guys whatever they want—on the house."

The brothers protested his generosity, but he waved away their objections. "Enjoy your evening," he said to them, then leaned in to Rox. "Make it fast and don't come back for a second round. I want them out of here quick."

Then he strode off to warn Heidi, furious with himself for dragging her into this world of borderline sleaze. Meanwhile, her uptight brothers were begging him to keep an eye on her. He had no business with a woman like Heidi. That truth hit him like a carjack in the gut.

Yeah, he was helping her now, but once she was back on her feet—in college or later, once she had a psychology practice—what would she want with him? She'd need a guy with ambition, not a bar manager with a music dream that might go nowhere.

She plain wanted more from the world than he did. He

didn't want to argue with her, disappoint her. He'd feel bad and then he'd get mad.

He found her at the bar, her tray full of beer steins. "We need to talk," he said, putting her load back on the bar. "Taylor, get someone else to deliver this." Jackson guided her into the break room, which was thankfully empty. "Don't panic, Heidi, but your brothers are here."

"My brothers?" Her voice squeaked and her eyes went wide.

He explained the situation. "They don't know you're here and I set them up at a back table."

"What a disaster." She tried to smile, but her pale face was blotched with embarrassment.

"You need to disappear. I'll take you home on my way to the audition."

"We're too busy for me to duck out. I'm not ashamed of being here." She jutted her chin, but bit her lip, too. "I'll just go over and make it a joke."

"Your brothers won't laugh. And they're right. This isn't the place for you." How had he been so stupid? "You should be working in an office or at least at a decent restaurant, not delivering shots to horny droolers who grab your ass and—"

"No one grabs my ass, Jackson. And until my brothers walked in the door, my being here was perfectly fine with you."

"I shouldn't have gotten you into this. Hell, I'm not even a decent landlord. The sink leaks, did you know that?"

"I asked for the job, Jackson. I'm here because I want to be. I'm going to talk to my brothers right now. Show me where they're sitting."

"Heidi, don't do this."

"I have to."

He took her arm to stop her, but she glared at him, so he let go. "What are you trying to prove?"

"That I'm in charge of my own life."

"They're at table forty-five and I'm going with you."

"Don't you dare." She shot him a ferocious look that made him step back.

He settled for trailing her, prepared to jump in and soften the shock if he could, offer her brothers his jaw to pound if it helped. He half wanted that. Hell, he deserved it.

14

HEIDI MARCHED TOWARD table forty-five, furious at herself for not handling the situation this morning at the house. She'd acted like a child and now Jackson was treating her like one. The last thing she needed was another protector. She'd chosen her job and her life and she might as well own up to it.

Except table forty-five was empty. "Where did the guys that were here go?" Heidi asked Rox, who breezed by.

"Yeah, that's choice. A wife called and the guy went white and they all decided they'd better eat dinner instead. Why…you know them?"

"Yeah," she said, filled with incredible relief. She did not want to tell her brothers about Moons. Not at all. She didn't want to tell them about Jackson, either. Not until she'd talked to him, sorted out what was really going on between them. She turned and saw Jackson coming toward her.

"They're gone," she said.

"Are you all right?"

She nodded, though she wasn't all right at all. And she could see Jackson knew that, too.

"Look, I have to take off for the audition, but I'll be back in two hours. Call my cell if you need me. I'm sorry I got you into this." He looked so grim and troubled and—this gave her a sick feeling—far away. "We'll talk later."

"Yeah," she said. "We'll talk." But what exactly would they say?

She went back to work and tried not to think about Jackson. An hour later, she stood at the bar. Taylor had just set off to fill her order when Dupree, the new guy, jerked up from behind the bar like a spastic jack-in-the-box. The guy creeped her out. Every look was a leer, every comment had sexual connotations and he was so jumpy he made her own heart pound.

"Do me a solid and put these away, babe." He thrust one of the plastic sacks that held bar towels at her. "Special delivery." He winked. The bag was tied shut, signifying the towels were dirty. Odd, since she'd seen Rox bring out a fresh sack just a bit ago. Must have been some big spills to use up all these towels. She noticed Duke's nephew Stan at the end of the bar watching the exchange with close attention. He weirded her out, too, and haunted the bar whenever Dupree was on duty.

She carried the bag of towels into the break room, but a commotion from the lounge made her lean into the hall to see what was going on.

Stan practically plowed her down as he ran past, a towel bag, of all things, in one hand. Behind him, she heard shouts, cries and running feet approaching. Behind her, the door alarm went off, so she knew Stan had ducked out the emergency exit.

A man thick with dark protective gear, straps and buckles burst into the hall, a gun extended. A *gun*.

She yelped.

"Stay in that room," he snapped at her. He tilted his head at the break room, then continued down the hall. She went where he'd indicated and more waitresses and dancers were ushered in, everyone looking scared. "I think it's a drug bust," Jasmine whispered.

A drug bust. Heidi looked down at the laundry sack that Dupree had just given her with a wink and remembered that Stan had taken off with another one. Why would Stan care about bar towels? Her stomach sank to her knees and the hand clutching the plastic bag felt clammy. She carried the towels to a grim-faced agent. "Officer, sir. You might want to look in this."

He took the sack, looked her over sternly, then emptied it onto a table. Dry towels were wrapped tightly around what turned out to be small plastic bags. She'd seen enough cop shows to guess the white stuff inside wasn't baking soda. She'd been holding a sack of drugs—coke or heroin or speed or some other illegal powder. She calmly explained about the bar towel procedure and showed the agent the hamper, which turned out to hold several more suspicious plastic bags.

She'd sounded as innocent as possible, but the agent insisted she come along to the station to "sort it all out," along with most of the Moons employees.

Could she be arrested for simply holding something? Maybe. Accessory after the fact or some terrible charge. Her blood ran cold as ice and she had the urgent need to pee.

She was led with her co-workers to the parking lot, where people stared and cameras flashed, and toward a police van. She felt like she was sleepwalking. *It's just a bad dream,* she told herself.

"Heidi?" Her brother Mark stood behind crime-scene tape, pale and horrified.

Make that a nightmare. "What are you doing here?" she asked.

He had the decency to look embarrassed. "My sunglasses fell out of my pocket, so I came back—guys from the conference dragged us here. It wasn't our idea. We tried— It's a long story...."

"Let's go." The agent urged her into the van.

"You're being arrested?" Mark asked, even more horrified.

"It's a mistake. I can explain." But how? She climbed into the back of the van and slid past the knees of worried employees on the benches.

"This is bullshit," the normally taciturn Taylor muttered. "It's Stan and that twitchy dick Dupree."

"What are we going to do?" Jasmine wailed, her voice high and shaky.

Heidi had no idea. She'd been *holding,* as they said in the movies. She could be arrested and charged. She needed an attorney. She needed a miracle. She had to get out of this.

What about Jackson? Sure. Jackson would save her. He was probably on his way back from the audition by now and could straighten this out before the van drove off.

She stopped moving and Rox banged into her from behind. "Sorry," Heidi said, reaching for her purse to get her phone. Except her purse was still in her locker.

She struggled to switch with Rox in the narrow aisle, banging into seated people, who huffed at her, so she could beg the officer outside the van to let her fetch her purse.

She was leaning out the door when she saw Jackson...wearing handcuffs and being led her way. Nevada was beside him, also restrained.

"You got my sister arrested!" she heard Mark shout at him.

"I'll take care of it," he called over his shoulder, then climbed into the van, pausing as he saw her. "I'll make it right," he said, then surveyed the worried group. "This is all a mistake. We'll straighten it out right away."

"What's with the handcuffs?" Taylor asked him.

But Nevada answered. "Jackson kept me from kicking that cop where it counts. I warned the guy to watch his hands, show some respect for the talent." She practically glowed with defiant pride. The van door slammed, an exclamation point to her words, and they began to move.

During the drive, Jackson took charge, asking questions and piecing together what had happened in a way that calmed everyone. Stan and Dupree had been taken off in a separate car, and, judging from what the agent in charge had said to him before Nevada got into a kicking match with an officer, they merely wanted to get everyone's statement at the station.

Jackson caught her eye. *I'll fix this. Don't worry.* She wanted to believe him, but she knew suddenly that her problems weren't his to fix.

How had she ended up like this? In front of her brothers, no less. She could still see Mark's pale and frightened face. Working at Moons was teaching Sunday school compared to a drug bust.

Her life was out of control, completely off the track. The idea rolled through her like sudden ice. The buzz of conversation slipped to the background and she did a long-needed reality check on herself. What the hell was she doing? She'd let her plan slip away. She wasn't pushing to get into school. She hadn't signed up for an online class. She'd barely touched the books Jackson had bought for her. Heck, he'd been more supportive of her dream than she'd been.

She'd been hiding from her future in the little world of Moons and Shear Ecstasy, turning them into her new small town, where she was doing amateur counseling behind a makeup mirror in a cloud of hairspray just like before.

She'd been hiding out the way Jackson had been doing when she met him. But he'd pushed on, put together the band, taken steps to change his life. She'd dropped off the path, distracted by the comfort of Moons. And Jackson. There was no forgetting the distraction of Jackson.

The truth was that she'd been relieved to be off the hook with school. School scared her. She'd hunkered down and gotten comfortable in her own Copper Corners. And as for Jackson, she'd latched onto him like a life raft in a storm.

Granted, he was a good guy, but she'd read far more into what was between them than ever could be. She didn't belong in his world. She'd landed there and let him rescue her. He'd been taking care of her just like her brothers wanted to. She'd invited him to, welcomed his help, cuddled right into it and escaped from responsibility for her own future.

But that was over. Starting here, starting now in this police van, she was taking charge of her life. As soon as she got out of jail.

HE'D MADE A MESS of his dad's rules, Jackson realized grimly, as the van bounced over the curb into the police station lot. Not only had he shredded the "something between you and the wolves" admonition, now he'd blown "watch out for the people you love." He looked at the tear-streaked faces and worried frowns of the Moons crew and realized he'd let them all down.

The worst was Heidi, who was trying to look brave and determined, but she was as shrunken and scared as a wet cat. Her brothers had watched her get arrested, for God's sake. They wanted to rip him a new one. As well they should. He'd promised to look out for her and he'd blown it. Jackson wanted to hit something. Hard.

What the hell had happened in the bar when he wasn't looking? That scumbag Dupree had been dealing drugs right under his nose. He'd sensed Stan and Dupree had been up to something, but he'd been too preoccupied with Heidi, then with the band, to stop and straighten it out. Charging after another dream, he'd let down the people he loved.

He'd screwed up big-time, but he would correct it—make sure everything was made right. Then he'd get Heidi a decent job, pay her damned tuition, if he had to, get her safely out of his life, so she could meet some solid, respectable guy who wouldn't get caught dead in a strip club. He'd only meant to help her, but falling in love with her had only caused her pain.

IT WAS SIX in the morning before Heidi was able to leave the police station. She was the last to go. Her situation was more complicated because of the drugs she'd been holding. Now she was clammy and sweaty, her clothes grimy and her eyes scratchy with exhaustion. The harsh clang of bars opening and closing, the yells and loud conversations, the scrape of feet, the hollow echo of the cold walls around them still rang in her ears. Not to mention the smell of metal and sweat and despair. What she wanted now was sleep and a bath.

She'd told her brothers she'd meet them at their hotel after their conference ended that day to explain everything. She dreaded their worried eyes, their I-told-you-so lecture. They were right, of course. She'd used bad judgment, gotten in over her head, expected Jackson to bail her out in too many ways. She'd tell them the truth and then she'd start over. Do it right this time. But first she'd get some sleep.

She would say goodbye to Jackson, too, but not until she was sure she could look at him without her heart filling up and spilling over. That was the hardest part.

An officer had her sign for her belongings and gave them to her. She balled up her apron with her order pad, clicked on her watch and poked her earrings into her ears. Just like her arrival in Phoenix, she was down to a few belongings, starting over again. She thanked the officer and headed down the hall to meet her ride.

Except there were her brothers. And Jackson. And all three were huddled together in loud conversation, too intent to notice her. Seeing Jackson rocked her, so she paused to collect herself before making her presence known.

"I talked her into the job," Jackson was saying. "It was totally my fault. And she's been an incredibly good influence on the strippers. She's got one of them looking at college and another one on a budget. It's been practice for becoming a shrink."

"Do you realize how ridiculous that sounds?" Mike said, his voice cracking.

"You got her arrested," Mark hissed, unusually hostile for him.

"She was in the wrong place at the wrong time, that's all, and her statement will help them get the real criminals doing time. She was only questioned."

"Why should we believe anything you say?" Michael asked.

"Because none of this is Jackson's fault," she said loudly, making them all turn to look at her. "He's done nothing but watch out for me." She sighed, then pointed at chairs along the wall. "Have a seat, guys. I have a story to tell and you're going to listen to it all."

The three men sat in a row on a bench. She wished

Jackson wasn't there, but it couldn't be helped. She sat across from them all and told her brothers about the stolen car, about Jackson offering her a room and the job she'd insisted on taking. She left out sleeping with him. That was personal and it was over, so it shouldn't matter to her brothers.

Every time her brothers or Jackson interrupted, she stopped them, and kept talking, ending with the laundry bag incident. "These were my choices, my decisions, and now it's my mess to clean up."

"If you'd told us in the beginning, gotten our help, none of this would have happened," Mike snapped.

"I wanted to make it on my own."

"At least you should have kept the money," Mark inserted.

"What would you have thought if I'd suddenly accepted a thousand dollars after all my insistence on doing it myself?"

"That something had changed," he replied, shrugging.

"That something was *wrong,* you mean, and you would have jumped into my life when I didn't want you to."

"But we knew something was wrong," Mike said. "You sounded funny on the phone. We assumed you were homesick. We should have demanded you tell us the truth. We should have come sooner and got you."

"The real problem," Mark inserted, "was that we made her so miserable at home, she felt better off living with some strange guy—"

"Hey," Jackson grumbled.

"—taking a trashy job."

"Hey," Jackson repeated.

"The *point* is that she was desperate to escape us," Mark insisted. "What kind of brothers were we being…really?"

"You were fine," Jackson jumped in. "You did everything you could. I was the one who let things get out of hand."

"You sure did," Mike snapped bitterly.

"But he's not family, Mike," Mark said. "It's our job to look out for Heidi."

"Would you all just stop it!" she shouted, startling herself with her vehemence. "Stop talking about me like I'm not here. This is my life. I screwed it up. I'm the one. Stop blaming yourselves. Or taking credit, or whatever it is you're doing."

They looked at her, as if surprised she was still there, then frowned.

"You're upset," Mike said. "We'll take you home now."

"I'm not going to Copper Corners, guys. Not now."

"I'll take you home," Jackson said, his eyes burning with emotion.

"But I can't go with you, either, Jackson."

The three men frowned and objected at once.

"Hello there!"

The voice made them turn to look up at Esmeralda, who waved elaborate nails their way. Bangle earrings jingled merrily and she snapped her gum. "Ready to go, hon?"

"This is Esmeralda Sunshine," she said to the three men. "The nail technician at Shear Ecstasy. She's renting me her guest room until I've saved enough to lease a place of my own."

"You can stay at the town house as long as you need," Jackson said.

"I know that, but I have to figure out what I want on my own." Just looking at his face made her want to cry. She would miss him so much. Being near him just confused her.

"There's no shame in reconsidering your decision," Mike said. "Don't let pride keep you from being happy at home. We won't interfere any more. We understand you want privacy."

"I know you guys would carve out a life for me with your fingernails and a toothpick if you had to, but it's not your job. I have to find my own way. Get back to your conference, guys. I know you have to straighten out the mess at Moons, Jackson." *We'll talk later,* she told him with her eyes.

"But, Heidi—"

"Heidi, you—"

"We can't—"

"I mean it," she said, waving away all three men's objections. "I'll call you all once I've gotten some sleep."

The three men glared at each other and she knew they'd start blaming each other the minute she walked out the door. She hadn't gotten through to them. Maybe she never would.

All she knew was that she'd strayed from her plan, leaning on Jackson, convincing herself she was in love with him. That had made her all too ready to set aside her dreams.

She had Esmeralda drive her straight to the town house for her things, so she could settle into her new life right away.

She was shocked to unlock the door and find Jackson there. She'd assumed he'd be at Moons. He stood in the doorway, his face full of shifting emotions—pleasure at the sight of her, followed by guilt and pain.

She was certain she looked similarly torn. How could a heart sink and rise and ache and sing all at the same time?

15

"WOULD YOU MIND waiting in the car?" she asked Esmeralda, who stood on the porch with her, looking from her to Jackson. "I'll get my things and be right out."

"Take your time." She snapped her gum. "Howard Stern will have something wild going. Lesbian nuns, housewife hookers, talking dogs." She shrugged, turned and toddled down the walk.

Heidi entered the town house, shut the door and leaned against it. "I'm sorry my brothers blamed you, Jackson."

"They had every right to."

"No. It was all me. I got swept up in everything…the bar…you…and I lost track of what I wanted."

He looked at her, his eyes red and sad. "I'm glad you didn't tell them about us. They would have ended up in jail for trying to beat the crap out of me." He tried a wry smile, but it came out sad. "You're right, though, about ending it." Jackson's eyes were a flat brown now. Gone was the golden warmth of love or desire. "You want more from the world than I do. I would hold you back." His Adam's apple bobbed up and down in a slow swallow that sounded dry.

"You've been so supportive." Too supportive. She'd fallen in love with the comfort of his big, safe arms. "What we had…what we shared…meant a lot." If she said she loved him, she knew she'd cry.

"Yeah."

"I hope you'll keep working with MoonDanz," she said. "That's a great move for you. There may be glitches and personality conflicts, but have faith in yourself."

"I'll be fine," he said.

They were different people and they wanted different things. When the time was right for her to settle down, she'd find someone more like her, right?

Right?

She would miss him like the sun.

"What are you going to do?" he asked her.

"Get an office job with regular hours, work at the salon weekends and evenings, save my money."

"If you want restaurant work, I know Duke can help."

"I can still do your housecleaning, if you'd like."

"Better not." He cleared his throat, and a muscle moved in his jaw. "You'll be busy."

She nodded. Better a clean break, she knew, though the idea of it made her ache. She didn't want to cut herself off from Jackson. Or from Moons, either.

She'd visit later. When it didn't hurt so much.

"I'd better get my stuff together," she said.

He offered to help, but she did it herself, filling just a few boxes with everything she owned. Jackson insisted she take some of the groceries she'd bought. He helped her carry everything out to Esmeralda's tiny Neon and then she walked back with him to get her purse and say goodbye.

She looked around the living room, took in the breast cocktail table, the nudie lamp, Tiki Town with its gently swaying hula girl, the bikini babe poster, the shiny engines. "It's funny, but I'll miss the look of the place," she said.

"That's hard to believe."

"I got used to all the breasts." It felt like home.

"Do you want a souvenir? How about that lamp?" He pointed at the hula girl.

"You love that lamp."

"But it'll remind you…"

Of that first kiss? When she'd slipped off the bamboo stool. Oh, Jackson. She wanted to take the whole living room, the whole town house, and stuff it into her pocket, carry it with her always.

"The bar would look empty without her," she said instead. "I have your Hawaiian shirt. That's my souvenir."

"It looks good on you. Better than it ever did on me." Heat flew across his face for a moment, then he quashed it. "Anyway… Hey, wait. I know what you need." He grinned and headed out of the room, returning with something in a fist. He uncurled his fingers to reveal the Hawaiian girl night-light.

She remembered the soft glow in the hall, the way it made Jackson's eyes gleam when he looked at her. "I love it," she said taking it from his hand.

Then he pulled her in his arms and buried his nose in her hair. "I wish things were different," he said. He looked into her face.

"Me, too," she said, stepping away from the warmth and security she longed for, but didn't dare accept. "Thanks for this." She held up the plastic woman with the Mona Lisa smile and the hibiscus in her hair. And the bare breasts, of course. "You were just what I needed." She backed toward the door, pausing at the threshold, not quite ready to leave.

"Wait!" he said, not wanting her to go yet either, it seemed. "Your tree! You want your tree, don't you?"

She followed him into the kitchen for the ficus, which looked dreadful. The few leaves that remained were yellow, brown or spotted. "It's dying," she said softly. "I don't know why. I watered it every day."

"I watered it, too."

"You did?" She reached down to feel the dirt, which was soaked. "We drowned the poor thing."

"Just trying to help."

"I know." They'd both tried to help each other and overdid it altogether. "Throw it away. Plant something else in the pot."

"I'll let it dry. If it bounces back, I'll call you."

"That'd be great," she said, not knowing whether she should hope for that or not. There wasn't much more to say. She glanced at the beer maid clock, at the neat kitchen, glass-front cupboards orderly and even, naked ladies turned to the back. The space where the bread maker belonged looked sad. "I'll make you some bread and drop it by," she said.

"Better not," he said, shaking his head.

And then she was just too sad, so she tightened her fingers around the Hawaiian lady, the breasts poking insistently into her palm, and left.

At the passenger door of the Neon, she turned and looked up at the porch, where Jackson stood looking out at her. The first time he'd done that, he'd felt sorry for her, offered her a beer because apartment hunting was thirsty work. Now she felt sorry for them both. She felt like she was leaving her best friend.

TWO WEEKS LATER, Jackson was deejaying at Moons as usual. In some ways, it was as if nothing at all had happened. In others, nothing would ever be the same.

Stan had confessed that his dealer had coerced him into allowing Dupree to deal drugs out of Moons. Duke was completely innocent. Because the new revue was mentioned so prominently, the publicity turned out to be positive and Moons's crowds grew even larger.

Duke had begged Jackson to stay on as manager, swearing he would never again hire a soul without Jackson's approval. Jackson did not need convincing. He wanted the familiarity of Moons while he licked his wounds. Moons felt more like home these days than the town house.

Without Heidi, the place was damned empty. After only a couple days, it smelled like beer and pizza again. It got so bad that on his day off, he'd attempted a peach pie just for the aroma. He'd bought a premade crust and steamed up the kitchen stewing the peaches in butter, cinnamon and sugar. The pie was nothing like Heidi's and, worst of all, it wasn't until the smell had leaked into every corner of the place that he realized it only made him miss her more.

The only thing that really helped was MoonDanz. He'd thrown himself into working with the band and that kept his mind occupied. He'd convinced Duke to invest in a demo CD in exchange for a cut of any deal they made. Jackson was circulating it with club owners in town and L.A. now.

That was exciting, but he still felt beat up—bruised as those peaches Heidi'd made into that first pie. He put on the song Heidi had stripped to on pain meds and sighed.

He looked out over the bar and caught Autumn frowning up at him. She shook her head and marched toward the stairs to his booth. What did she want now?

A few seconds later, she entered. "God, enough with that tune. You've played it three times tonight. Give us something fresh." She studied him. "What's with you? You've been mopin' around since the drug bust."

"I have things on my mind."

"Things?" She paused. "It's Heidi, huh?"

"I miss her," he said, surprised that he'd admitted it so quickly. He felt raw.

"You're in love with her…. Wow. I'm sorry, Jax. I never thought— I didn't think you— I told her you were a loner."

"I am a loner." He tried to laugh. "Except now I just feel alone." That raw, grated feeling spread throughout his whole body.

"Oh, Jax. You big lug. It happened. The true love thing. Did you tell her?"

"Of course not. What's the point? She moved on. She's getting a degree, becoming a shrink. What use would she have for a guy like me?"

"Heidi's not the kind of person who gets hung up on diplomas, Jax. If she needs you, she needs you."

"That's the point. She doesn't need me. I don't have a thing to offer her."

"She tell you that?"

"She said she wants to handle her own life."

"You did the big brother thing, didn't you?" She put her hands on her hips. "You know it makes us nuts when you do that. You operate from a male-dominant social paradigm. Paternalism infantilizes women."

"What the hell are you talking about?"

"I've been doing a little reading, my friend. Women's studies, along with accounting. Soon, I'll be vanquishing men's minds, along with their dicks."

He groaned, but he was proud of her for looking into school. He didn't dare say it or she'd slug him senseless.

"Heidi got me started, but she waited until I showed interest. She didn't say, 'You're wasting your brain, so take this class,' like you would have done."

He remembered how Heidi rolled her eyes when he dished out advice.

"Heidi needs your love and your support, not your advice. Now you, on the other hand, you could use a little bossing around. Already, she got you off your lazy ass and into the band scene. You need her to keep you going, my friend."

Maybe she was right. She at least had a point.

"Go get her. You need each other." She kissed him on the cheek. "Get her out here, too. Nevada's freaking out about the new routines—it's fear of success, I just know it. She's not due for a weave for a while. We can't wait that long for Heidi's help."

Jackson was still mulling over Autumn's words when he got home that night. The place smelled bad and felt empty. Heidi hadn't added one thing to the town house, except that shriveled-up tree, but she'd filled every corner so that he felt as if the place would be forever hollow without her.

His stomach burned, his heart ached. He wanted so badly to push through, figure this out in a way that would let him be with Heidi.

He had to be able to take care of her, keep the wolves away, didn't he? That's what men did for the women they loved. He felt the truth of that rule to his bones. Paternalistic, infantilizing or not.

He went into her room to grab some music to mope by, but he paused at the framed photo of his dad with his band. *Look out for the ones you love.* His dad had pushed back his music dream, relegated it to weekend gigs, passed it all by because of Jackson and his mother.

Personally, if his dad had asked, Jackson would have told him he'd rather live in tiny apartments all over the country than see his dad give up his music. It ate at him, he knew.

What had his mom thought?

I'm sure your dad courted her with music. Heidi had pointed that out. Maybe if his dad had asked his mom about it, she might have told him to go for it, too. Love and dreams could go hand in hand. Heidi had supported him with the band. Hell, she'd goaded him into it. Maybe he'd needed the push. Call it support. Maybe she wanted to look out for the person she loved, too.

She had bigger goals than he did, though. But so what? He could support her in whatever she wanted. And maybe she would do the same for him.

Pretty heavy, he realized, and his head began to hurt. But somewhere in him, deep, he felt his mom's smile. The one he'd loved the most. The one that said, *I love you more than life, Son, and I'm so proud of you.*

Maybe Heidi was right and his parents could see him after all. He knew one thing for sure. They would love Heidi.

A MONTH AFTER breaking up with Jackson, Heidi poured milk onto her corn flakes at Esmeralda's kitchen table and told herself to make it a good day.

"Goddess of light, the air in here sucks," Esmeralda said, waltzing in, sweeping her hands through the air as if to whisk away smoke. "Your aura is as gray as an English sky."

Esmeralda had turned out to be the perfect roommate—she'd given Heidi a spacious and tastefully decorated room and her own bathroom, she was neat, went to bed at ten, had healthy eating habits, and was fun to talk to, though she gave Heidi plenty of quiet time to think. Everything was perfect.

And Heidi was miserable. She missed Jackson. She

missed Moons. Even Shear Ecstasy didn't cheer her up. She'd recommitted to her plan, had sketched out a résumé and was booked for interviews at a temp agency, but she felt lost.

Esmeralda waltzed to the cupboard and brought back a pill container. "B vitamins, sweetie," she said, plunking them down on the table. She sat across from Heidi, and slapped Heidi's fingers out of her mouth. She'd been chewing her cuticles again. "They'll strengthen your nails, too." She grabbed Heidi's wrist. "Let Esmeralda look."

She thought it was her nails Esmeralda wanted to examine, but instead she flipped over her hand. "It's time. I'm reading your palm."

"But my life's still not set," she said, making a fist and pulling away.

Esmeralda locked on like handcuffs. "What have you got to lose? Your heart is broken, you're miserable. Besides, I only report things you can celebrate or fix."

"Okay, I guess," she said, and slowly uncurled her fingers.

Esmeralda pulled her hand onto her own palm and pressed the fingers out straight, then traced the surface creases with the kaleidoscope-painted nail of her index finger. "Long lifeline," she said, tilting her head, shifting Heidi's hand to catch the light streaming in from the window.

"That's good," Heidi said tentatively.

"Only if you don't waste it. Hmm. Deep understanding of people." She jabbed at a forked line, bending Heidi's fingers back hard.

"Ouch."

"Just seeing how deep. Hmm. Quite."

"So that means being a psychologist is the right career choice? Since I understand people?"

Esmeralda shrugged. "You do pretty good at the salon. Slippin' in zingers when your client's deciding if she likes it parted or back. Of course, with a degree, you'd get more cash."

So much for the prestige and respect of a credential. To Esmeralda, it was merely a matter of more money. Heidi smiled.

Esmeralda peered more closely. "Oh, and, you've got the Grand flippin' Canyon of a love line. One big love for your long, long life." She looked into her face. "Make sense?"

"I guess." Could it be Jackson? Her stomach jumped and her heart squeezed. She couldn't imagine falling any harder in love. But if he was her one love, what should she do about it?

Esmeralda went back to her work. "Aha. Look at all these options, but you only see one way…."

"I do?"

"Oh—see that little barbed wire fence?" She jabbed a spot near Heidi's thumb. "You cut yourself off from what you need. No woman's an island, hon. Where'd you get the idea you have to go it alone?"

"I don't know. I just—"

"Take help when you need it. It doesn't diminish you. Just use good sense." She patted the palm and let go. "That wasn't so bad was it? Want a yogurt drink to wash down the Bs?"

"No, um, thanks." She left her hand out, palm up, tingling from the scrapes and traces of Esmeralda's nails, while Esmeralda rummaged around the refrigerator.

Take help when you need it. It doesn't diminish you. Had she cut herself off from help just to prove her independence? Her brothers would loan her money for school.

Why couldn't she take it? She'd done some pretty great things already with Moons. Why did she have to quit?

And was Jackson her one love? Already? Barely a day into her new life? Sometimes it worked like that. And Jackson had been there for her, supporting her from the beginning. He wasn't perfect. He was different from her, but so what? She loved him. And, maybe, she needed him, too. Not because she couldn't handle her own life, but because everyone needed support. *No woman's an island, hon.* Did Jackson need her, too?

The phone rang, making her jump.

It was the detective who'd handled her robbery weeks ago. They'd found her car. He sounded as stunned as she felt and told her where to collect it. "Before you drive it, get a mechanic to look it over. It's been run pretty hard."

Heidi had her car back. Beat up, for sure, but it was back. She had a do-over, in a way. And she knew exactly where to tell the tow truck to go.

Three hours later, she climbed out of the tow-truck cab in the driveway of the faded-blue town house with the dingy-white gingerbread trim, her heart filled with familiar joy. She noticed the guys playing basketball again. Probably the very bunch who had stolen her car, but she didn't fear them. She'd keep her belongings locked up from now on. She was in the city. On the other hand, maybe she'd bake them some brownies. It'd be tougher to steal from someone they knew.

She'd figure it out later. Right now all that mattered was the big bear of a man she was about to roust from his usual late-morning hibernation.

She paid the tow guy and watched him drive away. She looked over at the Outback, no longer the shiny new dream vehicle. It might not even be worth saving, but she knew the best way to find out.

Dizzy from hardly breathing, she banged on the door. Nothing.

She banged again.

Still nothing.

This time she pounded with both fists and was rewarded by familiar thuds approaching from inside. "Hold your water," came that voice she loved. Jackson flung open the door. "Heidi?" His eyes widened and he looked so relieved and so full of love that her heart just melted.

"Jackson," she said.

Here was the man she wanted in her life forever. Sure he would keep big-brothering her, but she could live with that, now that she knew what she wanted for herself. Jackson's loving bossiness was a small price to pay for her happiness.

"Did I wake you?" she said.

"What do you think?" He couldn't even pretend to be pissed, she could tell, as he fought a grin, his eyes twinkling with delight.

"I need your help, Jackson," she said, taking a serious tone.

"You do?" He quirked a brow. "You need my help?"

"Absolutely. Look." She pointed at her battered car. As if on cue, the front fender dropped to the cement with a clang.

"I'll be damned. They found it."

"And I brought it straight to you. Can you fix it?"

"Let's take a look," he said, his grin almost taking over his face. He descended the porch and approached the car, then lifted the hood. "Looks pretty beat up," he said, leaning in, fiddling with some hoses, his voice muffled, but serious. "I'll do what I can."

Watching him dig in to rescue her made her heart fill up and spill over. "I love you, Jackson," she blurted.

"Huh? Ow!" He'd bumped his head on the hood raising up to turn to her. "You do? You love me?" He rubbed his crown. "Do you know what you're saying? Hell, Heidi, I manage a topless bar."

"And a band, don't forget. You manage a band."

"Who knows what will happen there? I'll be chasing music the rest of my life."

"So I'll chase it with you, while I'm going to school. I start next semester."

"That's good. About school, I mean."

"I was just scaring myself about it."

"Like I said, you'll knock 'em dead."

"You, too. You have to do what makes you happy, Jackson. Go for your dream."

He smiled softly. "I bet that's what my mom would have said if my dad had asked her about pursuing his music."

"I'm sure she would have."

He frowned. "How will your brothers feel about you being with the guy who got you arrested?"

"When they see I'm happy, they'll be happy. I acted insecure, so they acted protective."

"Still, your brothers…"

"They'll be fine. They had faith in me, too." Despite their small-town attitudes, their overprotective love for her, they'd let her go without much fuss. They'd kept their worry in check, except for a few frantic phone grillings and the occasional gift appliance or proffered check.

"Besides, I think we should invite them up for dinner and a show at Moons. I'm thinking Jasmine might give Mark a good run. And Autumn could teach Mike something about enjoying himself."

"Let's break 'em in easy, Heidi. See how this goes."

"I'm borrowing tuition money from them, by the way. It doesn't diminish me to accept what they can easily afford to give."

"As long as they don't smother you, right?"

"Exactly."

"Me, either, right? You want support and love, not a stranglehold? That's what Autumn said."

"Yes…."

"Also, she said that I need you to push me."

"Not too much, though. No drowning the ficus."

"Exactly." He grinned at her, love shining in his eyes.

"There it is," she said softly, "That way you look at me. I love that. It's like I fill up all the empty places."

"You do. You light me up, make me want to do more… to be more. I love you, Heidi."

"Me, too." Heidi's heart filled so big she thought she might burst.

Jackson seemed equally moved and had to look away. He squinted into the Outback. "So, is that your stuff I see?"

"It didn't work out with Esmeralda. Her furniture was too elegant. No breasts. No velvet."

"A shame." He shook his head. "There's no accounting for tastes."

"So, I was wondering if I could stay here. Just until my car gets fixed?"

"Hmm. Depends on how long it takes to do the work."

"How long do you think?"

"Not sure." His eyes twinkled at her, warm with love. "If I play my cards right, for as long as I live. Come here." He pulled her into his arms, giving her what she wanted and what she needed.

She felt safe and secure and sure of her future. She had

everything she wanted—a plan, a home, a man she loved
and all the confidence in herself she needed.

Heidi Fields had finally arrived.

* * * * *

*Look for the next Mills & Boon Blaze story
fron Dawn Atkins.* Don't Tempt Me...
is available in May 2007.

FREE!
2 Books
and a surprise gift!

We would like to take this opportunity to thank you for reading this Mills & Boon® book by offering you the chance to take TWO more specially selected titles from the Blaze™ series absolutely FREE! We're also making this offer to introduce you to the benefits of the Mills & Boon® Reader Service™—

★ **FREE home delivery**
★ **FREE gifts and competitions**
★ **FREE monthly Newsletter**
★ **Exclusive Reader Service offers**
★ **Books available before they're in the shops**

Accepting these FREE books and gift places you under no obligation to buy, you may cancel at any time, even after receiving your free shipment. Simply complete your details below and return the entire page to the address below. You don't even need a stamp!

YES! Please send me 2 free Blaze books and a surprise gift. I understand that unless you hear from me, I will receive 4 superb new titles every month for just £3.10 each, postage and packing free. I am under no obligation to purchase any books and may cancel my subscription at any time. The free books and gift will be mine to keep in any case.

K7ZEF

Ms/Mrs/Miss/Mr ....Initials ....
BLOCK CAPITALS PLEASE

Surname ....

Address ....

....

....Postcode ....

Send this whole page to:
UK: FREEPOST CN81, Croydon, CR9 3WZ